The Anarchist's Daughter

A Novel

Alba Ambert

iUniverse, Inc.
New York   Bloomington

The Anarchist's Daughter
A Novel

iUniverse books may be ordered through booksellers or by contacting:

iUniverse
1663 Liberty Drive
Bloomington, IN 47403
www.iuniverse.com
1-800-Authors (1-800-288-4677)

Because of the dynamic nature of the Internet, any Web addresses or links contained in this book
may have changed since publication and may no longer be valid.

ISBN: 978-0-595-48388-4 (pbk)
ISBN: 978-0-595-60479-1 (ebk)

Printed in the United States of America

iUniverse rev. date: 3/24/2009

Grateful acknowledgment is made to the following for permission to reprint copyrighted material: New Directions Publishing Corporation for a stanza of the poem "A Season in Hell (Un Saison En Enfer)" from *A Season in Hell and the Drunken Boat* by Arthur Rimbaud, translated by Louis Varèse, copyright 1961. Excerpts from *The Odyssey* by Homer, translated by Robert Fitzgerald. Copyright (c) 1961, 1963 by Robert Fitzgerald. Copyright renewed 1989 by Benedict R.C. Fitzgerald, on behalf of the Fitzgerald children. Reprinted by permission of Farrar, Straus and Giroux, LLC. *La Borinqueña,* the original national anthem of Puerto Rico, was written by Lola Rodríguez de Tió in 1868 and is now in the public domain.

Also by the Author

Poetry

Alphabets of Seeds
The Mirror is Always There
The Fifth Sun
Habito tu nombre
Gotas sobre el columpio

Fiction

A Perfect Silence
The Eighth Continent and Other Stories
The Passion of María Magdalena Stein
Porque hay silencio

Children's Books

Why the Wild Winds Blow
Thunder from the Earth
Face to the Sky

Non-Fiction

The Seven Powers of Spiritual Evolution
Every Greek Has a Story
Puerto Rican Children on the Mainland
Bilingual Education: A Sourcebook
Bilingual Education and English as a Second Language
Bilingual Education for Exceptional Students

This book is *dedicated to* Luisa Capetillo, Genara Pagán. Franca de Armiño, Concha Torres, Librada Rodríguez, Gregoria Molina, Emilia Vázquez, Ana Delgado, Tomasa Yumart, Luisa Torres, Paula Dávila, Julia Lind, Carmen Rosario, Juana Cofresí, Mercedes Dávila, Isabel Gatell, Rafaela López Negrón, Raymunda Otero, Paca Escabí de Peña, and the many other Puerto Rican women who struggled for the rights of all.

Chapter One

...But sing no more
this bitter tale that wears my heart away.
It opens in me again the wound of longing
for one incomparable, ever in my mind.

The Odyssey

I was born by the sea. Perhaps that's why I have always been comforted by the edges of things. I find solace in the scalloped rim of a shell, the lip of an orchid, the contours of silence. During my long life, I have kept close to the shores of oceans and rivers and the boundaries of time. As a child I learned to interpret the language of waves when they crested and crashed into rocks. I could easily read the delicate lace the waves sketched on the sand. By observing the sea's many transformations, I became proficient at deciphering the multiple faces of its language. My life as a translator and poet was possible because I was fluent in the language of the sea.

To tighten my bonds to the sea, my mother named me Marina. As a small child, I often gazed dreamily past the shore toward the horizon, imagining the lands and people that inhabited the other side. Even before Mamá read to me and taught me the meaning of distance, I always knew that there would be another side beyond the thick golden light spilling on the shantytown, across the dazzling turquoise ocean that stretched around the shore. I wasn't aware at that early stage in my life that I would be propelled away from the island I loved into the immensity of the world. I had no inkling then that an unexpected consequence of my mother's activism would take her from me. I never imagined she would be killed and her body found in the ocean I loved when I was only twelve, too young to lose her, too young to wander from a tiny Caribbean island to the improbable distance beyond my horizon.

I spent so many years trying to make sense of her death, reading yellowed papers at the library, talking to people, trying to fit all the puzzle pieces together. One piece always eluded me, slipping away like waves rolling out to sea.

But finally, it all started to fall into place.

One morning, I looked out at the crests of waves and the bright orange sunrise and was reminded of my mother. An ache that seemed to come from nowhere suddenly invaded my heart, and I felt unprotected, like an abandoned infant. For some reason, she had been on my mind all week. Nothing specific, just small, intangible things, like the way she arched her head back when she laughed or her smell of freshly baked bread fused with sea salt and lavender. It was like an aching sore that has not healed. A silence hard and transparent as glass overwhelmed me as I remembered a recurrent dream I had been having all week.

In the dream, I pulled apart the flaps of a cardboard box. Then I removed a bed of tissue paper and, with great impatience, pulled out the contents. But when I woke up, I never remembered what was inside the box.

When the phone rang, somehow I knew it had something to do with her. With the hole that had opened in the world when she died, that missing piece of the puzzle that prevented me from feeling whole. My heart pounded wildly, and I hesitated. On the fifth ring, I picked up the receiver quickly.

"*Buenos días.*" The woman's voice was deep and smoky. "Could I speak to *la señora* Marina Alomar, please?"

"I'm Marina Alomar. Who's speaking?" My shoulders tensed, and I felt a headache coming. I rubbed my forehead and listened.

"*Ay, mija*, you probably don't remember me, it's been so long. I'm Angelina Sánchez, Luisa Sánchez's daughter. Julián was my older brother, may he rest in peace. We were neighbors in La Perla."

Of course I remembered. When she asked if we could meet, I had no hesitation. I hung up the phone and looked out at La Perla, as I did every day.

I live on the second floor of an old Spanish colonial-style house on Norzagaray Street in Old San Juan. The coral house with turquoise trimmings is tall and narrow, built on a steep hill overlooking the Atlantic Ocean. It's a bit shabby and, like me, sagging at the seams.

My apartment is a sanctuary of marble-tiled floors and diamond-white walls, bound and held together by light. When I sit at my desk in the living room, the vast sea and sky lie ahead of me. On each side of the house stands an old Spanish fort. To the west, the shore curls like the pale arm of a young girl from the cemetery to the narrow point where San Felipe del Morro Fort has stood guard against foreign incursions for five centuries. To the east, the road bypasses La Perla, the shantytown that dips boldly down into the sea, and snakes purposefully toward San Cristóbal Fort at the entrance of the old city. No curtains or drapes shade my home, leaving exposed the expanses of glass that I slide open so sparkling light fills the corners of every room with white incandescence. In my home, light has nowhere to hide. I have always been reluctant to leave this haven of light, but that day as I locked my door with a determined click and ventured out into the morning haze of Old San Juan, there was an unexpected spring in my step.

La Bombonera was quiet; the breakfast crowd had left. A man sitting at the counter hunched over a heavy white cup, pouring spoonfuls of sugar into his coffee and stirring it noisily. He wore the baggy clothing of a homeless person who had access to a shelter to clean up and the skill to cadge enough change for coffee and cigarettes. In Puerto Rico, we call the homeless *los desamparados*, the forsaken ones.

We islanders are sensitive to the predicament of those who have no one to care for them, and we write songs about the heartbreak of abandonment. That's what those boleros in the jukebox are all about. A couple in the booth in front of me discussed the menu. The waiter, wearing a white open-collared shirt and black trousers, with a pencil poised over his pad, threw a look of long-suffering patience in my direction. I shrugged for his benefit, blew softly into my cup of hot coffee, and turned my face away from the mirrored wall as I sipped.

I'm old now, and I find it difficult to recognize the young woman who lingers in the deep folds of my skin. But the sensation of time passing, my awareness of its determined borders, is different from the margins I remember holding me together when I was young. What exists now is more a mirror image. The essential components are there, but the features are reversed and upside down. I feel young, and simultaneously I am heavy with time. The timbers of my body creak like an old wooden boat when I strain to get up in the morning. I'm like a leather suitcase full of rattling bones. Little fears creep up on me with age. Nuns, with their odor of incense and sanctity, grate on my nerves like a nail scraping on glass. Dread clutches at my throat on the rare occasions when I ride through the Dos Hermanos tunnel, struggling to adjust my focus from bright sunshine to the watery darkness that hems me in. The muffled swish of cars passing, the wind barreling through prefigure death.

At my age I have no choice but to contemplate an event that can take place at any moment. Each morning the sharp awareness of death retreats to the margins of my consciousness. The unremitting light speaks only of life.

Then night falls, and as my head drops on the pillow, I wonder whether I will ever wake again.

I glanced at the door. My thoughts shifted to Angelina, Julián, and, of course, my mother. I found myself gripping the edge of the table every time someone entered the diner. My heart thrummed. I could feel my mouth become dry. I had finished my second cup of coffee and longed for a cigar when a short plump woman struggled with the glass door, a large cardboard box the size of an old phonograph cradled in her arms. Her hair, closely cropped, recently dyed blonde and permed in tight clusters of curls, contrasted sharply with the thick dark eyebrows I remembered well. I stood up, plucking at the back of my skirt. In two long strides, the waiter was at the door helping her. Gingerly holding the old box away from his white shirt, he placed it on the table. Angelina thanked him profusely. When she turned around to look at me, her eyes welled with tears. We fell into each other's arms like broken twigs.

Little Angelina. I used to make rag dolls for her. We played *peregrina*, the native version of hopscotch, for hours on the squares I scratched on the hard soil with a white stone. I stayed at her house frequently, waiting for my mother to return from her many absences, and I used to read to Angelina until she fell asleep. When she was older, I made a book with scraps of paper from my mother's old leaflets and wrote a story I knew she would like, about princesses and castles and horses. She learned how to read with that book. When she started school, she returned home crying, vowing never to return. The teacher had been angry because Angelina was far ahead of the other children.

Angelina reached into her bag for a handkerchief; I plucked a paper napkin from the dispenser on the table. When we had wiped our faces, Angelina pointed at my red nose just as I noticed the black streaks of mascara smudging her cheeks. We bent over, the peals of our laughter echoing through the diner. The man at the counter turned around sullenly and the couple in front glanced at us and smiled. But what did we care? We contemplated the old Borax box, spotted with age, moisture stains, and soot, and our mood sobered. A frayed cord had been tied around it and secured with a double knot. The box sat between us like a boulder, taking up half the table. Angelina shoved the box against the wall. We slid into the booth facing each other, and I stretched my hand to touch hers.

"You should have told me the box was heavy. I could have picked it up."

"Oh, that's all right, Nana, I have a car and it's parked right next door. It's why I'm a little late. Had to go 'round a few times before finding a good spot."

Angelina spoke quickly, breathlessly. She continued to wipe her eyes with the man-sized handkerchief she had hastily pulled out of her bag.

Nana. It had been so many years since anyone called me by the name of my childhood, the nickname my mother coined for me.

"Nana." Angelina's voice pulled me back to the diner. "To think I've kept this old box for so many years. When Julián died and you left, Juan Carlos came by and brought this box. He said it was your mother's box, but he couldn't keep it any longer because he was about to be arrested. I asked him why he didn't give it to you. He said that you were in danger too. I was the only one who could keep it safely. Because I was not involved in politics and lived with the Pentecostal pastor and his family, no one suspected me. I cleared out everything before I got married, threw a lot of stuff away. But when I looked inside this box and saw all your mother's things, the books she wrote, her papers, I couldn't throw it away. I remember her giving speeches to the workers at La Perla. I didn't understand what she said, but I knew it was important. I could never throw out her box."

"How did you find me, Angelina? I've been away for a long time."

"Yeah, where were you?"

Uncomfortable, I tensed. How could I explain to her the great distance of exile, the expanse of hurt that lies between the place I was forced to live and the place where I belonged? I wanted to pull out a map, show her where I had been in relation to where we had been, how far across the ocean and seas, the great distance that stretched ahead of us, measurable in decades of unfilled voids, in trails of tears.

But I had no map, so I didn't need to burden her with the story of my leaving. She seemed to think that I had chosen to leave, that there had been options in my life, different paths I could inspect and then choose the most favorable. I didn't tell her there had been no choices for me. With pursuers at my heels, I sought refuge in New York; not the extravagant place that never sleeps, but García Lorca's city of sad kitchens. Exposed inevitably to the language of bards and movie stars, I consumed the spicy English invented in India, Africa, and the Caribbean and made it my own, to better soak up the scents and textures of Madras curry, sweet mango, and pulpy hand-made paper. English was the bond that fused us immigrants to the city like barnacles to a ship, salty kernels clinging to the steel-gray surface as immense as a planet.

As we clung to the ruthless geometry of the city's scaffolds and tasted the shame of its holds, we reeled from the asymmetry of the long shadows and found it hard to find a clearing, a point of reference beyond ourselves. Anger took hold of me then, and I joined other angry men and women, marching down urine-soaked stairways, racing through garbage-strewn alleys, in fierce denunciation of injustice.

Angelina finished her coffee. She squinted, the furrows at her eyes deepening. The tiny vertical lines above her lips pleated like a paper fan.

"It's really funny," she said. "I don't read much, my eyesight is so bad, but I was clearing up the kitchen table and saw your name on one of my granddaughter's books. Sandra's at the university now and likes to study in the kitchen. Close to the fridge. You know how teenagers are. When she sat down for breakfast, I said to her, 'I know this person. We grew up together.' And I picked up the book, but I couldn't understand, couldn't figure out how I could find you. So I asked Sandra, I said, 'You have to find her for me.' I thought it was so hard, but all she did was look up your name in the phone book." Angelina shook her head. "It didn't even cross my mind to do that. I saw it like something impossible, like swimming across the ocean to Miami or something. Anyhow, when you went away, to New York someone told me, I thought you'd never return."

"I lived in New York for many years," I said.

"Ay, Nana, why did you go away? I still don't understand."

I'm not sure I understand it all myself. My life of perpetual exile has consisted of leaving as much as staying.

All those years in New York.

Instead of coffee spoons, my life has been measured in soup ladles, mouthfuls of emptiness that drove me forward, beyond reason. It all began with my mother's death. If my mother had lived, I would never have had to leave. She was my fulcrum, the weight that kept my scale balanced.

When she was killed, I was rootless, uncontrollably adrift, like a speck of dust in the wind. When she died, I no longer had a place to stay. When I fled, I left behind a chunk of me. With pieces scattered in the void, I often wondered whether I'd ever be whole again. It's a question I no longer ask.

After so many years of flight and searching, having collected the bunches of memories that stood tall as cane at harvest, I returned to Puerto Rico several years ago, where I found, to my relief, that no one remembered my name. Except, I now realized, Angelina.

"Well, Angelina, let's say there was nothing for me here. My mother died and then Julián." I shrugged.

Angelina's eyes brimmed with tears again. She wiped her face with her big handkerchief and spoke softly.

"They didn't just die. They were murdered." Her dark brown eyes hardened with pain.

"I know."

"The police never found out who did it, either."

"They didn't want to."

"That's right."

We both turned toward the box, longing for answers. The clatter of dishes behind the counter drowned our thoughts.

"And here we are," I said finally.

"Here we are," Angelina smiled sadly.

Regrettably, I accepted a ride back home. Ensconced on a fat cushion, Angelina slid the driver's seat as far forward as it would go and assumed her navigational position, torso bent over the steering wheel, chin jutting forward, eyes squinting furiously. Her small feet barely touched the pedals. The car was a standard shift, and whenever we stopped at the top of the many steep Old San Juan streets, it would roll back before she managed to wield control of the clutch.

At the apartment building, she parked precariously, the car bolting so violently that the coffee in my stomach sloshed unpleasantly. It was like breaking in a wild stallion. My hands were chalk-white from clutching the door handle and the side of my seat, and my fingers were so stiff I could barely lift the box.

Angelina pushed it out the door from her side of the car and helped me bring it up the two flights of narrow stairs to my apartment. We were both out of breath when we deposited the box on my desk. Angelina looked at it tenderly, as if my mother's remains were collected there instead of in an unmarked grave by the sea.

Angelina turned her attention toward the window.

"The view is so beautiful," she said breathlessly. "Oh, there's La Perla." She pointed with her open hand, and her face gathered into a grimace that was in between a smile and a frown.

It was almost noon. Tourists were still struggling up the steep walk to El Morro. There was a time when this would be the siesta in Old San Juan, and a quiet stillness would settle on the city. The shops would be closed and shuttered for the several hours the sun was at its hottest, and people dropped off like flies after lunch.

Now, with air conditioning and the so-called tourist industry, it's different. Streets are lined with fashionable boutiques and tacky tourist shops peddling souvenirs of Puerto Rico made in China, kiosks displaying newspapers and magazines from all over the world, fusion cuisine restaurants, and contemporary art galleries. The shops stay open all day, regardless of the intensity of the sun. Lunch hour is whenever people can take a break. We don't organize our days according to the elements any longer. When it's hot we make it cold, and when it's cold we make it hot. At the flick of a switch.

"Stay for lunch," I said to Angelina and put my arm around her shoulders. It's at times like these when I despair at the inadequacy of words. She nodded and wiped her eyes as I went to the kitchen, mentally reviewing the contents of the refrigerator. I switched on the electric fan and poured salted water in a *caldero* for rice. I chopped up garlic, onions, and green peppers for a four-egg Spanish omelet. While the rice and omelet cooked, I prepared the vinaigrette for a simple lettuce and tomato salad. In the meantime, Angelina set the table in the dining area next to the kitchen.

"Have a doctor's appointment tomorrow," she announced and shook her head. "For these eyes. I can't read or sew or anything. All I can see are things that are far away. If I read something, I have to hold it way out there. My arms get so tired. I'm afraid they'll take my driver's license away if I don't get some eyeglasses or something." She screwed up her face in disapproval at the excessive demands of bureaucrats.

"Ay, Marina," she cried when we sat down to eat. "Why did you go to all this trouble, cooking so much food in this heat?"

"We have to celebrate our special day. It's too bad I don't have any wine."

She shook her head forcefully. "Oh, I don't drink, not even beer. Do you have any soda?"

"I'm sorry." I was truly devastated. I wanted to please Angelina, to give her at least a fraction of what she had given me that day.

"How about some pineapple juice?"

"Okay, that's good."

When we finally settled down to our meal, Angelina talked about her life after La Perla. She explained how poverty had forced her to quit school after finishing the sixth grade. She left school to work at La Colectiva, the tobacco factory where our mothers had worked. In the evenings and Sundays, she taught herself to type on the old Remington her mother Luisa inherited when my mother died. When word got around that Angelina could not only read and write with beautiful script, but also type, she was promptly promoted to the offices on the third floor, where she typed letters, filed documents, and handled the payroll for the factory manager.

"Remember the hours we spent practicing our handwriting at your house on scraps of paper with the yellow pencils your mother always kept lined up on a shelf?" Angelina took a sip of juice, wiped her mouth with a napkin, and continued. "Once for my birthday she gave me a black and white notebook and a bright yellow pencil with very dark lead. I'll never forget it. No one gave us birthday presents in those days. I wanted to write in that notebook every day, but I was afraid of using up the lead. Then Julián told me not to worry. He kept my pencil nicely sharpened with that pocket knife of his."

"You always had beautiful handwriting," I reminded her.

"I tried to imitate your mother's. It's the one thing that helped me get out of the hard work of stripping tobacco at the factory. People valued good handwriting in those days. It's not like today."

Angelina told me that after she was promoted to an office position, she liked to have lunch at a local *fonda*. That's where she met César Díaz, a construction worker who toiled at many jobs, from transporting and laying bricks to setting down wooden planks for floors. Angelina pulled out a picture of him when he was young. His skin was a sun-bronzed rich brown. His short-sleeved shirt revealed the hard biceps of a laborer. His dark eyes sparkled with kindness. He had four brothers and a sister named Violeta Isis. His parents, *doña* Lydia and *don* Félix, had been happily married for many years. They lived in the small wooden house *don* Félix had built with his own hands in Barrio Obrero for his wife and numerous offspring.

César soon saved enough money to open his own hardware store in Barrio Obrero. He and Angelina married, and she continued working until César could open a larger store that catered to the construction business. Besides the usual hardware items, he sold lumber, plumbing pipes, and electrical wiring. He was the first to introduce copper pipes to Barrio Obrero. Later, when the cement craze began, he sold sacks of cement, steel rods, gravel, sand, and cinder blocks with such success he had to build an annex. After a few years, La Colectiva went out of business, and Angelina settled into the new house César and *don* Félix had built and happily raised her four children.

"And my mother-in-law was wonderful, may she rest in peace," Angelina said as she pushed her empty plate aside. "She was a Pentecostal, you know, so we worshipped at the same church. She was surprised that I had converted from Catholicism. I explained that religion wasn't very important to us. You know how we were brought up. My mother hated priests and that skinny American reverend who showed up at La Perla out of nowhere and never left; remember him? She couldn't stand him! But she had us all baptized in the Catholic Church just in case." Angelina's eyes misted with sadness. "Then she died, and I converted when the Puerto Rican pastor's family took me in."

"Oh, you don't know how I loved being a member of César's family. My little sister died, then my mother. Julián was the only family I had left. Then he died too. It was so good to be part of a family again, and a big one. I think that's what I liked most about César, that big family of his. After we got married, I became a part of something I could count on. I was never lonely again. He was a good man, my César. He worked like a dog all his life to provide for his family. He died five years ago."

"Are your children all here?"

"The four of them graduated from university and stayed here. I'm so happy. Too many young people are leaving, going to New York, Miami, even California. But not my children. They're all married. I have six grandchildren and one on the way. Sandra's my eldest granddaughter and she lives with me because her parents are out in Mayagüez and she's at the university in Río Piedras, really close to where I live now. So she stays with me during the school term. They're all good kids; they help me out, look after me."

She nodded, sighed, and rubbed her full stomach. "Well, Marina, I hate to be like *San Blás* and eat and run, but I better go before the *tapón* starts. I hate to drive in that bottleneck, especially on the expressway. Those people drive like maniacs! Honestly, I don't know how they get licenses."

I almost burst out laughing, but I contained myself. I'm ashamed to admit that my first thoughts were not sympathetic. I was less concerned about the time she would spend in the crushing San Juan traffic than about the unsuspecting pedestrians and drivers she would terrorize as her car screeched, gears grinding, through the streets.

After Angelina hurried out, I pressed my back against the door and faced the box that had arrived to inhabit my world, another resident in my already crowded apartment. I don't live alone; I live with Giordano Bruno and Miguel de Cervantes y Saavedra, the big slate-gray cats I discovered, tiny and famished at the foot of the stairs, a few days after I moved in. They meow their demands for food and affection when I'm distracted, reminding me of the routine acts that constitute the essential stuff of living. Now, alone again, I looked around. As on other infrequent occasions when strangers came to the apartment, the cats were nowhere to be seen.

Before tackling the box, I lit up a cigar and let the aroma and sharp flavor suffuse my tongue, palate, and throat. Like the Taínos, the indigenous people of the island, I let the tobacco's medicinal powers engulf me and sweeten the room with the rich aroma of thick vegetation. I examined the photographs of rainbows that hang on the wall. With a rag, I wiped the smudges that mysteriously appear on the glass with annoying regularity. There must be an invisible smudge producer somewhere in the apartment. I shook my head and rubbed the glass vigorously. The rainbows reminded me of that line in *The Odyssey*: "Atlas, who holds the columns that bear from land the great thrust of the sky." That's exactly what rainbows are to me—immense columns holding up the sky.

Some people believe rainbows can't be photographed, but I keep a loaded camera in my desk drawer ready to capture those millions of drops of water that come together in the beams of sunlight, high and narrow as inverted *u*'s or curled into low, reaching arms, like the flying buttresses of a cathedral. As rainbows dissolve, they leave bright wisps of color in the sky, fragments of crimsons and golds tinting the whitecaps below. Long columns bear the great thrust of the arch in the sky. When the columns disappear first, a swath of color arches across the sky, but when the crest is the first to vanish, the columns shred into specks hovering close to the water.

I admired the rainbow images on my wall, their graceful symmetry, the way they sweep through the sky like comets and then shred and scatter in the light. They remind me of my mother's dreams, her hurts, and her disappointments. They remind me of my own moments of uncertainty and despair. They remind me of loss. Like a rainbow, I am open to everything, and I let pain get in too easily.

I started photographing rainbows to capture the impermanence of their perfection, the delicate beauty shaped by something as fragile as drops of water collecting in the sun. It's my attempt to hold on to the elusive, to not let reality, so liquid and fleeting, slip through my fingers like so many of my losses. After it rains, I photograph the single and double bows that arch across the sky, presiding over the ocean like sparkling necklaces. The beautiful symmetry of the arches, their colors dissolving into the sky like smoke, make me feel settled and at peace.

I stood in the middle of the living room staring at the box, puffing hard on my cigar, when a door banged shut and startled me.

My friend Soledad Beauchamp lives on the first floor. Often, she stops by to chat and offer to run errands for me. She knows that I hate to go out. Why bother? I've got the ocean like a cloth of sequins in front of me and the blue fullness of the sky. The world has nothing else to offer me.

Soledad orbits around a world that is very different from mine, more harried, marred by the tarnish of separations and the dead weight of unrealized expectations. She's in her mid-thirties, favors the bell bottoms, miniskirts, and fringed vests of the seventies. She calls it her retro look, and her honey-brown hair falls straight to the middle of her back.

She organizes the Casals Festival. Every year, before the festival begins, her brown eyes darken with pleated pouches underneath, the whites bloodshot from lack of sleep and worry, her slight frame sunk in and bony from all the weight she loses. I often watch her from my bedroom window at four o'clock in the morning, pacing the interior patio or sitting on a bench staring out at the black ocean, afflicted with worries about everything that could go wrong: the first violinist contracting dengue fever, the visiting composer caught in a snow storm at a foreign international airport, an important music critic mugged or, worse, stabbed in his hotel room. She runs through this catalog of horrors every night until the festival closes, when she falls into a dreamless sleep from dawn to dawn. When she surfaces, her eyes shine brightly; her smile is easy and alluring. Like a woman who has just had a baby, her memory wipes out the pain, and she begins preparations for the following year's festival with the verve and excitement of a child eager for the first day of school.

Braced for reviewing the box's contents, I had barely settled at my desk when the doorbell rang. Soledad walked in. It wasn't festival time, but I could see she was disturbed. It was too early in the day for a visit, and when she asked whether I needed something from the supermarket, I knew she really wanted to talk. She had those familiar circles under her eyes. She wore an old T-shirt and cut-offs, so she wasn't going anywhere, at least not that minute. I brewed some fresh coffee while she settled into my rocker.

Soledad tapped her fingers on the demitasse. She seemed lost somewhere far into the distance. I took a sip of my coffee and let the cup rest on the saucer.

"Has Rodrigo returned?" I asked quietly.

Soledad didn't say a word. She took a bite of a cracker spread with guava paste and looked out at the ocean, chewing slowly. A hush gathered around us, and I became distracted by my own thoughts. I don't know how long we sat there in silence, she contemplating the future, I imagine, in the blueness of the sky, the sharp turquoise of the ocean, and I overpowered by thoughts of the past that had resided in my mother's box for decades. I was so far into my thoughts that I was startled when she cleared her throat and finally spoke. Her voice was thin and soft.

"I can't be his mirror."

"You don't have to be."

"It's what men always want."

I plunged into silence again. What could I say without turning over in my own mind the many mirrors I had felt compelled to become so that men would love me? I shook my head slowly to get rid of the thought and where it was leading me. No, that was a place I did not want to revisit. Not then, not now.

Holding the arms of the rocking chair, Soledad tilted forward and pushed herself up, promising to pick up some milk for me (for the cats, really) once she found the energy to shower, dress, and leave her apartment. I put a hand on her arm. When she turned around, I hugged her. A tremor coursed through her body, and she let out a sob. I held her close as she wept into my shoulder. A light breeze lifted from the ocean. My blouse fluttered. The wetness on my shoulder chilled in the breeze, and goose bumps puckered on my skin. I touched her back and felt the knobs of her spine rubbing against the T-shirt. I threaded my fingers through her long brown hair and pushed it away from her face.

"I'm sorry, *doña* Marina," she said softly, and she glanced into the distance. Her face was loose as a turned-out pocket.

I've asked her countless times not to call me *doña*. It's so redolent of the class system and peonage, but she can't bring herself to resist the polite form of address when speaking to an elderly, therefore respected, person.

"Let's go to El Fogón for dinner tonight." I said this as enthusiastically as possible considering my aversion to refrigerator-cold restaurants, though I must admit that my mouth watered slightly when I thought of the tender *churrasco*, long and folded over like a blanket, on a plate as big as a skillet. Concerned with the suffering of animals as well as humans, my mother had been a vegetarian; I never ate meat as a child. Though I've lapsed on a few occasions, I try not to be tempted even by El Fogón's deliciously broiled steaks. But I knew it was one of Soledad's favorite places, and it was obvious she needed to talk. Soledad shook her head, her lips set in a bitter line.

"Rodrigo told me the truth, *doña* Marina."

"His truth?"

"My truth is totally different. That's why I couldn't be his mirror." She sighed and lowered her head. "The jerk married me so he could get U.S. citizenship. He was about to be sent back to Argentina. Now he has a green card and doesn't want anything to do with me. I should report him to Immigration. That's what I should do."

Ever cautious of nefarious government officers, Immigration and FBI at the top on my list, I was tempted to advise her against it. Not because of Rodrigo, but her welfare. Those pitiless agents were perfectly capable of putting her in prison, citing some obscure law that hasn't been active for two hundred years, while Rodrigo, of course, goes free. They might even hold her friendship with me against her. But prudently I said nothing about this.

"I'm so sorry, Soledad."

"I really love him, you know."

"I know."

She kissed me on the cheek and, pressing the palms of her small hands against her face, stepped out. I stood at the door until the sound of her hurried steps faded and her door slammed shut.

I inspected the delicately tinted rainbows on my wall again. The photos always manage to console me when I'm heavy-hearted. Reproaching myself for taking on other people's burdens, I regarded the satiny sheen of the single and double arches, brighter than any jewel. There are not enough words for the many colors of pain, but as my eyes settled on the violets, indigos, light blues, greens, golden yellows, oranges, and dazzling crimsons, a drift of comfort and quiet lassitude slipped into me.

I tried not to think about Soledad's doomed marriage, but I couldn't help recalling how Rodrigo had wooed her relentlessly until, exhausted by his attentions, she fell in love. That's a secret men harbor and exploit. They know with absolute certainty that if they pursue their quarry long and vigorously enough, especially if they've detected a weakness—the soft spot of low self-esteem, the open sore of frustration—they will eventually ensnare the object of their pursuit. All it takes is patience, an intense attack, and pushing the right buttons.

Persistence is all Rodrigo can brag about. He has the short, stocky legs of a bulldog, Popeye arms, and a big unattractive head on a thick neck. His face is broad and empty. But after a siege that lasted over a year, pretty Soledad relented. She should have been treated like a delicate rainbow. Instead, his empty face puffed up with spite and cruelty, and he twisted a knife in her chest with his words.

But let me get back to the box waiting patiently on my desk. After my anxiety and procrastination and now the interruption, I couldn't bring myself to open it. Instead I sat at the desk rubbing my fingers against the old box, reading the details about weight and contents printed on its sides, wondering what avoirdupois means, lacking the energy to look it up in the dictionary. I was annoyed with myself at this unexpected reluctance. At my age, I'm accustomed to waiting. Most of the impatience of youth has faded with time. A sudden fear pressed against my heart as I thought of what might be inside. I rummaged through my drawers for a penknife or scissors. The clatter of pens made me wonder about the silence in the apartment, a silence that distracted me again.

Now, where are those cats? I wondered.

Up to no good, I was sure. I shut the desk drawer and looked around me, suddenly concerned about their absence. I hadn't seen them since I returned with Angelina two hours before. To think they find places to hide in such a small apartment … Sometimes they disappear for hours and I worried myself sick, thinking they fell out the window.

To my relief, the minute I got up, Bruno and Cervantes appeared. Bruno stretched out on a sunny patch on the floor, and Cervantes licked his paw. As if in agreement, they then both moved toward the kitchen entrance, looking at me resentfully as they went. On this most extraordinary of days, I had forgotten to feed them. Weighed down by guilt, I entered the kitchen, and they licked their whiskers in anticipation of the meal they knew I would set out for them. After I fed the cats, I went back to the living room, ready. I was now determined to confront the memories, to bring them back to life.

I sat at my desk again. Light shimmered on and brightened the shabby box. It's amazing how everything looks better in the light. Since learning of the existence of Mamá's box, I had felt poised on the dark rim of an infinite night. I guess I was afraid to fall off.

Finally, a need I had never felt before seized me. I took a deep breath, cut the cord with the scissors, and pulled the carton lids apart. My mother's life waited in there. I promised myself to piece it together like a giant puzzle.

The Spanish word for jigsaw puzzle is *rompecabezas*—head breaker. But it wasn't my head that was breaking as I searched once again through the immense hole at the center of my mother's life. Instead, my heart broke when I noticed the tenderness with which she inscribed my name on a strip of paper, when I thought of the hardship she endured to write each essay, every poem. I struggled to discover her world, to fill in the chasm and make her life whole again.

With care and heartbreak, I stitched her meager biography together and hoped, against all hope, that I could find a solution to the puzzle that had beset me throughout my long life. I needed to know, finally and without a doubt, why she had been killed and who was responsible for her death. I had held this question at bay long enough. I wasn't aware of the exact contents of the box, but I had a feeling deep in my womb that I would finally find the answer to the most desperate questions I ever faced.

I fingered the slender books and pamphlets Mamá had published, mold-spotted pages dotted with tiny holes where silverfish had burrowed through. I found a straw-colored envelope full of sepia photographs of my mother holding up banners during worker demonstrations, carrying a *jacho*, the torch that symbolized the worker's struggle. In one photo, she sat at a desk, papers and books spilling onto the floor. In a portrait, my father stared out with a hesitant smile, handsome in a dark suit and a broad-brimmed hat, one arm resting easily on a tall stand that read *Te Amo*. I turned it over and saw his large, awkward script. "To my beloved Isabel, from your *compañero* who adores you, Bolívar."

Pressing the tips of my fingers against his handsome face, I then traced his slender body down to his white shoes then back up to his face. A shadow cut a line diagonally across one eye and climbed into the darkness of the background. I've often wondered as I've looked into the dead eyes in photographs if they will ever again see the moment passing as the camera clicks. But then, a photograph is not a true image of reality, is it? It's more a specter caught in light before it vanishes into the world of shadows. An impossible boundary exists between photographs and the reality they represent. A frozen split second, never to be repeated, never to exist again. Maybe nothing is real, after all, and what we experience is a series of disappearances, fading into the nothingness of time that slips irreversibly away.

I unfolded a weathered article published in *Unión Obrera* in 1907. The paper tore between my fingers at the weakened folds, and I held the paper together gingerly with both hands.

> *Comrades from Ponce inform us that on the evening of Tuesday, the 26th of the present month, our compañera Carmen Rosario entered into a free and loving contract with comrade Francisco Santiago. The act was presided by comrade Eugenio Sánchez. It is the first free love contract to be celebrated in Puerto Rico and it heralds a happy era. We congratulate the couple.*

My mother's comrades lived in their daily ceremonies among the theories conceived by Russian and French and Italian theorists. I wondered whether Kropotkin, Proudhon, and Malatesta had ever entered into free love arrangements. I wondered how authentic their lives were, how faithfully they held to their written beliefs in the ordinary days they lived as fathers and husbands and sons.

A lock of curly black hair had been carefully wrapped in paraffin paper with my name and a date written on it. My first haircut. Infant locks preserved over seventy years, a testament to our instinctual hunger to preserve the remains of the past for future interpretation.

In conserving bits and pieces of the past, buried in layers of time and circumstance, we sustain a disturbing archeology, delectable material for voyeurs to touch and worry with dirt-encrusted fingers. I wondered, *Whose reality am I looking at?* as I dug through my mother's mementos. Would I be able, through her objects and writings, to understand her past, a past that was so inextricably bound to mine? In understanding her better, would I understand myself, or would I discover instead an archaeology of silence?

Loneliness engulfed me as I read a poem my mother wrote. She didn't sign it, but I recognized her small, delicate script, set firmly enough on the creamy paper to survive almost a century. She wrote it in the third person singular, perhaps to distance herself from the pain and loneliness of my father's absence. As I read each word, I ached with her as she lingered by the sea, expecting my father's return.

As She Waits

The bugle taps of war

score a distance
of sand and roar
as her gaze drifts
to the blade-sharp ships
that slice the sea.

Time bunches
like mussels
on salt-crusted rocks.
Twilight thickens
round her shoulders
with a purple fold of light.

She strokes the sparkle
on her finger
and remembers
the dip of his knee,
the crest of his head,
his unexpected promise.

As she waits,
eagle wings
kiss her loom,
held up so high
she knits stars
into the moon.

I retrieved a rustic wooden box, the size of a tobacco carton. It was made of pine, pale and knotty like the coffin of a poor person. Its scent of sea salt and humidity brought a sudden rush of nostalgia that made my heart turn. The box had been lost for years, passed on from hand to hand, inhabiting the dusty spaces of oblivion.

Carefully, almost reverentially, I dipped into the box within a box and pulled out the first thing my fingers touched. I unfolded my mother's birth certificate from Our Lady of the Rosary Parish in Camuy.

> *I hereby certify that Isabel Pagán Ginés, native of Camuy,*
> *natural daughter of Paula Pagán Carrión, daughter of Rafael*
> *Carrión and Cipriana Ginés, was born on the 15th day of*
> *December of the year 1893, as attested in Book 21, Folio 349,*

Number 629 Baptism of this Parish Archive. Camuy, Puerto Rico, January 26, 1931.

The parish priest, Father Alberto María Sorli of the Carmelite Order, had signed it. The document, thin and fragile as the wing of a moth, was firmly stamped with the parish seal.

I placed the birth certificate aside and sorted through stacks of photographs with names I could not recognize penciled in the backs. I pulled out my mother's thick journal. There was a manuscript too. She had been writing an autobiography that included my father's life. So many holes were filling in, so much emptiness infusing the dark spaces of my memory.

I remembered that I'd often wake up late at night to see her hunched over a notebook, her brows pressed together in concentration, her lower lip tucked between her teeth. I could hear the soft scratch of the pen on paper as she wrote deliberately, in her precise script, under the light of the kerosene lamp.

When I was satisfied that Mamá was there, I'd drift back to sleep, comforted and safe. Now my hands trembled as I held the diary. A folded sheet of paper fell out of it and landed at my feet. My heart pounded as I unfolded the letter and read the large, tightly spaced handwriting. I could imagine the writer sitting at his ample desk, composing swiftly while rain pelted against the windows and lightning glowed in the darkness of the room. I finished reading the letter, and my hands shook violently. There was a roar in my ears as I searched for the diary entry my mother had made after the date on the letter. A hard knot rose in my throat. In her small, neat script, my mother had written:

"Julián brought a letter to me. It's a bomb waiting to explode! If they discover that I have it, they will kill me too."

I read the letter and my mother's entry several times, the words tumbling through my brain like loose rocks. I folded the letter carefully and tucked it in Mamá's journal. I held the book to my chest. My heart thumped so hard, I felt sick and had to hold on to the edge of the desk for balance. My mind raced as I thought of running down to Soledad's place, telling her the story, asking for advice. I thought of Angelina, with her dyed curls bouncing as she maneuvered through the streets, terrifying pedestrians and stray dogs. I shook my head repeatedly, regretting the loss of friends, of family. Everyone I knew intimately seemed to inhabit spaces of memory and imagination I could not, at that moment, reach.

I put the diary back inside the pale unvarnished box. With a click of the latch, I pushed the slit on the small hasp through a metal loop daubed with stains of time. I slid my fingers across the grain of the wood. A dark stain curled and streaked on its side. This memory box contained the things that helped me remember all that I thought forgotten. It showed me all I had not known. The objects in the box bound me more than ever to my mother as I touched what she touched and read what she wrote. As I understood details of her life and lived them through her words, she and I were again one.

Thinking about my mother's murder, I couldn't sleep. Now that I knew the truth, anger and loathing grew inside me like the gnarled roots of alien plants. I've always tried not to fall prey to hatred. I know it's a poison that can hurt me more than anyone else.

But that night I found it difficult not to hate. I padded barefoot to my bedroom window and lit a cigar, its ashes glowing in the dark. The reflected gleam of a full moon shimmered on the water in bands of light. The sea was calm and murmured gently as the waves came into shore and pulled out toward the beams of the moon. I decided to tidy up the spare room where I keep all the things I had meant to organize or throw out but never got around to doing. It's what I do when I'm trying to work through a conundrum, to find a fresh metaphor, grasp an idea that eludes me. I was on the brink of letting my anger boil over again, of spewing vulgarities, like vomit, in all the languages I know. Of somehow letting the anger and hatred vault out of my heart.

I thought it was best if I drowned the anger with forgetfulness, distraction. I rummaged through old photo albums, books, folders stuffed with newspaper clippings. I found notebooks with scrawled poems I couldn't remember having written. One of the poems was about love. I tried to recapture the ache and yearning while its memory lingered at the brink of my mind, yet I couldn't name it. Calling it love alone would not do. After so many years alone, my heart lurched at the mere thought of it.

I read a few lines. The poem was not only about love; it was also about staying and about leaving. Then a couple of lines—"I would like to have the day/to live in a different language"—somehow triggered a need to act, to bring up my fist in condemnation of the terrible injustice done to my mother, to me.

At that moment the idea hit me, sudden as a sniper's bullet. My best revenge, I decided, was to write a book. I would find a receptive publisher and tell him or her the story. Once the story was printed, this old case would see the light once more. I would bring it out from the shadows, where it had been condemned to live for too many years.

So it was on that sleepless night when I examined the yellowed papers and faded ribbons that I resolved to tell my story and the many parallel stories that ran alongside it.

The moment I made the decision, the love and the hurt and the losses came flooding back, and I was immobilized by fear. Why in the world would I want to subject myself to this? Had I gone mad?

It's not easy to tell such a story. It's hard to go back in time and feel your own presence as a younger, different person. It's like seeing yourself as a stranger in a disturbing dream. I considered putting the box, with its old poems and remnants of dreams, away. I considered letting go, but I wavered for only a moment.

Embarking on this journey, I know, will free me at last.

Every journey has a reason, every tale a purpose, and this, I guess, is mine.

Chapter Two

Of these adventures ...
Tell us in our time,
lift the great song again.

The Odyssey

My father, Bolívar Alomar Seguro, learned to build things with his father Epifanio, a country man made morose and quiet by excruciating work with the sugar cane.

The Alomars had long ago settled the mountains and valleys of the Cordillera Central. On November 19, 1493, on his second voyage to the New World, Columbus and his men landed on the island of Borinquen, Land of the Great Lord, the name given to Puerto Rico by its indigenous inhabitants, the Taínos. It wasn't until 1508 that the Spaniards returned to colonize the island.

On this second incursion, Damián Alomar, Bolívar's forefather, left the barren countryside of Andalucía and, in pursuit of gold and the limitless power he believed it would give him, joined Juan Ponce de León's crew in Cádiz to embark on the looting of Puerto Rico. The Spaniards moved swiftly to control the island, dividing up the land and enslaving the Taínos to scoop out the gold and plant and cut the cane in the fields. The conquistadores exercised their superior authority by killing and burning, roasting men, women, and children and tossing them to the wild dogs. Over several decades the entire nation of thirty thousand Taínos was decimated. Yet their strong seed remained in the offspring of Spaniards and Taíno women.

So it was that Damián Alomar, with the blessing of the Catholic Church, wed a Taína who had been baptized and given the Christian name of María. She bore eight sons and two daughters of various shades and dispositions. Those who survived scattered their sons and daughters throughout the island, fusing with other *mestizos* and the iron-strong African slaves who were dragged to the island in chains to carry on the backbreaking work of the mines and plantations. Taíno blood lingered in the slight slant of an eye, the copper glow of skin, or hair as dark and thick as forest vine.

In Epifanio, Bolívar's father, the Taíno blood was almost imperceptible. He was an angular man, with small bones and slender lips. Yet his dark brown eyes had slight folds in the inner corners and looked like almonds set on a bed of hay. Along with those almond eyes, he passed on to his sons the knack for finding planks of wood, shot through with rusty nails and bits of wire. Gripping a claw hammer firmly, he pulled out the nails, pounded them straight, and with an old weathered stone scraped off the rust. He sanded the planks of wood and squeezed the damp sawdust between his fingers. With these discarded bits and pieces found in the thistle that he combed regularly, he repaired the weatherworn boards of the family shack and built a cooking shed at the back.

Bolívar's mother, Andrea, was a thin, threadbare woman, dried out by the demands of ten births and the raising of six survivors, all boys, sent early to work at the sugar plantation and unable to help with the household chores that kept her leashed tightly to the shack. She held her head down as she stumbled through a life that was like a dog's dream, colorless and bland. She never thought about her grandmother's harrowing trip across the Atlantic from the island of Corsica to the false promise of a new world. She never saw her grandfather's knuckles, tough as bark from working another's fields.

Andrea went about her life without questioning. When decisions were necessary, others made them for her. When each boy was born, the priest consulted his dusty *Calendar of Saints of the Holy Roman Catholic Church* and christened him according to the saint of the day. These were severe names; it was hard to wrap the tongue around their multi-syllabic, consonant-heavy forms. In an attempt to shorten and lighten those intractable names, the parents distinguished their sons with short and simple nicknames. Obdulio, the oldest, became Yuyo, while Faustino was rebaptized Tino. Bernardo answered to Nando, and Liberato was called Lato. Daniel's first nickname of Danielito was too long and unwieldy, and the parents eased it into the simple Lito.

By the time Bolívar was born, Andrea was angry at God. When she felt with despair the familiar quickening in her stomach, the nausea that rose up her throat in the morning, she fell into bed with a fever for the first time in her life. She had thought she was done with bringing up babies and suckling them at her withered breasts. She refused to get the priest for the christening until she had named the child herself. Bolívar, he would be called. She had heard somewhere, maybe in church when people gathered to gossip after mass, that there was a hard man out there in Perú or Venezuela, she was not sure—a hard man who was a revolutionary. No, this child would not be named for a saint. She shook her head resolutely; he would be named for a hard man.

Andrea often stared at her youngest with silent resentment for his flagrant theft of her last days of peace, which would have been spent darning the seats of old trousers, stirring a stew pot dreamily, or perhaps sitting in the coolness of the mountain air searching through the gathering dusk for the first star of the evening. Frayed as an old collar, she died when Bolívar was nine, her dreams of peace and quiet unrealized. When she was about to expire, she called for her husband and every one of her sons but Bolívar.

The child squatted outside the shack, tears washing down his cheeks, wondering why his mother had forsaken him.

Two years after his wife's death, Epifanio removed Bolívar from school so he could work with his brothers on the sugar plantation clearing stubble, repairing palisades, piling the cane high in carts to be carried to the giant sugar mills where the sweet sap was squeezed from the crushed weed. He ignored the deep ache of his muscles as he cut the cane with a swift swipe.

Cane rats and termites scuttled through the rows of sweet reeds when he stripped away the leaves and lopped off the top of the stalk just above the last mature nod, leaving the stubble on the field to swell and burst into a new generation of cane that would make his work begin anew in a never-ending cycle.

When Epifanio, old and worn by the age of forty-eight, died clutching his chest under the worst of the noon heat, Bolívar was sixteen. No longer attached to the plantation through their father, the Alomar brothers soon moved on. Two went as far as New York City, risking the holds of old ships to work in factories. One of them died in a sugar processing plant accident. No one knew what happened to Lito, the fifth son. A neighbor saw him pack a bundle on the family donkey and head down the mountain road. Many peasants reported seeing the ragged shirt on his back as he fled from a hut, ripe banana or mango in his hand; he was spotted climbing the branches of a *yagrumo* for shelter during a rain squall. Some people claimed to have been startled by his bright brown eyes staring from the thick leaves of a *majagua* bush. Rumors persisted for years that he had died fighting with the Cuban insurrectionists against the Spaniards.

Left to his own devices, Bolívar, the youngest, was the last to leave. His angular body, all sharp corners and rectangles, followed the long trail of flight of thin and tired young men from the harrowing work of the cane. He too packed his meager belongings in one of his mother's kerchiefs, flung it over his shoulder, and headed down the stubbled road from the mountains, hitching rides on ox-carts piled with sugar cane or trucks or horse-drawn carriages weighted with luxuries the plantation owners found impossible to live without.

At the shore of San Juan, his heart stopped for a second when he saw the blue immensity ahead of him for the first time. When he looked out at the immeasurable expanse of blue light, its waves curling softly into a band of sand, smelled the sea-wrack scent, and observed the hard glare of the wheeling sun that lifted into his skull like an old ache, he wished he would never have to leave this place of blue infinity.

He settled happily in San Juan and soon found work in the cigar factory, at first doing the menial task of unpacking bales of tobacco while he trained for the more lucrative and prestigious position of cigar roller. The minute he took in the lichen scent of tobacco and stroked the broad leaves traced with delicate capillaries, he knew he would discard his identity of lowly sugar cane cutter and transform himself into a proud artisan. During all the years he worked in San Juan, rolling cigars, building things for Isabel, his past tucked away somewhere deep and unreachable, he would often wake up at night to the swish and hiss of a machete swinging in the air just before coming down to cut into the juicy flesh of the cane.

Isabel had always been poor. From her birth, from the birth of her mother, from the birth of her mother's mother, as far back as time could be traced and counted and retold, her family had been poor.

Her mother, Paula Ginés, never talked about the father who sired her. It was rumored that he was the impoverished son of an emancipated slave who had been caught in the middle of a drunken brawl and killed by mistake. Paula never discussed him, but she often told stories of her own mother, María Dolores, Isabel's grandmother, driven by poverty from the Canary Islands, a sad kerchief on her head, to clean the houses of the rich Creoles of the island, to cook their food and bear their children, a destiny she had no choice but to hand down to her daughter. But Paula was not content with this state of affairs. Since childhood, when she punched the son of her mother's mistress for putting his hand up her skirt in one of the dark rooms of the big dark house, she wore a constant scowl of rebellion, distaste flowering on her lips when she was ordered to be quiet, obedient, subservient.

For decades she had been the laundress for *doña* Elena Gautier, the overbearing wife of a plantation owner. Paula swore her daughter would live a better life, which in her mind meant a life of independence from the whims of the predatory rich. After a long day of work, pressing the heavy coal-filled iron hard over fine linen shirts and trousers, she returned to her tiny wooden house to embroider bed linen and *guayaberas* for the wealthy women who knocked on her door. The women sought the delicate bits of fabric they could bring to their noses in virtuous shock at some breach of established mores or in the sadness brought about by their husbands' refusals to allow a luxury purchase.

With this money, Paula paid for private lessons with the local teacher, who taught Isabel to read and write, to work with numbers. She knew that an educated person could not be enslaved, not even a woman. José Esteban Alvarado de Godoy was a good teacher, and Isabel learned rudimentary literacy quickly. But more than the letters he taught her to string together into meaning, much more than the numbers he taught her to connect and reconnect in multiple variables, José Esteban stoked her mind with stars. Once Isabel learned to read, José Esteban could not feed her books quickly enough, and when she had read his entire collection in Spanish, he taught her French so she could read the heavy volumes of literature and the slender books of poetry he had brought across the Atlantic in a sturdy shipping trunk. Finally, she learned English, and she read through José Esteban's trilingual library several times.

José Esteban Alvarado de Godoy had returned from university studies in Paris fortified with notions of equality and the restorative properties of lyrical poetry. Every day he ambled from the big house where he lived with his widowed mother toward his schoolroom full of boisterous boys. In the heat of the morning sun, he sported a heavy European-cut suit and tie and mopped the sweat from his face with a fragrant handkerchief bearing his initials, finely embroidered at no cost by Isabel's mother.

At the age of fourteen, Isabel was fully developed. She was small-boned, but her breasts were full and well-defined as ripe mangos. She was not strikingly pretty, but her hips rounded from a slender waist and her thighs, lengthened and muscled by long walks, pushed against her long full skirts, their strong contours like the hill slopes. She knew that José Esteban, a bachelor still at the age of thirty, suffered the most terrible lovesickness, which she had unwittingly provoked.

Although Paula had stopped paying for private lessons when Isabel was twelve, José Esteban would not relinquish the precious time he spent with Isabel. While alone in his room, his thoughts invariably turned to Isabel as dawn slipped through the window, rustling the muslin curtains with cool air. She had a startling intellect, though she didn't have the voluptuous beauty of Concepción López de Victoria, the heiress his mother was so eager he court and marry. Concepción could take a man's breath away with her brown curls and huge green eyes, among other endowments. But José Esteban considered her beauty harsh in a way and a trifle vulgar. It was like having too many sweets at one sitting. Besides, once the woman opened her mouth, her enchantment was dispelled like the fog in the wind. Not Isabel. Her mind had no equal. There were times, in fact, when he felt that his own intelligence, dampened by lack of stimulation in the small provincial town, was no match for the young girl's ability to rapidly assimilate knowledge.

One morning in the dawn light, José Esteban surveyed the quiet street from the veranda. It was no later than five in the morning, yet already there was movement in town. Farmers drove carts loaded with fresh avocados, green and ripe bananas and plantains, and sacks of flour and dried beans to the marketplace south of the main plaza. A cart wheel squeaked piercingly and cast sparks of dust into the still air. A whiff of freshly brewed coffee awoke in José Esteban a deep longing. At a distance, the church bell summoned parishioners to the morning mass; he saw the bread women glide along the blue mist with golden brown loaves on their heads. Morning would break soon in a sudden hot breath of humid air. All he could think of was ripe mangos and hard, sloping hills.

At that moment, Isabel was hurrying in the opposite direction from José Esteban's big house. Paula was thirty-nine and slowing down with the burden of hard work and worry. Isabel often helped her with the more laborious chores her mistress imposed on her. That morning Isabel had gulped down a cup of black coffee and, loaded with a bundle of soiled clothing and a bar of tallow soap, retreated to the river, her favorite place. Isabel scaled the hill, weaving through the prickly bramble that lay low on the ground. She clambered down the other side, pounding hard with her bare feet on the matted earth, the tough grasses, lichen, and creamy-flowered mosses. She stooped under the bowers of vine and the *clusia* roots that hung from the branches of the tall forest trees and crossed into a small clearing where she sat down to rest. She gazed dreamily at the tangle of moss-covered almonds, flamboyants, and tamarinds. It was peaceful there away from the din of the constant, pompous demands of Paula's mistress. Years later, she would still hear the grating voice of *doña* Elena, who habitually called Paula to the kitchen before she changed from her starched uniform into the frayed cotton dress she wore for the long walk home, Isabel always at her side.

"Well, Paula," *doña* Elena sniffed. "I don't know how many times I have to ask you, when are you going to let me have Isabel?" Her eyes slid with ill-contained displeasure toward Isabel, who stood slightly behind Paula and pulled uncomfortably at her skirt.

"You know Isabel isn't done with her studies." Paula spoke softly, but Isabel recognized the intimation of anger in her voice.

Doña Elena sighed loudly and pressed an embroidered handkerchief to her cheek. "I don't understand, Paula, why in the world you insist on educating a girl whose role in life is to be a maid. Like you. And what's wrong with that? Are you unhappy with your lot in life? I mean, why should you? As far as I can see, you have that nice little house that we rented to you, and clothes on your back. You eat your meals here every day. We treat you more than fairly. What more can you possibly want for Isabel? "

"Something better."

"Well, I never!" Doña Elena's meager lips were ashen. Angrily, she waved an accusing finger at Paula. "You're making a big mistake, I'm telling you right here and now. Isabel is going to think she's too big for her britches with all this reading and writing with that kind-hearted *don* José Esteban. You know he's just being nice, allowing Isabel the privilege of being his so-called student. The poor dear, he came back from Paris with some absurd ideas, but he'll get over it. Just wait until he marries Concepción. She'll take care of those preposterous French notions. In the meantime, you better let Isabel start working. It'll take me years to train her properly, you know. If you wait any more, it'll be too late. And don't turn to me then for help."

By the river, Isabel shook her head to clear the image. She let her mind soar to a place far removed from *doña* Elena's barrage of criticism. She rose to the high reaches of thought. A line came to her, like a dart, then another and another, until she had composed a poem in her head. She was repeating it aloud to set it in her mind until she could write it down later when she was startled by José Esteban's deep voice. He stepped into the clearing, his eyes moist with a desire that Isabel recognized as forbidden, a desire that was worse than forbidden because it was uninvited and unwelcome. She shrank from his gaze.

"After all these years, Isabel, are you afraid of me?" His eyes brimmed with hurt and disappointment.

"How did you know I was here?" She gave him a hard look.

"I ran into your mother on her way back from the market." He shrugged helplessly.

"Well, I have to go back home. I forgot the soap."

José Esteban pulled out a slender book from his shirt pocket. "I just got this in the mail. From Paris." He brandished the cover tantalizingly. Rimbaud. Her eyes brightened, and she snatched the book from his hand. She sat on the bundle of dirty clothes and flipped through it hungrily, resting at a random page. José Esteban, the insistent chirping of a *ruiseñor*, and the forest itself fell into the background.

Le loup criait sous les feuilles
En crachant les belles plumes
De son repas de volailles:

Comme lui je me consume.
(Howling underneath the leaves
The wolf spits out the lovely plumes
Of his feast of fowls:
Like him I am consumed.)

Isabel glanced up, inflamed by the boundless reach of poetry. She was excited by the idea of consuming oneself, a notion that relentlessly clung to her thoughts. When she saw José Esteban's lust-filled face, his eyes burning with need, his lips slack and hungry, she got up quickly and brushed her skirt with a hand.

"Let me kiss you, Isabel," José Esteban pleaded awkwardly, his voice stuck somewhere in the back of his throat. "I'll give you the book." He smiled nervously. "I'll give you anything you want." His voice was like a mournful guitar note.

For a moment Isabel struggled with the possibility of choice. She looked down at the slender book, its creamy cover embossed with leafy letters, delicately tipped in red. Then she shook her head forcefully, pressed the poetry book against José Esteban's hand, gathered the bundle of clothes, and raced home.

Paula was sitting on the tiny porch, drawing bright red thread through white linen in a cross stitch, tucking in seams and pulling out pins. Isabel flew up the steps. Paula drew in her breath when she pricked a finger. She put the finger to her mouth and stood up in expectation. She knew someone else was coming, someone who had followed Isabel. When José Esteban approached, her shoulders relaxed. He hesitated for a second when he saw Paula, but he gathered his composure and politely tipped his hat. He glanced into the house hoping to catch a glimpse of Isabel, who he was sure was hiding inside.

"*Buenos días, don* José Esteban," Paula said. "Would you like some lemonade? You seem a bit warm this morning."

"Why, yes, *doña* Paula." José Esteban pulled out a handkerchief and mopped his face. "As a matter of fact, there's something I wish to discuss with you."

"*Ya me pareció*, I thought you might," Paula mumbled as she poured the lemonade and brought it to the porch on a wicker tray.

Paula picked up the embroidery she had been working on and drew the needle through the edge of the fabric. She folded her hands on her lap and waited.

"Well, *doña* Paula, this might seem a bit abrupt, but I'd like your permission to marry Isabel." José Esteban's voice was low and quick.

Paula repositioned herself on the seat of her chair, looked out at the distance for a moment, and then faced José Esteban.

"I don't understand. Everyone in town is talking about your marriage to *la señorita* Concepción López de Victoria."

"Those are my mother's wishes, but they aren't mine. I don't love Concepción."

"Ah, but she's beautiful and very rich."

"I don't care about that. I love your daughter, who may not be beautiful, or rich, but she's kind, independent, and so intelligent. Her mind takes my breath away."

Paula looked down at her lap and studied her fingers. She smiled to herself when she thought of Isabel, who had certainly crawled under the porch with the chickens to listen to their every word.

"Well, *don* José Esteban, excuse me for saying this, I know it's not my place, but I think you may be acting too hastily. You know very well that my permission doesn't matter one hoot. First, you have to talk to your mother. When you discuss this with *doña* Isaura, then you can come back to this house and we can have our talk, if you still want to." She nodded. "Isabel is the dark-skinned natural daughter of a simple servant, and her intelligence and the other things you said about her don't mean a thing in this society. Money, light skin color, and the right family names are all your family and their friends are concerned about."

"None of that matters to me," José Esteban said desperately.

"Maybe not. And I'm very grateful for everything you've done for my Isabel, but I don't think your mother will approve of this marriage."

José Esteban stood up stiffly.

"I will speak to Mamá, and I will return to ask for Isabel's hand in marriage," he said with formal conviction. "I give you my word of honor."

A week had passed with no word from José Esteban, when Padre Francisco summoned Paula to the parish house.

"*Doña* Isaura Alvarado has taken to bed with a fever. She has asked me to speak to you. So has *doña* Concepción's father, who has practically married his daughter off to *don* José Esteban with a fine dowry, I must add. The town is up in arms about this. What were you thinking, Paula, encouraging a well-born young man to marry your daughter?"

In the weeks that followed, stone-throwing youngsters pursued Paula and Isabel as they returned home from the market. Isabel fell on her knees, packages strewn on the ground, blood streaming from her forehead. Obscene notes wrapped in rocks were thrown into their house, breaking the meager dishes and water glasses they owned. The rich women who had gladly paid for Paula's exquisite embroidery stopped placing orders, and Paula was asked to leave *doña* Elena's house, where she had served for over twenty years. José Esteban never had the courage to face his society of family and friends. His marriage to Concepción at the cathedral in the most extravagant event the town had ever witnessed pitched Paula into bed. A month later, she died in her sleep, and Isabel moved to San Juan to live with a distant relative.

Chapter Three

Begin when all the rest who left behind them
... had long ago returned.

The Odyssey

Isabel and Bolivar met at La Colectiva, the two-story tobacco factory in Puerta de Tierra. After General Nelson Miles invaded Puerto Rico and changed the spelling of the island's name, it was officially named the Porto Rico Tobacco Leaf Company. The General, better known as "Indian Fighter" for his ardor in repressing Native Americans, found himself unable to draw the spare line of his lips over his broad set of teeth and stretch them out again to shape the diphthong in *puerto*. Without hesitation, he changed the spelling of the island to Porto Rico, undeterred by the fact that *porto* is a Portuguese word that does not exist in the Spanish language. So it was that in a cigar factory with a misspelled name, each tobacco worker contributed two cents a week to have Isabel, well known by the workers for her union activities, read at the cigar rolling galley for an hour in the morning and two hours after lunch. The workers met with her weekly to select the reading material by vote.

Isabel was small and had a squarish face, closely set dark eyes, and a wide nose that flared at the nostrils. Her mouth was large and sensual, her lips thick and dark. Her skin had the deep golden glow of walnuts. Perched on a wooden rostrum high above the workers' heads, in a clear and resonant voice, Isabel read from the local newspapers *La Correspondencia, El Tiempo,* and *La Democracia* during the morning session and political tracts and literature in the afternoon. The stark language of the workers' favorite authors—Bakunin, Herzen, Diego Abad de Santillán, and Malatesta—was tempered by the entrancing stories of Victor Hugo, Benito Pérez Galdós, and Fyodor Dostoevsky plus the local drama of Zeno Gandía.

Each day she opened a book or unfolded a newspaper to read as the *torcedores,* or cigar rollers, sat in rows at long tables, handling the dark leathery leaves. Every morning she openly observed handsome Bolivar as he took his position at the front bench and arranged the various implements of his trade on the table. Carefully avoiding looking up at her, he began his work when the stock boy deposited a variety of tobacco leaves on his bench.

True to the *torcedores'* routine, Bolivar sorted the leaves carefully. He kept the wrapper leaves moist and pliable by covering them with a dampened cloth. Isabel read Bukinin's piece on the rise and decline of the bourgeoisie while Bolivar smoothed a binder leaf on the palm of his left hand and filled it with long filler leaves, blending different types of tobaccos, from sweet to bitter, to reach the flavor combination required by La Colectiva.

Once he assembled the variety of leaves in the palm of his hand, Bolivar broke off the filler to the length of a cigar. He kept adding tobacco to this bunch until he had a feel for how much he needed. When Isabel paused from her reading to take a sip of water and glanced at him, she was overcome with tenderness as Bolivar smoothed the tobacco gently with a lover's caress, feeling the thickness of the bunch as he formed it and the tightness or looseness of the leaves as he folded one into the other, using a precise amount of pressure as he pressed and formed the leaves.

She closed her eyes and rubbed them with the tips of her fingers as he made the "open head" work. This was a delicate task that required the sweeter, tenderer tips of the filler leaves to be at the tuck, or lighting, end of the cigar so that the smoker's first puff held the best flavor.

When she opened her eyes, Bolivar had already shaped the filler and was placing the bunch on the corner of the binder leaf and curling the edge around the filler leaves, rolling them up inside. Isabel could see his frown of concentration as he performed this essential movement, which had to be done meticulously. She knew that the shape and form of the cigar developed and was maintained at this crucial point. The shape Bolivar had already given the filler, combined with the delicate pressure he applied while rolling the binder leaf around the filler, helped him to contour the cigar into the trim shape that was the hallmark of La Colectiva cigars.

Beads of perspiration dotted Bolivar's upper lip, and Isabel looked away. She was aware of the importance of the bunch-making stage of cigar rolling. It required great skill and sensitivity because the actual smoking value of the cigar depended on it. A wrong twist in the leaf or too many leaves crossed at one place produced barriers for smoke and flavor detectable by the experienced smoker. In a good cigar, all the flavor had to reach the smoker, and the "draw" had to be smooth and complete. A cigar packed too loosely was like a chimney with too much draft, allowing excessive amounts of hot air to pass through too quickly. If the smoke traveled too fast, the cigar would be harsh or burning. It was important, too, that the smoke travel at just the right pace so the smoker had only to puff and not pull on the cigar.

After Bolívar finished the bunch and laid it aside, he cleared the board with a swift stroke and reached under the moist cloth for the large, velvety wrapper leaf, rich brown like fertile soil. He had been working quickly to this point, but he slowed his pace; this was the most delicate leaf on the cigar and had to be handled carefully. A hole or tear would ruin the cigar's appearance. The wrapper he chose was moist and pliable for working.

He stretched it out on the wooden block with the glossy outside facing down, smoothing it with his moistened fingertips. Then he cut the wrapper to shape, long, thin, and slightly curved, with his *chaveta*, the flat, semicircular knife he kept immaculately clean and sharp. He had selected a "right" leaf, one with veins that moved out from the stem to the right, and he began rolling from the left toward the right. If the leaf had been a "left," he would have had to move in the opposite direction. At the tuck, he expertly rolled the bunch up inside the narrow wrapper in a spiral motion, coiling it around toward the other end, gradually covering the entire bunch.

At each turn, he overlapped the leaf slightly until the head was perfectly rounded, so that the wrapper covered it completely. He then made a flag on the end of the leaf, dipped his finger into a cup of clear, tasteless glue, and took the remaining piece of leaf between his thumb and forefinger, sliding on the paste as he turned the cigar and wound the flag smoothly over the head. The seam in the wrapper leaf almost disappeared from sight; Bolivar examined the cigar and carefully placed it on a pile to his side. Isabel could see that Bolivar was adept at the subtleties that *torcedores* learned through experience over the years.

He worked rhythmically, shaping and rolling, looking intently at his hands until Isabel resumed reading. Then he ventured to glance up at her shyly, hoping she would not notice his attention. His almond-shaped eyes sparkled with excitement, despite himself, and he held his lips tightly clenched. Except for a mumbled "*buenos días*" or "*buenas tardes*," in the many months she had been a reader, he had never said a word to Isabel. One day Isabel, who always took charge when events slowed down or, as was the case with Bolívar, refused to budge, decided to take the matter into her own hands.

The day Bolivar was vanquished was a day of discussion, discord, and dogs. Isabel would always remember the discussion that ignited among the workers that afternoon when she read about Bakunin's concept of spontaneous revolutions. It was a humid day, and the room was thick with the strong leathery scent of cured tobacco. The foreman Gustavo Ortiz , a tall corpulent man with a huge handlebar mustache, black as tar, strode through the aisles and between the rows of tables picking up a random cigar here and there, hefting its weight in the broad palm of his hand, scrutinizing it for size and smoothness. If Gustavo spotted a *torcedor* making a sausage, what cigar rollers called a poorly made cigar, or if he calculated that someone was not making enough cigars to fulfill the day's quota, he would hand out a pink slip. To get around this, workers sometimes bribed Gustavo, well known for the unusual practice of eating meat every day.

That afternoon, Gustavo circled Benito's bench like a hungry shark. Benito had already received a pink slip that week, but when he glanced up at Gustavo, a trace of a smile wavered on his lips. Soon after he arrived home from work the day before, Benito had selected his best layer and put her in a cage.

While the chicken squawked, he tore off a bit of cardboard from a box, scrawled a number on it, and attached it to the cage with a bit of string. This was the number assigned to him and which he had to place on the bundles of cigars he rolled at the factory. That evening, stealthy as a thief, he tossed the chicken into Gustavo's backyard. He was sure the boss would remember his recent gift when the time came to evaluate his performance. Gustavo's scrutiny now failed to unsettle Benito as he rolled and listened to the cadence of Isabel's voice, though he knew he was slower than the other rollers and his cigars more likely to be returned as unfit to box and sell.

When Isabel finished reading Bakunin's text on spontaneous revolutions, without missing a beat in the cigar he was rolling, Demetrio Castro's deep voice echoed through the large room.

"Things have to be planned, and planned right, if they're going to work! Do you think whoever built this factory didn't plan where the hooks would go to hang tobacco leaves so they wouldn't dry out, how and where the workers would sit to make us roll cigars faster and more efficiently? How about the foreman, *don* Gustavo here? Do you think the owners would have let us supervise ourselves?"

Demetrio clamped his lips and placed a freshly rolled and expertly shaped cigar on the fragrant bundle in front of him. He was a small, narrow-faced man with the rust-colored fingers of tobacco rollers. He wore a wide-brimmed hat pushed to the back of his head and puffed on a fat cigar as he worked. Gustavo Ortiz looked up from a cigar he was inspecting and scowled. Demetrio shrugged and ignored him.

Sergio, stretching out a tobacco leaf smooth as veined marble, contributed to the discussion. "What're you talking about, Demetrio? Bakunin is right. Things happen when they're ripe to happen. Most of the time, no matter how much you plan something, it doesn't come out like you thought. It's like planning for rain. Even better, it's like having a baby. When the time comes, it just pops out."

"Ah, but you're too far ahead of things," Nico responded from the back of the room, where he was setting a large stack of tobacco leaves down on the floor for the women to strip and remove the stems before they were sent to the *torcedores*. "Having an infant requires the love of a pretty woman." Nico stood up brushing the sweat from his forehead, an impish twinkle in his eye.

Carlota, one of the tobacco strippers, scowled.

"That's disgusting!" she said angrily. She pointed her knife at Nico before pushing the blade through the tobacco leaf and pulling out the thick vein. "All you men think about is that." She took a sip of the lukewarm water she had paid Gustavo for that morning and cleared her throat.

"What?" Nico asked, though he knew perfectly well what she meant.

"You know."

"No, I don't," he insisted.

"Yes, you do. You just want me to say it."

"So why are you so afraid of mentioning something natural? Do you think it's some kind of sin?"

"Who said I'm afraid?" Carlota responded angrily.

"Why won't you say what you mean, then?"

"You know perfectly well what I'm talking about. The act," she finally said, her neck and face reddening fiercely.

"Now that's a euphemism!" Demetrio shook his head. The walls boomed with his laughter.

"*Don* Carlos," Carlota said softly. Her cheeks were still red with embarrassment. "What was that word *don* Demetrio used?"

Carlos glanced up quickly. He was in his seventies, and his face was weathered as bleached driftwood. He'd been rolling cigars for over fifty years, and he was adept at looking up and rolling at the same time without missing a beat. On the table at his side, he kept the fat *Diccionario de la Real Academia Española* that he consulted when there was any doubt about the definition of a word. Everyone said it weighed a ton and warned of its potential to fall on and fracture a hapless toe.

"A request has been made to look up the word *eufemismo*," Carlos announced in his husky, smoke-filled voice. He was in charge of looking up words the workers were unfamiliar with during readings and discussions. To make up for the cigars he did not produce during this task, the other rollers contributed their own cigars to his quota.

"*Sí, don Carlos*," several voices responded. Glancing at the supervisor, Carlos consulted the dictionary and read the definition. Then he gave an example. "Does everyone understand?" He glanced around the galley.

"Yeah," Demetrio said and glanced up quickly, "It's using a nice word for something that's not so nice."

While the discussion rumbled through the room as workers vied to make themselves heard, Isabel's gaze settled on Bolívar. Her head swam when she looked at him. It reminded her of the first day she walked into La Colectiva, when the thick, intoxicating odor of tobacco had made her giddy and nauseous at once.

Bolívar's eyes were fixed steadily on his work while he fidgeted uncomfortably. Seated so close to her, he was unable to hide behind anyone, no matter how much he wanted to escape her piercing eyes. He was twenty-two years old, slim and angular. He had light brown hair and yellow streaks in his chestnut-colored eyes. His pale face was thin, set off by high cheekbones, sharp as the blades of the cane, and a pointy chin he liked to stroke on the rare occasions when his hands were idle. He wasn't much of a speaker. Isabel had rarely heard him say a word, but he listened attentively to everything that was read and discussed while he concentrated on the cigars he rolled with nimble fingers. She couldn't help regarding him intently as he "worked up" the tobacco, as cigar makers called their trade. Throughout it all, he felt the weight of Isabel's eyes on him, and his heart felt light, yet inexplicably uneasy.

Isabel sighed and looked away. She smoothed her long skirt and gathered books and newspapers into a copious straw woven bag before moving on to her other work. After reading at La Colectiva, she composed pamphlets, distributed them in factories, and attended and spoke at workers' rallies. Late at night, when the family she boarded with in an old wooden house in Santurce slept, she sat by an oil lamp and wrote the poetry she kept in a Sultana soda cracker tin under her bed.

"Well, *compañeros y compañeras.*" Her voice projected like an actor's over the discussion that had suddenly veered from spontaneous revolutions to Jean Valjean's woes.

"Why did Balzac name this character Jean Valjean?" Sergio asked. "Tell me that. It sounds awfully funny! You'd think a famous writer like him could come up with a better name."

Don Demetrio shook his head.

"Writers always give meaningful names to their characters, and I'm sure Balzac had good reason to name him that. Think about it, Sergio. Maybe what he wanted was to show how Jean lived like a mirror of himself. He was who he was, but then he wasn't. Do you see what I mean?"

Sergio shook his head, an expression of confusion on his serious young face.

"I don't think so, *don* Demetrio."

"*Mira*," Demetrio continued. "His name is like an echo, like his past life always calling to him even in the present. You're young, Sergio, and don't have much of a past, but one day you'll understand what I mean."

There was a pause, and Isabel called "*Hasta mañana*" to the workers and waved. She stepped down from the rostrum and purposefully dropped a book in front of Bolívar's post. The book fell with a hollow thud, and without a moment's hesitation, he leaped from his seat to pick it up.

In his haste, he knocked back his chair. Bolívar brought a hand to his forehead as the chair toppled noisily against Diomedes' table behind his and the older man's neat bundle of cigars tumbled to the ground.

"*Oye*," Diomedes whispered while Bolívar scrabbled on the floor strewn with tobacco shreds and nervously picked up the cigars. "Don't be so clumsy in front of the *compañera,* or she'll never give you the time of day."

In the meantime, Isabel had deftly tucked a note under Bolívar's *chaveta* and, skirt rustling as she straightened her back and smoothed her long sleeves, she strode firmly down the aisle.

Isabel usually wrote her pamphlets and articles and met with labor leaders at the gouged cedar table at the Worker's Union, but it was difficult to concentrate that day as she scribbled nervously on a sheet of paper. Her heart quivered with every clank of the printing press while she waited for Bolívar's shift to be over. She imagined him covering his tobacco leaves with the moist cloth at the end of the long day so they wouldn't dehydrate, sweeping tobacco scraps into the pouch in front of his bench, removing his long apron and collecting the "smokers," the three free cigars workers received each day. She imagined him putting on his hat and walking out to meet her.

With impatience, she poked her head into the other room where Isidro was feeding paper into the plate cylinder and rotating the printing wheel. He was a small man and looked dwarfed by the machine. Isabel touched his shoulder gently. He turned around, perspiration dripping down the warped wood of his face.

"What's this?" Isabel yelled above the noise and picked up one of the leaflets he was printing. When she finished reading, she waved it in the air like a flag.

He stopped the machine and collected the leaflets. The silence was thick and unexpected. "That's for the next rally." He wiped his wide, sun-tarnished forehead with an arm.

"What rally? How come I don't know anything about this?"

His dark eyes moved away.

"We had a meeting last night," he mumbled.

"And I wasn't notified? I was at La Colectiva most of yesterday. Fermín could have told me something."

His nose twitched as if he had smelled something rotten. "You better ask the boss."

"Who?"

"Reinaldo."

"Oh, so now Reinaldo's 'the boss?' I thought we were anarchists, the whole point of which is to do away with authority, not create it."

Isidro shrugged and turned out his ink-stained hands.

"And what is this?" Isabel waved the leaflet in the air. "It's an invitation to riot! We're supposed to be pacifists, aren't we, against violence and all of that?" She shook her head angrily. "And what is this now? What is this?" In her anger, she kept countering Isidro's uncharacteristic silence with the same question. When he spoke, Isidro's voice was hard and brittle as pork crackling.

"There's been some changes, *compañera*. We're gonna change tactics. We were getting nowhere fast with this commitment to peaceful solutions. We can't wait for the revolution to come on its own. We're gonna die waiting. What we gotta do is take it."

"Take what?"

"Control."

"Impose control, you mean. Just like everyone else is doing. So what's the difference between you and them?" Isabel sighed and pressed her lips together. She crumpled the leaflet in her fist. "True anarchists detest violence and destruction. It's not right to treat anyone violently. It's what we've been struggling against all these years. All that violence everywhere, in war, execution, imprisonment, the grinding down of the worker's natural goodness in a monotonous round of work and more work; the sexual and economic exploitation of women and children. Aren't we supposed to be against violence in all its forms?"

"Not all anarchists are your kind, Isabel."

Isabel closed her eyes and rubbed her temples with her fingertips.

"Listen, it's not as if I haven't seen this coming. I knew Reinaldo was up to something. Give him a message for me when you see him, will you, *por favor*? Tell him I'm submitting my letter of resignation to the Union and I'll be joining la *Federación de Trabajadores*. *Don* Demetrio has been asking me to join for ages. I'm not staying where I'm not wanted. Besides, you don't represent my ideals any longer."

"I'm sorry, Isabel." Isidro said before leaving the room.

Angrily, Isabel threw the crumpled leaflet on the floor. She took several deep breaths and sat down at the table, head in her hands. When she had calmed down, she looked out the window that overlooked the bay. She composed the letter for Reinaldo and the rest of the committee in her head before setting it down on paper. She felt oddly relieved once she wrote it and, with firm hand, scripted Reinaldo's name on the envelope. She propped the envelope against a ledger on the table.

As soon as she was done, her thoughts turned to Bolívar. She hoped he would be at the Plaza to meet with her. Had he read her note? she wondered. Or did he have someone, Demetrio maybe, read it for him? She hardly knew Bolívar, couldn't even recall whether he could read and write. How stupid of her to have taken his literacy for granted! If he couldn't read and asked someone indiscreet, like Nico, for example, to read her note, she was doomed. Nico would torture her with his idiotic teasing forever. Thoughts hurtled through her head. Maybe she shouldn't have been so impulsive. Maybe she should have listened to *doña* Ana, the owner of her boarding house, who had been encouraging Isabel to stand a small statue of Saint Anthony on its head so she could find a husband.

"*Por favor, doña Ana*," Isabel would cry impatiently. "I don't believe in religion, or saints. You know that!"

"*Ay, mija de mi alma*," Ana invariably responded, making the sign of the cross quickly. "How can you be so sure?" She nodded her small head knowingly. "Just think." She poked her forehead with an index finger. "What if … what if," she repeated for effect, "there truly are all those saints and archangels up there helping us out." She turned her eyes up to the ceiling dramatically. "You could miss a great opportunity. Just ask, *mija*, just ask. Those who don't cry, don't suckle, you know."

One morning, Ana had gone to the market and met a Brazilian woman, who informed her that in Brazil they first boil San Antonio and then stand him on his head. This made San Antonio's gifts more potent and was, therefore, a much more effective technique, the Brazilian woman assured her. It was the dry season, so that evening while Isabel helped her prepare dinner, Ana boiled poor Saint Anthony in the pot of beans she was cooking, to save water. Then, deaf to Isabel's protests, she pushed the saint into the young woman's hands and made her promise she would take him to her room and stand him on his head. Isabel turned up her nose when the smell from being cooked with the beans hit her. The beans also smelled bad, and they tasted even worse later that evening.

"Don't make faces!" *doña* Ana cried impatiently. "You're gonna get all wrinkled and then nobody's gonna marry you."

"But I don't want to get married."

"But you want a nice young man to make you happy, don't you? That's not against your party."

"It's not a party; it's a way of life."

"Whatever it is ..." Ana waved her hands impatiently. "It doesn't say you have to be a nun, right?"

"*Sí, doña* Ana, you're right."

"So take San Antonio, *mija*. Do it for me and for your dear mother, may she rest in peace. You don't have to believe anything; you don't even have to say a prayer, which wouldn't be such a bad idea, by the way." She threw a disapproving glance at Isabel. "Just let San Antonio do his work all by himself, *el pobrecito*."

To quiet Ana down, Isabel reluctantly agreed. She wrapped the small statue in a handkerchief, and, because it toppled over whenever she tried to stand it on its head, she stood it on its feet on the windowsill, where she hoped the fresh air would take away the odor.

The next morning, the odiferous saint had mysteriously disappeared.

Ana shook her head sorrowfully, lips tightly clenched, when she heard of the saint's disappearance.

"You'll never find a husband now, Isabel," she said with conviction, nodding repeatedly.

Isabel picked up the crumpled leaflet she had thrown on the floor, smoothed it out, and read it again. She stuffed it in her bag angrily. She would show it to Demetrio later when she discussed joining the Workers' Federation. At the moment, she itched to be outdoors; some movement might help the long and difficult afternoon pass quicker. Before leaving, she picked up the book she had been reading, *Middlemarch,* and, glancing at the title, she was reminded of Reinaldo and Isidro's lack of vision. Then her thoughts drifted toward Ana's efforts and the boiled San Antonio. She wondered whether his disappearance was some kind of omen and turned quickly toward San Juan Bay.

The port swarmed with people, stray dogs, and canvas-covered trucks as Isabel hurried through the piers. The steady clop of horse hooves on cobblestones cut through sailors' conversations and orders barked at the stevedores. A soldier held the reins of a fractious black horse. It glinted with sweat, baring its teeth. The horse's irises turned upward, flashing the bloodshot whites. Reins tightly in hand, the soldier rubbed his other hand under an armpit. He pressed his sweat-drenched hand to the horse's twitching nostrils. Isabel watched in amazement as the animal took in the odor and in a matter of seconds calmed down, allowing the soldier to mount and steer him into a brisk trot. She wished it were as easy to calm recalcitrant foremen, factory owners, and landowners. She smiled to herself, imagining Benito rubbing his armpits and calming Gustavo with his body odor.

Shreds of afternoon light swathed the muscular bodies of stevedores as they grunted under the weight of crates, barrels, and sacks. There was a time when cargo surfaced from tired fleets of brigantines, barques, and schooners, their tall timbers creaking wearily in the ocean air. The pier had seen the *Aurora* bringing in wheat and wine from Barcelona, the *Victoria* of Málaga laden with wood and hides, the *Anfitrite* bringing fruit and mail from Santander.

One of these, from Cádiz or Sevilla, neatly docked after dropping anchor and securing itself with shackles and cable, had brought the shameful cargo of Isabel's ancestors and pitched them from its dank hold. Isabel could almost hear the clank and scrape of chains on the ship's plank as she imagined the African slaves dragged from the hull squinting at the blanched sky, a greenish tint lurking under their skin after the endless voyage to nowhere.

Now purely inert cargo surfaced from a tired fleet of ships, immobile in the breeze. A bunch of sailors and dock-side vendors clustered around the captain of the *Belencita*, a Spanish ship Isabel had seen moored at the docks before. Isabel, who had a journalist's nose for incidents, approached the knot of tired men. The *Belencita*'s captain, weather-beaten but spirited, regaled the crowd with a detailed account of the dangerous journey he had endured through three days and three nights of storm.

"But there are worse fates than that," he hastened to emphasize, with the superstitious fear of those who defy the elements and live to tell their stories. The captain then launched into lively tales of Greek and Italian ships in the Black Sea, blinded by brooding fogs, laden with black caviar and salt fish from the Russian ports, which sought entrance to the straits of Constantinople, only to strike the shoals and sink helplessly in the dark night. Isabel was enthralled by the stories and would have stayed there for hours listening to the captain, but the Alcaldía clock tower rang on the hour, and she remembered why she had been hurrying to the Plaza.

Isabel sat rigidly at a bench in the Plaza de Armas, turning the pages of the book she had brought to pass the time. *Middlemarch* lay open but unread on her lap. Even Dorothea's struggle for reforms failed to sustain her attention. She bit her lower lip and glanced at the men and women walking purposefully down the cobblestoned streets that circled the plaza, stepping aside as horses, heads rising and falling like hammers, clattered through.

A small boy ambled slowly under the hot sun, selling *niñitos*, sweet bananas the size of a man's thumb, in a large wicker basket. A red and white trolley clanked and stopped at the corner. A woman, wearing a colorfully printed cotton dress, stepped down. She carried a caged hen like a suitcase, and her other arm rested on the thin shoulders of a little girl. The girl had long black hair held back with a white ribbon tied in a bow. Neatly dressed but spindly, she had the ashen look of someone stricken with *bilharzia*. The girl tripped and fell at the feet of two Spanish nuns who were rushing to the Convento de los Dominicos before vespers. Their white starched wimples were as pale as their skin, and their cheeks were sagged and lined by years of prayer and renunciation.

On the ground, the girl looked up at them with fear in her eyes and started to cry. The nuns pinched in their faces, as though sucking on limes, and glanced down at the girl disapprovingly.

When the mother put the caged hen on the ground to help the girl to her feet, the nuns pressed white handkerchiefs to their upturned noses and quickened their steps.

Isabel made another effort to read, but despite herself the print swam before her eyes, and she was unable to distinguish a word. She might as well have been illiterate or blind. Everything distracted her as she searched around her for Bolívar's familiar face. The nuns glided up San Justo Street. Her gaze followed the mother and daughter as they disappeared into one of the many alleys of the old city, when the whiff of salt air and the brackish water that collected in the gutters punched her stomach. A filthy white and black dog, ribs nearly poking through his sides, sniffed at her skirt. Isabel frowned and clicked her tongue, but the dog lowered his skinny haunches and settled at her side. She rolled her eyes to the sky and sighed.

Throwing a quick glance at the clock, Isabel dug into her purse. Dog at her heel, she dashed to one of the food vendors lining the plaza. The dog whined when he caught the meaty scent of the *alcapurria* in Isabel's hand. Isabel rushed back to her bench at the other side of the plaza, the dog whimpering beside her. She blew on the turnover, kept hot by the vendor's coal brazier. When it had cooled, she broke it in half and fed it to the dog. Then she settled on the bench again, smoothed her skirt, wiped her fingers with her handkerchief, and opened her book. She glanced at the clock and wondered why Bolívar was late.

Maybe he hadn't seen the note.

Maybe he gave it to Nico to read, and Nico, typically, made up something else and sent him scurrying in the opposite direction.

In her effort to conceal the note from the eyes of the other workers, she may have hidden it too well. Her thoughts were interrupted by something wet and spongy that seeped through her dress and soaked her leg. She leaped up, and as her book fell on the ground, the stray dog that had marked her with his pungent urine cringed back in fear, tail between his legs, ears flat against his head.

"Oh, no!" she cried, holding her hands to her head. "What am I going to do now? You wretched ingrate! Why did you do that?" She paced up and down, angrily addressing the dog, who stared at her with the fear of old whippings in his brown eyes. "I feed you and this is what you do, *sinvergüenza?*"

She bent down and shook the urine from her skirt, her nose wrinkled at the caustic smell. When a pair of shiny black shoes, gleaming like papaya seeds, appeared at her side, her heart faltered. She raised her head slowly, and, as she feared, there stood Bolívar, hat firmly in place, hands in his freshly ironed linen trouser pockets, dashing in his crisp, dazzlingly white long-sleeved shirt. He had gone home to change, she was pleased to notice. He smiled shyly and, with a dip of his head, removed his broad brimmed felt hat.

"*Buenas tardes,*" Bolívar said, his voice strong and firm. "May I help you with something, *señorita?*" His speech was stiff and formal as a starched shirt. It had the strong guttural accent of the countryside.

"Oh, no, no," Isabel responded firmly. She pointed her chin at the dog, which was wagging its tail furiously, and shrugged. Bolívar held out an arm, his handsome face perfectly composed. She gave one last swipe at her skirt and tucked her hand under his arm. When she realized that the soiled side of her skirt grazed against his trouser leg, she switched to his other arm. As she pinched the fabric and held her skirt away from her leg, she noticed that a pack of stray dogs, tracking the scent of urine, had joined them, sniffing the air greedily. Regarding the mangy pack of dogs, her drenched skirt reeking of dog piss, she felt an uncontrollable spasm rise to her throat. She tried to contain it, pressing her lips together hard, sucking her cheeks in. Her eyes watered as she finally let out a burst of laughter.

Bolívar stood still and smiled timidly, while Isabel held her sides and roared.

"I apologize, Bolívar," she sputtered. "This isn't making a good impression on you, is it?" She flicked at the tears streaming down her cheeks with her fingers, and Bolívar drew out an immaculately clean handkerchief from his pocket. While Isabel wiped her face, he examined his shoes pensively. Isabel took a deep breath and, determined to carry out her intentions, slipped her hand through Bolívar's arm, and they set out on a walk around the plaza.

Isabel, Bolívar, and the pack of dogs rounded the plaza several times. Isabel, who was never someone who waited patiently for anything, had done most of the talking, while Bolívar listened. Isabel glanced furtively and with intense longing at his long, strong fingers, noticing the way his shoulders sloped easily under his shirt, that his lean chest felt strong against her arm. She took in the scent of soap and tobacco on his skin, and she knew that this was the man she wanted. He wasn't a confrere—she didn't even know whether he was literate—but her heart thrummed joyously whenever she set eyes on him, and that feeling he aroused in her went a long way in compensating for his insufficiencies.

Soon after the dog day, as they would always call it, they became a couple. She moved into Bolívar's bright shack by the sea. Bolívar assured his new companion that this arrangement would be temporary. They would save enough money to buy a small plot of land where he would build a solid wooden house, preferably of *ausubo*, the strong, insect-resistant iron wood so plentiful at the foot of mountains where he had been born and raised. They would live happily forever, he said. She was amused by his optimism, and somewhere deep in her pessimistic heart, she was conquered by it.

Chapter Four

The sun rose on the flawless brimming sea.
The Odyssey

Isabel lived in two worlds.

In the physical world, she darted in and out of dank meeting rooms hazy with cigar smoke. In this world, she attended worker demonstrations and composed union pamphlets and articles for the workers. But often her mind detached itself from her surroundings and held onto a thought that would not let go, an idea that fascinated her. She wanted to pick at it, like a sore, like the bits of stone in dried beans. On those occasions, she forgot to eat or drink, and she emerged from her reveries famished and dry as bone.

Sometimes it was difficult for her to surface from her mind, to swim out of the deep swells and take a long breath so she could make the difficult transition into the physical world and engage a gaggle of workers and persuade them to move in a single direction.

Often in the dark recesses of the night, she woke up with a jolt while Bolívar snored softly at her side, and she worried about what would become of her. She never told him about the threats she received because of her political activism, about the harassment by her political enemies when they knew Bolívar was at work. Bolívar slept innocently, a man incapable of hurting anyone, a man of simple tastes and gentle disposition. No matter how long they lived together, she knew he would never understand the storms that raged inside her head, the worries that kept her awake.

Every evening he hurried home from the tobacco factory under the golden rim of the evening clouds, the edge of light on the rocks. When he caught a whiff of the salty air, he knew he would be home soon, and his heart missed a beat. Hungry and anxious to see his young *compañera,* he quickened his step.

After a simple meal of rice and pinto beans, they settled in the plain four-poster bed he had built for them. He would blow out the oil lamp and lay his hand on her tentatively, as though approaching a temple, a sacred place he had never felt he had a right to desecrate, but he entered it nonetheless, feeling excited and apprehensive at once. He quivered with hope and desire when his rough hand reached under her cotton nightgown and felt her smooth skin, her body compact and warm, her bones small and delicate. He curled down to kiss her feet, the instep high and smooth like the flanks of mountains, his fingers threading through her toes. As he worked the ribbons of her legs, he mumbled a wordless melody, like a seahorse singing while he mates. His lips moved up, exploring the lean surfaces of her body. When her legs parted, he knew she too was ready.

In the daytime, Isabel inhabited her other world. Most days she pecked at the small, round keys of a rusty Remington. She liked to say that Columbus brought the typewriter to Puerto Rico on his first voyage. Despite the Remington's arthritic episodes, her fingers darted deftly across the keyboard and pushed the carriage return to the beginning of a new line with a screech, while her eyes stared intently at the white paper gathering words that had moments before only existed in her mind. Her tempo was broken when a key stuck stubbornly to the ribbon as it hit the paper and she had to dislodge it with a fingertip or when a finger lodged stubbornly between two keys. She clicked her tongue impatiently while pulling it out, often drawing blood. When she capitalized a letter at the beginning of a sentence, the carriage would rise with a clank; once the letter was typed and the shift key released, it fell with a thud.

Clack, clack, clack, clack, screech, clank, thud, clack, clack, clack.

She mumbled as her ink-stained fingers pecked. She shook her head, often turning back to hit the *x* key many times to delete what she would eliminate or rewrite. Keys had to be hit with consistent pressure so the letters would be packed with an even amount of ink, making them smooth and uniform. But weaker fingers tended to hit weakly, and her *a*'s and *ñ*'s were often lighter colored than the others. Typed thoughts assumed a permanence that did not exist in hand-scripted writing, and Isabel liked this fixedness. Letters engraved on white paper, almost embossed, lent words an official air, an aura of objective facts and detachment.

Amid the noisy *clack, clack, clack,* she stopped suddenly and paced around the tiny shack. She needed a verb, a strong one that would compel the reader into action. She chewed and sucked on a segment of sugar cane until the reed was dry as hay. Then, she plucked out a handkerchief from her skirt pocket and wiped the books on a shelf Bolívar had built. Her brows furrowed with deep thought, her underlip caught between her teeth.

Distractedly, she pressed the handkerchief against her forehead, and the dust made her sneeze. When she opened her eyes, the perfect word slipped into her mind like a drop of rain. She tapped on the keyboard five times and sat back. She rolled the paper forward to read the neat, tightly bundled five-letter word. *Seize*. It looked so perfect, embossed on the thin paper, like a battle scar, a sign of courage and determination. Isabel completed the line with a vigorous period and smiled. She loved the ruthless symmetry of a good sentence.

Isabel sat in a patch of sunlight that streamed in through the narrow opening that served as a window. She lifted her ankle-length skirt over her knees and positioned herself in front of the old Remington again. She rubbed her eyes with the heels of her small hands. She was uncomfortably hot sitting in the sunlight, so she moved the chair to the side. Dust motes swirled. She sighed when she realized she also had to shift the table with the heavy typewriter out of the sunlight.

"There," she mumbled, as she wiped her forehead. A slant of light fell on the paper she was typing, and she slid her fingers across the chair Bolívar had restored. It was so like him to make her feel comfortable, to try to anticipate her every need and whim.

Often he went about his chores, replacing a worn-out board on the wall, repainting the house, sawing and hammering, without saying a word. He could spend an entire day, glancing now and then at Isabel while she ardently set forth her views with a mix of confusion and admiration in his eyes, without opening his mouth.

When she asked him what he thought about *Moncho Reyes*, the nickname given by the islanders to the American governor E. Montgomery Reilly when they found his name unpronounceable, or when she asked his opinion on the war that was raging across the ocean, Bolívar invariably shrugged one shoulder and said, "You know, *mi amor*, that I don't know about those things. I work hard all day, I come home to you every night, and I'm happy. Who wants to think about politics? All I can think about is what a lucky man I am."

"Oh, Bolívar," she would sigh. "Aren't you concerned about the oppression of the workers?"

"The bosses are working me to death too. Look at these hands." He thrust his palms out. His hands were big and calloused like *coccoloba* leaves, permanently dyed by tobacco, toughened by cuts that had scabbed over and split again. "I can't change these things, even if I wanted to. No one listens to me. I'm nobody."

"Well, it's a good thing everyone doesn't have your attitude," Isabel would counter angrily. She sighed noisily and folded her thin arms across her chest, determined once more never to speak to him again.

But then he would stretch out his coarse, tobacco-stained hands and present her with a gift, something he knew she wanted without having to ask, like the simple pine box with a hasp, where she could keep her papers and journals, and her anger dissolved like sugar in a jar of warm water. When she smiled warmly at him, grateful for his care and generosity of spirit, he wondered once again about his monumental luck, for it was nothing other than that, he was convinced, that had made Isabel love him.

Chapter Five

He went ashore and kissed the earth in joy,
hot tears blinding his eyes at sight of home.
But there were eyes that watched him from a height.

The Odyssey

I, Marina Alomar Pagán, was born on March 1, 1917, in La Perla, a shantytown in San Juan, Puerto Rico, to Isabel Pagán Quijano, the labor activist and anarchist, and Bolívar Alomar Seguro, the expert cigar roller, on a hot afternoon that predicted a long drought.

I've been given many names: Marina, to start, and *doña* Eugenia's secret name, a name I will never know, and Nana, my mother's sweet call. Names are important definers, I suppose. But often after a name catches on, people no longer remember the reason why something was called what it was. Then the bare name, the defining name, remains with nothing behind it for support, like a sheet of paper drifting in the wind.

Before I was born, my father cleared a narrow passageway that led from our shack to the ocean. After he died, it became known as Widow's Path. And I, who was always at Mamá's side until that awful day when she was killed, though I have been motherless for most of my life, always think of myself as the anarchist's daughter.

My birth was witnessed by my mother's friend and neighbor Luisa Sánchez, the spiritualist *doña* Eugenia, and a chorus of shantytown women. It was also witnessed by the scarred man.

I was registered with my father's name, though children born to unwed women were legally required to assume their mothers' surnames. But official birth certificates on the island were kind. Rather than branding us illegitimate, the certificates proclaimed us "natural." I like the designation *natural*. It conveys everything my mother believed in, her commitment to the idea of nature as good and honest, her understanding that people are inherently honorable. Remove the chains that bind them and the oppression that makes them mean and, she thought, people will be and will do good, given the opportunity.

I was born at home in a canary-yellow shack that glowed like gold in the sun.

On the day of my birth, my father was at the tobacco factory rolling cigars. My mother, Isabel Pagán, big and awkward, gripped the sides of the doorless entryway and lifted herself into the shack, determined to finish an article she was writing for the union periodical. She eased into the chair my father had found lying on its side on a slice of brown grass near El Morro Fort.

My father was always making something from nothing.

One day, he finished work early, his fingers seizing up from a ten-hour day of rolling eight hundred and fifty cigars. The sun, low and pale against the blue sky, lit the chair's wooden frame, and Bolívar could see that though it was thick and sturdy, the seat caning had unraveled and been torn off by stray dogs. Bolívar carried it home. The next day he cut some palm fronds with a machete, sliced them into ribbons, and set the strips out in the sun. Once they had dried to the color of honey, he twisted the ribbons into the long, strong cords he wove into the chair's seat.

With a swipe of her arm, Isabel pulled the paper from the black roller. She leaned back in the chair to reread the article, pencil in hand for final amendments. She was on the second paragraph when she felt a shift in the balance of the room, a shadow darkening the spot of light that had spread evenly on the table, as though the wing of a giant vulture had shrouded the house. Her heart turned over, and she was heavy with dread. A shiver ran through her when she glanced up to the window and saw a man, his face heavily scarred, watching her.

The article slipped from her fingers and floated to the floor. Arms at her sides, she looked down at the paper. It was upside down, and the words seemed like tiny black ants marching to a feast. Isabel tried to get on her feet, but her huge stomach weighed her down like a sack of iron nails. Pedro Mauleón y Castillo, face crosshatched with the scars of frenzied street fights, flung his head back and laughed when he saw the fear and surprise in her eyes. Isabel was rarely at a loss for words, but that hot afternoon, swollen with humidity, she sensed violence in the air. The harsh scent was so strong she could taste it. Fingers clutching at her thighs, she heaved herself up determined to find a stick and push Pedro's ugly face away.

When she turned around, he was at the entryway.

"What do you want?" she asked angrily.

"You and me gotta talk. Come out here. I won't bite you. Cross my heart." Pedro's eyes were filled with mockery.

Isabel glared at him. He was like something she might find under a stone. Pedro was a cigar maker by trade, but recently he had begun earning his living intimidating those opposed to the Puerto Rican Republican party. He headed *Las Turbas*—officially known as the Committee for the Defense of the Republican Party—and orchestrated demonstrations that always ended in violence. He was fearless and stubborn and that, perhaps, was what made him so dangerous. Indifferent to pain, he had no regard for his own life. Born snarling at the world, with an eerie inability to empathize, he was blissfully unconcerned with the pain of others. Heedless to the loss of lives, he felt no remorse for the many deaths he had caused. On the contrary, he was often heard at the local bar bragging about the many men he had killed with his bare hands.

"What in the world do we have to talk about? You're on one side of the fence and I'm on the other."

"That's exactly it, Isabel," he said quickly. "We should join forces. I'm not as bad as I look, you know."

"You're as bad as you act."

"You know, Isabel, I don't like the way you look at me, like you're better than me. You anarchists are all the same, thinking you're so superior because you read books and write junk people don't even bother to wipe their asses with."

"Unfortunately, we're not the same. You might want to talk to Reinaldo now. He's more involved in your brand of politics."

"I wanna talk to you. That ridiculous pacifist *mierda* that's pouring from your mouth is getting on my nerves, you know. I don't want you giving any more speeches in the barrio. *Basta ya.* I've tolerated you long enough. And this is my territory, don't forget that." His gaze slid over her from head to toe. "Don't think that because you're a woman and you've got a man to protect you I won't go after you. I'll take care of both of you. Two for the price of one. That's even better! "

Blinded by anger, Isabel forgot the discomfort of her huge abdomen and wagged a finger in front of Mauleón's scarred face. "How dare you threaten me? And leave Bolívar out of this. He has nothing to do with anything." She tried unsuccessfully to compose herself. "And who the hell are you to tell me where I can or can't speak? That's none of your damn business."

"Watch your language, *señora*." Pedro let out a shrill laugh. "And you're so wrong about that. Whatever you do is my business, Isabel, when you're working against me, telling people to rally peacefully, not to vote. That ain't getting us nowhere. We need to revolt against all those who are against us, and for that we need people with machetes and guns. It's the only way we can win around here."

"You sound just like Reinaldo! And you're not even an anarchist. Not that he's one either." Isabel smiled sarcastically. "And what are your goals, anyhow, besides putting the Republican Party into power? There must be something else."

"Like what?"

"Like money, personal power, authority—all those things you men are willing to kill for and even die for."

He ignored the comment. "The Republican Party is the only way, and I'll crush anyone who's not with me on that."

"Listen, Pedro. I don't want to get into this discussion right now. I don't think I want to have a discussion with you ever. We really have nothing to talk about. So please, just go down those steps and never, ever come to my house again."

Isabel felt a shift in the room as her head felt suddenly light, almost weightless. Her stomach bunched up in a knot, and she thought she would faint. She wiped her face and licked her parched lips before she spoke.

"Get out of here, Mauleón. Just leave me alone."

"No, I ain't leaving you alone. That speech you gave the other day against the American landowners, that was more useless propaganda, you turd. Who's gonna protect us if the Americans don't? We're gonna be real Americans soon, or haven't you heard the news? So you better get over it. They'll really protect us, you know. I mean, who else will do it? Who's gonna protect the world? Not you, with those phony Communist ideas you're always putting into people's heads." His voice sliced through her dizzy head like the swing of a machete.

Isabel trained her eyes on a blaze of scars that dissected Mauleón forehead and the tiny slashes nicking the skin under his blue eyes. With a look of intense distaste, she drew a deep breath.

"I'm not a Communist, you idiot," Isabel cried. "I'm an anarchist and a pacifist and I'll never join someone like you. All you care about is destruction for destruction's sake. It's not about the Republican Party, is it, Mauleón? It's about you wanting to be the boss, you wanting to be a tyrant so you can stomp on everyone else."

"You'll be sorry you wouldn't cut a deal with me," Pedro said angrily. "You'll be real sorry." He stepped down, dredged something thick from his chest, and spat on the ground.

After a minute, Isabel stuck her head out of the entryway to make sure he was gone. When she turned back inside, a bolt of pain coursed through the core of her body, like the poisoned tip of an arrow. Water gushed between her legs and puddled at her feet. Her knees buckled and she clutched at her stomach. She crawled into bed, face soaked with perspiration and tears. She squeezed her eyes shut as the pain surged through her in tidal waves that ripped the air from her lungs. She gripped the edge of the bed and gasped as the pain rolled along her body and crushed her. A sharp cry broke through her lips.

The sound of the wind echoed through the room, and Isabel was seized with a deeper volley of pain. Her throat was tight and hoarse, her chest heavy. She moaned, a tight guttural sound from the depths of the womb. The hot tar of pain burned her insides. She pitched with the blunt punches of hurt. The wind brought in the rotting smell of pig swill, and her stomach clenched like a fist. Thin saliva dribbled from the sides of her mouth, and she turned her face toward the wall, away from the world.

In the brief space between the sieges of pain, Isabel's mind split in two. A part of her felt every kick that battered her insides when she breathed. The other side of her, detached and in control, inhaled deeply, turned her face to the entryway, and let out a blood curdling screech that was so loud and high and full of ferocity that the shantytown pigs began to squeal with her.

At that moment, Luisa Sánchez was returning to her place next door, an old soda cracker can filled with water from the communal pump at her hip. Every day after working as a tobacco stripper at La Colectiva, she brought water home for cooking and washing. She was in her early twenties, a wide-hipped woman with light brown skin, raven-black hair curling at her shoulders, and sparkling dark eyes, wide as a child's. Her tender face was oval and smooth as a washed pebble. When she heard Isabel scream, she dropped the can and broke into a sprint. She turned the corner of Isabel's shack and was startled to find Pedro lingering in the shadows.

"What the hell do you think you're doing sneaking around here, *desgraciao*?"

"None of your business, *pendeja*." Pedro scowled. Momentarily, Luisa was taken aback, an undefined fear cut through her like a bolt of lightning in the night sky. She narrowed her eyes and rushed into Isabel's shack. Isabel was moaning softly, scraping the walls with her fingernails. Luisa's fear metamorphosed into anger when she suspected Pedro's motives. She stuck her head out the entryway.

"Get out of here!" She flicked her hair back and went into the shack. A pair of scissors gleamed on Isabel's table. She held them like a knife, missed the steps as she jumped from the entryway to the ground and lunged at Pedro's face. He ducked swiftly and grabbed her wrist, squeezing it hard until she dropped the scissors.

"Help! Help me, someone, *por favor*, before he kills me!" Luisa cried.

Neighbors gathered around as Luisa ran to the back of the shack, shoving people aside to see where Pedro had gone. She saw his white shirttail flapping as he ran toward the slaughterhouse. When Luisa dashed back to the house, Isabel let out another scream. Luisa knelt at her side, gently prodded her knees apart, and examined her.

All meaning collapses with pain, and Isabel could only feel the boulder crushing down from her chest to her thighs. A steel-white iron mass pushed against her intestines, her bladder, and she felt an overpowering urge to urinate and defecate at the same time. The mass bore down fiercely, splitting her back in half. Her legs parted wide, knees bent, feet digging like shovels into the straw-filled bedding.

"The baby's coming fast. No time to get the *comadrona*." Luisa shook her head. "I'll have to do this myself," she said to herself quietly.

Luisa glanced over her shoulder and, with a great sense of relief, saw two women who were wending their way through the crowd of women that had gathered outside the shack. Eugenia, the imposing spiritualist, was often consulted by the shantytown dwellers for everything from love potions to healing to the exorcism of evil spirits. She came forward with determination. She wore a red turban tied with a knot on top of her head and an immaculately white cotton dress. Five bead necklaces draped over her breasts. She smoked a fat cigar, and the pleasant scent of sandalwood mixed with tobacco billowed from her skin.

"Thank the Virgin you're here, *doña* Eugenia," Luisa said to the woman, who had arrived with a younger version of herself. "I think the baby's coming fast."

Luisa stepped aside to let the spiritualist examine Isabel. But Eugenia merely glanced at Isabel's protruding stomach and nodded. She turned to her daughter.

"Emilia, get the fire going outside and boil some water."

Just as the young woman turned to leave, Isabel grunted and the baby slipped out, sticky with blood and trembling. Eugenia blew on the top of the infant's head and put her mouth to her tiny ear. Softly she called her true name so that she would enter the body. The name she whispered was an occult name, the name that no one could use to harm her. Only Eugenia would ever know the baby's secret name. She brought out a small knife from her ample pocket and severed the umbilical cord while mumbling a Yoruba prayer under her breath. The baby let out a wail.

"A girl, Isabel." Eugenia smiled, her white teeth gleaming.

"It's what Bolívar and I hoped for." Isabel's voice was spongy and wet. "My little Marina," she said, and she dropped her head on the pillow.

"Get me that water. What are you waiting for?" Eugenia said to Emilia, who stood in the middle of the room gaping. Eugenia took a pinch of scented powder from a pouch in her pocket and dropped it into a basin of warm water. She gently bathed the baby while Luisa cleaned the afterbirth. While the baby lay in her mother's arms wailing, Eugenia propped Isabel's head up and tipped a tea she had brewed into her mouth.

"This will help with the pain," she whispered.

Eugenia lit a candle and prayed. She took the umbilical cord outside and buried it by a palm tree. When Eugenia looked up, Pedro was poking his head into the shack. He christened the baby with yet another name, the name she would always be called by her mother's enemies.

"So, the anarchist's daughter was born with a big mouth." He nodded spitefully. "Just like her mother." His voice was like the grating of chains, hard and relentless. "Another goddamn troublemaker, I bet."

Luisa was ready to pounce on him, but Eugenia shook her head and motioned her to stay still. The tall woman approached the scarred man, fists anchored on her wide hips. She looked around at the women who had gathered around the shack to comment on the exciting developments in Isabel's home. Then Eugenia glared at Pedro.

"You know who I am, don't you, Mauleón?"

Pedro looked at her warily. The woman's deep voice had wiped his cocky grin clean off his face. For a second, the women thought he had gone deaf and dumb. He caught himself soon enough and sneered.

"Sure I know who you are. Don't think you can scare me with that mumbo jumbo you're always mumbling. You're crazy, that's what you are. Someone should lock you up in the nut house."

Eugenia's daughter squatted in a corner and began to weep quietly. Eugenia turned to her angrily.

"You be quiet, Emilia. You hear me?" She turned back to Pedro.

"I don't ever want to see your ugly face around here again, Mauleón. If I so much as hear that you've been bothering this nice lady," she wagged a finger in his face, "something uglier than your face is going to fall on your head."

A shade of fear tracked across the scars in Pedro's face. He attempted a snicker but couldn't quite manage to shift his lips into a crooked smile. He brushed his forehead with his wrist and elbowed through the women gathered around the shack. Without a word, he slipped quietly into the hazy afternoon.

And so it was that on the first day of March, 1917, I arrived on this tiny rectangle of sea and salt. On the day of my birth I was considered Puerto Rican.

The next day, we were compelled to become U.S. citizens, and I, together with all the people on the island, became something we were not. Something undefinable and vague, for we were never full-fledged Americans with all the rights and obligations that entailed, nor did Puerto Rican citizenship exist. Even today, almost a century later, we are not a commonwealth, not a territory, not a state, not an independent nation. We are a people defined by what we are not.

Chapter Six

Here the newly dead drifted together, whispering.

The Odyssey

A lot had happened in Puerto Rico by the time I was born. The Spaniards had already been defeated in the Spanish-American War in 1898. The Americans had bombed San Juan in the north, while General Nelson Miles, who had just waged successful campaigns against Crazy Horse and Geronimo, led the ground troops that invaded the island from the south. Not only did General Miles rename the island Porto Rico, he promptly mandated what the island newspaper editors could and could not publish.

But war and repression weren't all that had brought devastation to the island. Hurricane San Ciriaco pitched thousands of people to their deaths and pelted the island with thick sheets of rain and gusts of wind that destroyed the coffee crop and the sugar cane and tobacco fields and plunged islanders further into the desolation of unremitting poverty. The faces of sunken-chested adolescents flushed with the malarial fevers that blighted the island. There was no escape from hookworm, anemia, tuberculosis, and influenza.

I was six months old when my father was conscripted into the U.S. Army and shipped to Europe to fight in World War I. The need for more soldiers to fight in the war prompted conferral of our new political mis-identity. In discharging the formidable burden of his newly imposed citizenship, my father was mobilized to the 77th Division, later known as the "Lost Battalion."

When he received the little blue card that commanded him to report to Fort Buchanan, my mother urged him to refuse enlistment as a conscientious objector. But he insisted that he would rather die in war than live in prison. She sent pleas to the governor and the War Department asking to exempt him as the sole supporter of his family. When that didn't work, she wrote to the president of the United States of America. (She never called it the U.S. or the United States or, heaven forbid, America. It was either the United States of America or the Metropolis.). But they weren't legally married, so she had no right to make claims on his behalf.

I can imagine the pitch and roll of the ship to Liverpool; the Channel crossing to Le Havre; my father's hands, accustomed to the velvet smoothness of the tobacco leaf, loading a hard British gun, intended to kill. Slaughter surrounded him as he traversed the bomb-pocked roads, throwing sulphur on the dead who had been in shell holes so long their clothes had rotted off. In the company of ruined men he camped in ruined cities, the iron ground jam-packed with horses and men stiff from the cold and the wet. He dodged German machine guns by zig-zagging through fields, crawling under barbed wire to load bridge timber and dead bodies into five-ton trucks. He slid down muddy hills, ran knee-deep in mud and frozen water while planes strafed the ground, dropping bombs around him, the air so full of dirt and dust he couldn't breathe; the noise so loud his eardrums rang like giant cowbells. Plodding through the sludge, sleeping in wet dugouts, he was exhausted as he marched in the night, lantern in hand, toes frozen in his boots. Shivering with fear and the bone-deep cold of dawn, he skirted sink holes flooded with green water and stumbled on soldiers dying in the dirt from the poison gas.

When his battalion cut the Sedan-Mézière railroad out of tangled woods and underbrush, rats swarmed everywhere, attacking the wounded, eating the dead. But that was just the beginning of the horror, the true horror that happened in that unfathomable space between the Muese River and the Argonne Forest. The place smelled badly of the dead, the woods were shot to pieces, and the ground was torn up with shells. Bullets buzzed by his ears, like a swarm of hornets he couldn't shake away. Smoke loomed ahead, and the woods looked like a terrible hurricane had swept through them. Fighter planes zoomed above his helmet when the order came to set out before daylight and take the Decauville Railroad from the Germans. He survived the gas by wearing his mask all day, pressing through the shells, ducking enemy fire. He crawled through the trenches with Lorenzo, a light-skinned Puerto Rican. He and Bolívar hadn't been sent, like their dark-skinned companions from the island, to the French Army with American blacks. When the battalion of five hundred-fifty filthy and dog-tired men reached the ravine, they slid down the mud to the railroad tracks. As they hit bottom, they were surrounded by Germans.

Bolívar shot at the red sparks burning in the wind and watched the men get gassed, shot up, blown to pieces. The enemy was powerful, swinging machine guns, pumping volleys, striking with hand grenades, charging with bayonets. The ravine was thick with the scent of blood and death. No one believed they would survive the siege, and the name Lost Battalion would always be attached to the 77th. Hundreds were killed by hard German shells. After three days of spitting fire, the dead falling everywhere around him, Bolívar was hit, not by a German, but by the American artillery that, given the wrong coordinates, trained their guns on the precise spot where the Lost Battalion fought. Dozens of men were killed before the Americans realized their mistake. Bolívar never saw the soldiers who finally saved the remaining hundred or so men. When the Armistice was signed a month later, he didn't hear the mournful French sing *Finis La Guerre*.

My mother spoke frequently of him, her voice sunken to a whisper, her face etched with deep sadness. My father's friend Lorenzo survived the Lost Battalion and came to the little house by the sea to tell Mamá what a brave man Bolívar had been. He himself had buried him on a hill overlooking the ravine where he died in the Argonne Forest. Lorenzo never told her about all the horrors he saw, but he didn't have to. Isabel had seen many animals being led to slaughter at the bottom of La Perla. She could easily imagine the terror of death in my father's eyes.

Sometimes she would stand by our bright yellow shack and look out at the other sun-washed shanties clustered on the barren slope that overlooked the sea, as if waiting for his lean frame to appear on the horizon, his large hands jammed in his trouser pockets. His corpse was never returned for burial in Puerto Rico and I knew there was a time when she believed he wasn't dead, that Lorenzo, shell-shocked and anguished, had buried the wrong man. It wasn't her Bolívar buried in the Argonne Forest, she convinced herself. Even his lifeless body could not exist far away from her. On some nights I stood with her as she waited for a sign of him. From our yellow shanty on the crest of the hill, La Perla, with its jutting tin roofs, planes of cardboard, and grid of dirt roads winding through the shacks to the sea, resembled the open mouth of a shark.

The first shacks of La Perla, built by the butchers and peons of the slaughterhouse, were close to the eastern walls of La Perla Castle, on the other side of Santa María Magdalena de Pazzis Cemetery. With the opening of the tobacco factory, waves of tobacco workers and their families moved in. When my father came to San Juan from the countryside, the lower parts of La Perla were built up, and he staked claim to a tiny spit of hardened soil at the top of the slope. He cobbled together a shack from tin gasoline cans, soap boxes, and any discarded bits of wood that he could scrape together. That's what everyone did; they fashioned their shacks with spit and sweat. Later, when he found work in the cigar factory, he rebuilt the one-room shack with used planks and a corrugated zinc roof. Twice a year he touched up the yellow paint continuously faded by the sun and salt air. Mamá always said he had been good with his hands. Except for string hammocks, some crates, and the intricate designs of spider webs, most of our neighbors had very little in their shacks, but we were the proud owners of the wooden four-poster bed my father had built. He fastened a white mosquito net my mother had sewn to a beam on the ceiling, and draped it over the bed. There were also a small table, a couple of chairs, and some shelves for my mother's books and papers.

One day after a long reading session at La Colectiva, Mamá stood with me facing the ocean. The sky was thick with gold-rimmed clouds. The wind came from the south, and we could smell the fear of the animals driven to the abattoir at the bottom of La Perla. Every afternoon at five, the shrill order to kill smote the wind, and we could hear the anxious bellows of cows, the low snort of pigs, and the faltering cry of sheep dragged to the channel at the shore of the Atlantic. Hands clasped over my ears, I could still hear the last animal shrieks as they died and the clank of pails when peons hurried to collect the blood for sausages. The animals were quartered on a cobbled path built for that purpose. Years later men would have their throats slit on that path and their bodies thrown into the sea like the entrails of the abattoir animals. I didn't know then that this very sea would also be my mother's executioner.

The wind lifted and our skirts snapped like flags as we looked down from our home at the staggered shacks on the slope, which slanted steeply into the coast of the Atlantic. I gazed at its waters shimmering like sapphires. I pushed the salt-sprayed hair away from my face and realized that even the smells and sounds coming from the slaughterhouse could never diminish the pleasure I felt when I looked at the sea.

That evening, as the sun was going down like the thick orange egg yolk, Mamá turned to me.

"Nana," she said softly. She only called me Marina when she was angry at me. "I don't think your father will ever return."

Chapter Seven

He'll make you fight —for he can take the forms
of all the beasts, and water, and blinding fire;
but you must hold on, even so, and crush him
until he breaks the silence.

The Odyssey

The morning my mother was arrested for the first time, the wet scent of dew evaporated in the sun's morning rays, replaced by the pungent scent of sea salt and brine. I was seven years old and remember it well. I sat outside on a wooden crate shelling pigeon peas, the *gandules* my mother had brought that morning from the Old San Juan market. I picked at the tiny knob on top of the pod and pulled down the silky thread that held the two halves together. In the distance, seagulls cawed before they dipped into the sea.

Mamá was at the cooking shed chopping kindling for the stove.

The sun was already pounding hard when I heard the unmistakable scuff of boots. A man's voice, deep, loud, and peremptory, rumbled through like a drum. Startled, I leaped up, and the pigeon peas in my lap scattered onto the ground. I was momentarily bewildered. *Gandules* were an expensive treat, and I struggled against an impulse to kneel and gather them into my lap again. But the commotion beckoned more urgently than the *gandules,* and I ran to press my hand into Mamá's. Her face was drawn with fright. Wrinkles like razor nicks accented the corners of her mouth.

A tall, bony policeman shoved me aside and dragged her away from me. The rest of us perspired in the afternoon heat, but he was cool as a river in his black uniform, his black knee-high boots glinting in the sun. His dark eyes were full of cruelty, and I shrank from his gaze.

I bounded back to Mamá and held on to her hand mutinously. She had recovered from the surprise and was shouting, waving an arm in the air. An icy fear filled me as my heart pounded wildly against the wall of my chest. I was suddenly aware of the barefoot women with naked children riding their hips who crowded around our house to catch a glimpse of my mother as the policemen handcuffed her hands in front of her. The policeman with the cruel eyes pushed me aside again. When I stumbled, an iguana scurried away, swishing its long tail, and Luisa's chickens squawked in fright.

Suddenly, I was petrified of our own neighbors, afraid that taking an egg from under one of their chickens or throwing stones at their water barrels were illegal acts. I was convinced they had brought the police to punish my mother for my wicked wrongdoing. I closed my eyes and hoped it was all a dreadful mistake. I promised myself never to be naughty again.

I yearned to hear them say, "Oh, *doña* Isabel, we made a mistake. We apologize to you and your darling daughter."

But when I opened my eyes, the officers were shoving Mamá forward, and she was fending them off forcefully with her bound fists. It didn't help matters that instead of lowering her head as was expected of her, Mamá fixed her eyes on the policemen with that sharp look she wore whenever she knew she was right.

"Do you think you can silence me so easily?" She shook her head and raised her manacled arms. She stumbled a few times, but kept her head erect. When she spoke, her voice was clear and hard with anger. "You can shackle my body, but not my mind or my tongue. Do you understand?"

The bony policeman let out a burst of laughter.

"Don't give us any ideas, *doña* Isabel, or we might chop off that sharp tongue of yours."

"Yeah," said the fat policeman, laughing. "And what's an anarchist without a tongue? It's all you know how to wag anyhow."

"What's going on here?" Luisa pushed through the crowd, shading her eyes from the hot sun. Her words resonated with anger, but fear hid in the tiny creases at the corner of her eyes.

"You better watch it and mind your own business, or we'll put you away too." The cruel-eyed policeman stood close to Luisa, his boots shining like the scales of a snake in the light. He stared openly at the fresh breast milk stains on her blouse.

"We might have some fun with that one," the fat policeman sneered. He laughed and grabbed Luisa's arm.

"Pig! Take your filthy hands off me, *cabrón*!" Luisa screamed and pulled away.

The bony officer let out a belch of laughter.

"All right! Give me a woman with a temper any time. Now that's a wild mare I can break in!" He turned to the crowd that had gathered around us and opened his arms expansively, his face drawn back in a smirk.

The shantytown dwellers regarded the police with suspicion. The men coughed and shuffled with a noncommittal air while the women pretended to be distracted with their children.

Tomás, who was usually found at the plaza slapping dominoes on a stone table, poked an elbow into his friend's ribs.

"Look at him, strutting like a young rooster around pretty women. He thinks we don't know about the stuff he plants in people's shacks so he can cart them off to La Princesa."

"Or get paid off with a nice fat chicken, some pork chops, or a dozen eggs," his friend nodded.

"Yeah," Tomás agreed. "Luisa better be careful, or he'll want some time with her in her hammock."

"Dead baby or no dead baby."

"*Así son las cosas.* That's right!"

"Get out of the way, will you?" the policeman yelled at Luisa. "We have to deal with this crazy *anarquista* who thinks she can break our *cojones.*"

Luisa stared at him stonily, fists at her hips.

"I'll deal with you later," the policeman said with a lizard's lazy blink.

Luisa's smooth face wrinkled with anxiety, and she reached up to touch her throat.

"Why me? I haven't done nothing." Tears of anger and frustration washed down her face. "Neither has Isabel," she added.

Mamá, who should have been more cautious given the unfavorable situation she was in, was not dissuaded by the handcuffs or police mistreatment from expressing herself at the top of her voice.

"What're you accusing me of anyway? Just tell me that. Demanding some freedom, some justice? Is what I've done that's so wrong. The values you stomp on with your boots?" She tossed back her head contemptuously.

"Shut up, I said." The policeman clenched his raised fist.

"That's the police's true role, isn't it? You're nothing but the henchmen of the government, of the rich, squeezing the people until we're dry. You shouldn't be taking me to La Princesa. You're the real criminals."

The fat policeman shoved Mamá forward. His colleague clasped her tightly by the arm as he led her away from La Perla to the main road that ringed the old city. Luisa and I ran behind them.

Suddenly, I felt Luisa's hand squeeze tightly around mine. She let out a gasp.

"*Ay Virgen María*, that's Pedro Mauleón."

My gaze darted from face to face among the throng that clustered on the road, following the irresistible scent of scandal. Even Jacinto and his crippled son, whom he drove around the shantytown in the wooden wheelbarrow my father made for him, were there. Then my heart lurched when I saw a big man, face crisscrossed with scars, who stood slightly removed from the crowd. Luisa looked at me with fear. She pressed her finger to her lips.

"Shh," she advised. "We can't let your mother know who's behind this."

"Take care of *la nena*, Luisa," my mother turned around and shouted.

"Nana, don't cry," she said to me, her eyes tender and warm. Somehow she found the strength to pull away from the policemen, and I ran up to her.

"Be strong, Nana. Don't let them see you cry," she said just before the policeman pulled out his billy club and swung. I squeezed my eyes shut and pressed my fists against my ears. I twirled with the Earth around the sun. When I opened my eyes, I cast a quick glance at the sea for consolation. Luisa's arm was around my shoulders. The last I saw of Mamá that awful day was her thin back as the police shoved her into a black car.

That night as the ocean pounded against the stone walls that contained it, I had the strange sensation that everything was standing still, even time. The sky was drained of light, and I felt a terrible ache in my temples. My eyes welled with tears of dread and unbearable desolation. My chest was tight with hurt. My knees could barely sustain me as I dropped to the straw mat I would share with Luisa's daughters Angelina and little Gloria.

I wanted to be somewhere dark, comforting, but I had nowhere to hide from my shame. For worse than the fear, worse than the terrible sense of isolation, was the inexplicable shame that burned through my heart. My tears moistened the hard mat where I tried to sleep among the tangle of legs and arms of Luisa's girls. I was ashamed of my mother, of her loud speeches, the pity I saw in the neighbors' eyes when they looked at me, how instead of my name they called me the anarchist's daughter. I saw the contempt in their eyes as they turned their faces, coiled like wire, when the police took my mother away. I bristled with shame and anger.

Why did she have to do this? Why couldn't she live happily with me without having to go around giving speeches, marching in demonstrations, writing books? Wasn't it enough that my father had died? Did she want to be killed too?

As long as I live, I'll never forget that long night waiting for Mamá to return, and I'll never forgive myself for being ashamed of her, for not understanding her courage and the terrible danger she was in. But I loved my mother more than anything in the world. She was my universe. I wanted her with me, reading a story before I fell asleep, stroking my hair gently, kissing me good night.

On that long night of my mother's first arrest, I lay on a straw mat at Luisa's and stared through the window at the sky. Angelina, Luisa's five-year-old daughter, swung a bare leg over my chest. Her three-year-old sister Gloria curled into herself like a cocoon, a thumb wedged deeply in her mouth. Julián, Luisa's eldest, was on a mat at our side. He slept deeply, and I could see the glitter of saliva on his lips. Julián was nine, only two years older than me, but he already worked at the tobacco factory hauling bales of tobacco leaves, sewn together and bundled in dry palm fronds. The four of us struggled for some space on the narrow straw mats. Luisa was sound asleep in a string hammock in a corner of the small room. I wondered whether she dreamed of the stillborn baby she had buried at the foot of La Perla only a week before.

Luisa had always been unlucky in love, the one thing she desperately sought to find. She was so lovely, her shoulder-length raven-black hair with a center part held high behind her ears with little conch combs. She was small, but big breasted, with wide voluptuous hips and strong legs. Men stared at her when she walked to the trolley stop to go to work or when she slung a can on her hip to collect water at the pump. She still kept the Whitman's Sampler box of chocolates Julián's father had given her the Christmas before he disappeared. Angelina and I loved to play with it, pretending we were rich little girls who could sit in a room called a parlor, like the Spanish heroines we read about, and munch on nut-filled chocolates all day. The box said "Merry Christmas" and had a beautiful Christmas tree full of lighted candles drawn in cross-stitches, like fine embroidery, on the cover.

Luisa and Mamá talked about Julián's father many times. His name was Alfredo Cordero. He worked at the abattoir. He told Luisa he was sick and tired of working like a dog for so little money. He planned to join the Merchant Marine so he could earn enough to send for her and the boy. Soon after making this announcement, Alfredo boarded a ship to New York. That was the last time Luisa saw him. She always became teary-eyed when she got to that part of her story, and, frankly, I had to dab at some tears myself when I saw her eyes stunned with grief and heard the weariness in her voice.

Once I overheard *don* Tomás while he played dominoes with three other old men near our house. He claimed to have seen Alfredo nattily dressed *tirando flores*, casting verbal compliments at the young women who walked by the *Alcaldía* unescorted. When Tomás waved to him, Alfredo hastily put on his hat and scurried into the nearest alley.

Angelina and Gloria's father stayed around longer, but his eye was always straying. My mother never breathed a word of this to anyone, but one night I woke up and heard Mamá whispering angrily in the dark.

"Get out of here," she said to the shadow of a man. "You're drunk, so I won't mention this to Luisa, but you better not come in here again. Do you hear me?"

"*Pero mamita*," the man responded, in a slurred, whiney voice that made my hairs stand on end. "Don't you need a man around here to keep you warm? I'm man enough to keep both you and Luisa happy."

When he mentioned Luisa, I realized who he was. I knew I wasn't supposed to be listening, so I lay quietly on my side ready at any moment to protect my mother if the man Luisa lived with got any peculiar ideas.

A few months later, Luisa was sobbing in my mother's arms.

"He got that girl pregnant, *el sinvergüenza*. And she's only fourteen! Her father came with a machete and dragged him out before the first rooster crowed. He has to marry her or else. And what am I going to do now, Isabel? I've got three kids to take care of and no one to help me." She rubbed her eyes and sniffed. "*¡Qué desgraciada soy!* I'm the most ill-starred woman in the world when it comes to men. No matter what I do, they always leave. Aren't there any decent men in this world? Or is it me? What am I doing wrong?"

Mamá drew her out of the sun. When she had made some coffee, they sat on the steps talking quietly.

"Why don't you come to one of our meetings?" my mother suggested. When she said this, I raised my eyes to the sky. It was so typical of her to always look for solutions in her anarchist beliefs.

"We could use your help, and you might meet someone interesting and nice."

"Oh, no, I'm not getting involved in politics." Luisa shook her head forcefully. "I've seen all the trouble it's gotten you into." She stood up like a bolt and smoothed her skirt. "I'm never, ever going to fall for another guy as long as I live. *Se acabó.*"

Her resolution lasted until a handsome bricklayer working at a construction site near La Colectiva spotted her. It was he, she confided to my mother when she thought I was sleeping, who was responsible for the dead child. When she told him she was pregnant, she never saw him again. No one except my mother knew about the dead baby's father. Rumors were rife throughout La Perla. Some suspected Gustavo, the foreman at La Colectiva. Others thought it was the American Protestant preacher, who kept hounding people with his bible talk.

I was stunned by Luisa's grief when she held the tiny bundle in her arms, tears streaming down her cheeks as she stumbled down the hill to the bottom of La Perla. Julián was with her, holding a small spade in his hand. I followed them, clasping Angelina and Gloria on either side of me. Luisa and the little girls fell to their knees and prayed while Julián dug a hole in the sand. I didn't know how to pray so I moved my lips and mumbled.

Mamá believed organized religion, especially Catholicism, supported the system of exploitation of workers and the enrichment of the bourgeoisie. Every time she saw a priest or a nun, she reminded me that the Church did nothing but encourage ignorance by promoting dogmas.

"Catholicism," she said frequently, "is based on social inequities."

So on that sad afternoon, as I mumbled a wordless prayer, Julián dug open a hole and Luisa held the baby up, chin lifted, her voice torn with grief.

"*¿Por qué, Dios mío, por qué?*" It was a question we would all ask ourselves after every senseless death, every instance of injustice.

We helped Julián bury the baby with our bare hands. On the tiny mound Julián sunk a small cross he had made with scraps of wood and rusty nails. Luisa's eyes were swollen, and she stared at the mound in silence. Her blouse was wet with breast milk. The children, respectful of the dead and the pain of the living, didn't speak. The wind kicked up whitecaps on the turquoise waters, and a sooty tern slashed into the waves. I could smell the warm saltiness of the sea. When I pressed my hands together, bleached powdery grains of sand slipped through my fingers. I closed my eyes for a second and listened to the waves crashing like thunder on the shore. I imagined the baby, light as the wing of a sea gull, floating away with the wind. I imagined it smiling at us from above.

I suppose that was my prayer.

After Mamá's arrest, we helped Luisa cook some rice and finish off the kidney beans that had been soaking in a gourd bowl on the table. Luisa prepared our meal in the outside cooking shed, and we sat on the steps to eat. Of all her children, only little Gloria had inherited her looks. Angelina and Julián were olive-skinned. Julián had dark, curly hair and Angelina's was blue-black, thick, and straight.

"Mami, aren't you eating?" Julián asked.

Luisa shook her head and stared out at the ocean until night fell with a thud. She was worried about Mamá, but when she looked out at the gathering darkness, I knew she was thinking about her dead baby. When we went inside, Julián rummaged through a tin can full of candle stubs. He lit one and stood it on a tin plate. Luisa's shack was smaller than ours and more spare. It was a square box scraped together from old pieces of wood, tin gasoline cans, and soap boxes. There were two small benches, a shelf with a roughly carved *Virgen de la Providencia* and an empty *quinqué*, a kerosene lamp. The lamp's chimney and the wall behind it were black with soot. We brought out two rolled straw mats and a folded string hammock from a corner. Luisa hung the hammock from the walls. Angelina, Gloria, Julián, and I unrolled our mats and fell into them.

Outside, I could hear the wheel of Jacinto's wheelbarrow squeaking. He must be taking his son out for a final ride before turning in.

"Jacinto." The sea air carried *don* Tomás' voice loud and clear through the shantytown. "When in heaven's name are you going to oil that wheel?"

"It doesn't bother me," *don* Jacinto said softly. I heard him clearly, so he must have been close to our shack.

"Well, it bothers everyone else. That damn thing squeals like a pig having its throat cut."

"But I like it when it squeaks. It's so quiet around here, especially at night, that sometimes I think I'll go crazy."

Don Tomás slammed the shutters hard.

"I don't know why he's so het up about this," *don* Jacinto said to his son. "I don't like it when it's so quiet. It makes me think."

The squeaking became fainter as *don* Jacinto pushed the wheelbarrow farther away from us.

Aníbal, *don* Joaquín's son, was born with shriveled legs. They hung from his body like wet ribbons, the feet swinging in different directions. Aníbal's mother Carmen died in childbirth. Everyone said she had been a beautiful woman, *don* Joaquín's pride and joy. While she lived, Joaquín never went out with his fellow workers at the slaughterhouse for a drink on payday. He never played dominoes with *don* Tomás at the small plaza at the bottom of the shantytown. Every evening, after long hours of butchering, he came home to press his ear against his wife's belly, to hear the heartbeat of what he hoped would be his first son.

His mistake had been not to call for *doña* Eugenia as soon as his wife fell ill. At first Joaquín believed her lack of appetite and paleness, the indifference she showed when he brought her a favorite mango glistening with dew, were the natural results of a difficult pregnancy. It was their first child, and they had no experience in these matters. By the time *doña* Eugenia had been called into the neat shack, it was too late.

The *mal de ojo*, the evil eye everyone dreaded, had already poisoned the fetus. There was nothing the shantytown spiritualist could do but pray to her pantheon of Yoruba gods and goddesses for some relief from Carmen's pain during her long and arduous delivery. Relief came with death. Carmen was gone, and Joaquín was left to witness the death of his hopes for a sturdy son and a long life with the woman he loved. Through the years, he would plead with *doña* Eugenia to tell him who the culprit was, who had blighted his child, his beautiful wife, his very life with the terrible *mal de ojo*.

"It's envy," she said finally after much insistence. "Envy is one of the most destructive forces on Earth, and it can come from anyone."

Don Joaquín spent years scrutinizing people's eyes to see if he could detect the evil power of envy in them. He never trusted anyone again.

When little Aníbal was about four, it became difficult for Joaquín to carry him around the shantytown. He had quit his job at the slaughterhouse, and my father helped him build a wooden stand with a crank-operated honing wheel. With this contraption, Joaquín was able to earn a living as an *amolador*. People came from all over the shantytown and even Puerta de Tierra with knives, blades, machetes, and scissors that needed sharpening. But still little Aníbal's mobility was a problem; Joaquín could make much more money if he were able to go to his clients.

"Your father saw Aníbal helplessly lying on a cot," my mother once told me, "and he immediately went out searching for discarded planks of wood. With his own money, he bought nails and a set of wheels and built a cart, so Joaquín could take his little boy with him when he went out." Mamá rubbed her eyes with the heel of her hand. "So much of Bolívar's goodness remains." Then she turned and hugged me. She planted a big kiss on my cheek. "But of all the goodness he left behind, you're by far the best."

Luisa and the other children slept soundly. But I lay awake listening to Anibal's squeaky wheel and the sounds of the night. I missed our house, the big raft of a bed occupied only by Mamá and me. I missed helping her wash her long black hair in rainwater. Every time I thought of it, my tears began to flow. I tried to take my mind off things, recalling the story Mamá had started reading to me the night before she was arrested. Whenever she was tired, she said that I was too old to be read to every night, that I could read to myself, but I always managed to persuade her to read to me. I loved listening to her soft voice in the night with the sweet background music of the waves and falling asleep with my mind full of people and places I had never seen, but who seemed as familiar as the tips of my fingers.

Chapter Eight

Dawn came stitched in gold.

The Odyssey

I ran down a long corridor of sand, walls of sea towering on either side of me, white nightgown snapping in the wind.

Mami, mami, I cried, and I hurried into a squat house, thinking it was mine.

It was empty except for salamanders and lizards scratching on the dirt floor. I raced down the wind-scored sand again and saw several small houses packed together. As I ran towards them, the houses became broader and taller. The melody of palm fronds rustled in the breeze.

That time I recognized the house I'd been looking for; yellow and bright like a gold coin flashing in the sun. As I ran through the house, I discovered the comforting sight of a wide four-poster bed. The flowing white sheets hid a figure beneath them.

Nana, Nana.

Swirls of cloth muffled the gentle voice. The hidden figure lifted the sheet like a parasol, and I was sheltered in its warmth.

I woke up with a start. Thunder rumbled in the distance, and thick pellets of rain fell heavily on the tin roof. Luisa stumbled sleepily around the room, cursing each time she bumped into a wall or the wooden crates used as seats. She positioned a tin bed pan on the floor to collect the water that leaked through a large hole in the roof.

She fell back in the hammock, and soon I heard her soft snores.

Lulled by the cadence of the rain dripping into the pan as the wind moaned with sadness, I drifted gently into the sounds and colors of dreams. I let go, falling quickly into sleep once more.

Nana, Nana.

My mother's dreamy call chimed above the thunder and over the rain that pounded on the tin roof, beyond the wind that seeped between the thin wallboards. Angelina turned toward me in her sleep and flung her arm across my chest. Pulled back to wakefulness, I pushed Angelina's arm aside and dashed out of Luisa's shack, soaked by the eely water, the wind roaring in my ears.

A bolt of lightning whitened the sky, illuminating my mother like a marble sculpture, hand clutching the doorway, hair studded with raindrops. Her drenched figure cut against the electric whiteness, lips pulled into a tight line, eyes shining with something I could not recognize.

I had never seen her afraid.

A few days later, I hopped down the steps. I had just landed on the ground when I saw him.

Pedro Mauleón sniffed the air like a hungry wolf. He was dressed for something important in a white short-sleeved *guayabera* and white trousers that had a knife-sharp edge. An angry seam curled like a scythe across his right cheek, and his hands and arms were tattooed with dark blue cords. His scars were more noticeable as he stood in the sun near our house, looking around as if he were minding his own business, eyes alert to every movement in the shantytown.

"Hi, little girl. You the anarchist's daughter, huh?"

Quickly, I glanced back inside the house, hoping my mother wouldn't hear. The sea churned noisily that afternoon. Maybe the scarred man would go away before she noticed, before he frightened her the way he was frightening me, with his scars, his crooked smile, the mockery in his eyes.

"I saw you being born. Bet you didn't know that, huh?"

I shook my head, staring at the ground.

"You show respect when I talk to you. Good, that's good. I like that. Not like your mother, who looks me in the eye, with no respect for a man whatsoever. You know what? Sometimes I think the problem's that she doesn't know who I am." With this pronouncement, Pedro Mauleón straightened his back and nodded vigorously.

"Where's your mother? She inside?"

Just as I was going to shake my head with all the sincerity I could muster considering the lie I was telling, my mother came up to me and put her arm around my shoulder.

"What do you want, Mauleón?"

"*Buenas tardes* to you too!" Mauleón snickered and turned his head to the sides to see if anyone was looking.

"I'm very busy, so just tell me what it is that you came here to say and leave."

"Just wanted to know how they treated you in jail, Isabel."

Although I knew it was rude, I couldn't help staring at Pedro Mauleón. The ugliness of his malicious face coupled with his scars was fascinating. From the corner of my eye, I sensed the presence of *don* Tomás inching closer and Luisa poking her head out of her doorway.

"What business is that of yours?"

"Don't you know I put you there? It's nothing but my business, or didn't you know?"

"Why are you doing this, Mauleón?"

"Because I enjoy it."

"You like telling lies about innocent people to the police?"

"What do you mean, lies? Are you crazy? You're breaking the law left and right promoting communism, telling people not to obey the law. And those letters you write for people. The devil only knows what you say in those letters. A lot of filthy propaganda I bet. I'll turn you in as many times as I have to until you see things my way."

"That's never going to happen, so don't waste your time."

That's when he pulled out the gun.

I stared right into the barrel, a shiny black hole that seemed to go on forever. Luisa let out a scream, and dogs began to bark in the distance. My mother did not move. I was so scared, neither did I.

"How about if I put a hole in your head? Or that daughter of yours, huh?"

I remember vividly my mother's arm tensing across my shoulders, slipping down to my hand and tugging at me. Slowly, almost as if she were dancing a bolero, my mother turned, positioning me in front of her, her back toward Mauleón. Without a word, she pushed me gently up the steps into the house. I don't know how I managed to make my legs move that unfathomable distance between Mauleón's gun and our house.

Once I was safe, my mother turned around. Mauleón was still pointing the gun at her, a frightening smirk on his face.

"Don't you ever threaten me or my child," she said and went into the house.

It must have been six in the morning when I opened my eyes and looked toward Mamá, as I always did first thing after I woke up. She was lying next to me moaning, a wet rag soaked with witch hazel on her forehead, arm thrown across her eyes. With the gradual clearing of the sky, I heard the last notes of the *coquís* before their diurnal silence. Those few moments of silence were

73

broken by the insistent chirp of invisible *pitirres*, deep in the thick fronds of yagrumos and cocoteros. I knew their chatter would strike Mamá like a sledgehammer and wished they would stop.

Huge gray clouds lay low on the horizon and contrasted starkly with the silvery sheen of the sky. The ocean's dark blue waves rolled to shore with a low murmur. The day, different from the sudden fall of night, took its time to unfurl its light over the world. Houses were sharp against the gathering luminosity of dawn, their colors defined, planes stark in the light. Palm tree fronds swayed gently with the breeze as the clouds whitened, the pale light from the east turning into a bright yellow glow through the clouds.

Mamá moaned.

I rushed to *doña* Eugenia's. She was the only one who could help Mamá with her headache. Deep herb aromas wafted along the path, so I knew that Eugenia was already up. She was in the brown patch in front of her small house wielding a bundle of dried herbs in her hand. As she waved the fragrant wand in the air, embers glittered on its tip. *Doña* Eugenia breathed in the smoke that curled in its wake and passed the herbs around her body while she mumbled prayers. I waited respectfully for her to complete her ritual, feeling lifted into the air by the intensity of sage and lavender.

When she finished, *doña* Eugenia lit a cigar, and with a half-closed eye, she waved for me to come forward.

"*Doña* Eugenia," I said breathlessly. "Mamá has another migraine. Please come and help."

"*Ya mismo, mija.* Go back home and I'll be there in no time. *Vete con Dios y las once mil vírgenes.*"

That phrase almost made me stop in my tracks. Who were these eleven thousand virgins that *doña* Eugenia was always talking about? I made a mental note to ask Mamá as soon as she felt better.

Silently, I hovered around Mamá, helplessly bringing water to her lips, soaking the rag with witch hazel when it dried out. I knew sound magnified and pounded painfully inside Mama's head.

Doña Eugenia arrived, cigar clamped firmly in mouth, wielding a leather pouch full of miracles. She rubbed oil on an annatto leaf and stuck it to Mamá's forehead.

"The leaf will dry out and become powder. We'll brush the powder away and your headache will be gone."

Then she brought Mamá's feet out from under the sheet and, standing at the bottom of the bed, put her hands on the arches. She closed her eyes and held Mamá's feet for a long time. My mother fell into a deep sleep, as if someone had given her a narcotic. I could tell because her eyes were tightly closed and her lips slightly parted. *Doña* Eugenia moved her large hands from Mamá's feet to her knees, the hips, belly, chest, and finally her head. At every point, *doña* Eugenia held her hands for a long time, her eyes closed as if she were listening to a voice deep inside her. I was very quiet. Somehow whatever it was *doña* Eugenia was doing had reached me. It was so peaceful and still in the room, I wished I never had to leave it.

Julián poked his head inside and startled me when he spoke.

"*Buenos días*, Nana." Quickly, he surveyed the scene. "What's wrong with your mother?"

"Migraine." I whispered and fanned my hand in the air to indicate that Julián should lower his voice too. He nodded and with a gesture asked me to step outside. He squeezed my arm with urgency.

"*Don* Celestino told me to find out what happened. She's supposed to give a speech at the workers' rally soon."

"I know, I know, but what can I do? She's really sick. She even threw up." I shook my head morosely. "I don't think she's going to make it, even with *doña* Eugenia helping out."

Julián poked the dry dirt with his toe, looking dejected and concerned.

"Where's Luisa?" I asked, surprised that she hadn't come by as she usually did in the mornings.

"She's at the rally already. Everyone from La Colectiva's there, even the foreman. Lots of policemen too."

Julián and I stared at the distance, trying to find a solution to this problem in the wide expanse of the sea or maybe the fat clouds that sat on the horizon, when *doña* Eugenia called. We rushed in. Mamá sat at the edge of the bed. *Doña* Eugenia was brushing off the annato powder from her forehead and placing it carefully in a white handkerchief.

"We don't want this to fall on the floor and give someone else your headache. I'll get rid of it now," she said. "No sense bringing any more pain into this world."

"Thank you, *doña* Eugenia."

"May God be with you."

Mamá combed her long hair with a conch comb and pinned it back in a tight bun.

"What're you doing, Mami?" I could barely contain myself. "You can't go to that rally. You're sick!"

She turned her head gingerly, holding her hands to her ears. "Don't shout, Marina, please. Do you want to give me another migraine?"

I lowered my voice just enough to keep a hint of concern in it.

"You're going, aren't you?"

"I have to." She turned to Julián. "What's happening now?"

75

"The speeches started. *Don* Celestino wants you to get there pronto before people start leaving. They all came to listen to you, he says."

"Can't disappoint my fans, then, can I?" She grasped the bedpost and heaved herself up. She closed her eyes and settled her body to the ground.

"Thanks to *doña* Eugenia, the pain's gone, but I still feel a little weak."

"Do you want some water, Mami?"

She raised her hand and shook her head slowly. "Nothing can pass through these lips until after the rally."

She looked around, pale and drawn but determined.

"Where's my umbrella, Nana?"

"I'll get it."

When we stepped out into the blazing noon sun, Mamá stumbled, and for a moment Julián and I thought she would fall. Julián held her arm, and I waited for her to unfurl the umbrella and then held her other arm. Slowly we made our way out of La Perla to the main road that would lead us to the Plaza Colón. I was now holding tightly to her elbow and felt how with each step she seemed to get stronger, her gait faster and livelier. By the time we reached the plaza, she had recovered the usual bounce in her step.

A few men turned around and recognized her as we reached the edge of the crowd.

"*Aquí está*, she's here," they whispered and moved aside to let her pass.

Mamá snapped the umbrella shut and handed it to me. With a faint smile, she waved at the people and slowly climbed up the wooden steps of the temporary platform. A cordon of policemen surrounded the crowd. Others were stationed at the front corners of the platform, and at least a dozen formed a line behind the speakers' seats. The shifty glances of some demonstrators warned us that there were plainclothes policemen pretending to be workers among the crowd.

Four men and a woman sat at the platform, wiping the sweat from their faces with big white handkerchiefs. An older man was addressing the crowd through a loudspeaker in a low, ponderous voice. His speech was coming to a conclusion now that Mamá had arrived. People waved white and red Federación de Trabajadores flags and shouted "*Viva el trabajador. Abajo la injusticia*" (Long live the worker. Down with injustice). *Don* Celestino promptly got up and extended his big hands to quiet the crowed.

"*Compañeras y compañeras*," his deep voice thundered, and everyone became still, listening carefully. "In solidarity with the workers struggle at La Colectiva, we have the honor of presenting *la compañera* Isabel Pagán, relentless worker, labor organizer, author, and anarchist, who will address us with her words of wisdom."

Those who knew *don* Celestino were aware of his ability to grab a loudspeaker and drone on for hours, enjoying the sound of his own voice. To avoid any further delay to Mamá's speech, a voice rose above *don* Celestino's, then others joined in the chant:

"Isabel! Isabel! Isabel!"

When they managed to drown *don* Celestino's stentorian voice, he was forced to shout to be heard over the chanting crowd.

"Well, I see you are impatient, and I can't blame you. Without further delay, on this very important day, I am proud to present *la compañera* Isabel Pagán from the Federación de Trabajadores to address the workers."

The sound of clapping and yelling was deafening. I looked up at Mamá as she approached the microphone. Her smile was radiant, her eyes luminous and clear. The migraine had been vanquished. My neck hurt as I looked up at her, my mouth open in amazement. Julián, who had been fidgeting throughout *don* Celestino's introduction, now stood still, eyes wide as saucers, gazing up at Mamá adoringly.

"*Compañeros y compañeras*," Mamá began softly, and like a wave, the crowd pressed forward to hear her every word. "Today we are assembled here to demonstrate to the owners of La Colectiva, through their lackeys," at this point she threw a look of disdain in the direction of Gustavo and the other foremen who hovered uncomfortably at the periphery of the platform, "how strong we are. That without the workers, they are nothing." Her voice was like the murmur of flowing water.

Wild applause thundered and strong voices cut through the air.

"*¡Arriba los trabajadores!*"

Mamá waited a few seconds for the voices to peter out, the faint echo of applause still in the air. Julián craned his neck and wobbled on the tips of his toes so he could see better.

"We can't allow the payment of starvation wages any longer. For there is no freedom if one class of men can starve another with impunity. We all want freedom, don't we?" She looked around at the crowd; her eyes seemed to focus piercingly on every upturned face. The crowd was with her.

"*Sí, libertad ahora*" (Yes, freedom now).

"Well, how can we have freedom, I ask you, when the rich man violates our freedom with his freedom to sentence the workers to life or death?"

When the cries and yelps died down, she continued.

"Are the rich owners willing or even able to harvest the tobacco leaves, transport them to their drying sites, pierce the central veins of the leaves with fine threads, and then hang them to cure? Can they ferment them turning each one constantly, taking care not to damage the delicate leaves, with just the right amount of moisture and light? You tell me, can they?"

"Nooooo!!"

"Can the owners collect the tobacco from the farms, bale and transport it to the factories?"

She paused and looked around at the people shaking their heads, throwing clenched fists in the air.

"Can the owners do what our *compañeras* do so well, rolling up the large leaves with one hand and stripping out the vein with the other, day in, day out, flicking their wrists beyond the pain? And when they get thirsty, do the owners have to pay for the water they drink as the tobacco strippers do?"

This comment brought out the fury in the crowd, and a howl of disapproval coursed through the plaza.

"Are these absentee owners capable, I ask you, of sitting for hours and hours like our compañeros the *torcedores* do at long, hard work tables, meticulously selecting the right filler to be placed in each cigar, judging with a glance the coloration and bouquet of the leaves? Can the owners roll the filler, select the proper broadleaf, chosen for elasticity and brightness, and wrap the perfect cigar? Could the owner do this in two minutes? Could the owner do this over two hundred times a day?"

"So *compañeros y compañeras*, are the rich owners capable of taking those perfectly grown and cured tobacco leaves and cutting and rolling them into fragrant cigars that are sold in the Americas, in Europe, all over the world."

"¡¡*Noooooo*!!!"

"Then who does all this work?"

"We do!!"

"What happens if you don't do the work?"

"¡*Nada!*"

"Without your work, will the owners be able to amass riches?"

"¡*Noooo!*"

"Do they need you more than you need them?"

"¡*Síii!*"

"So, isn't what they're doing to you a gross injustice?"

"¡*Síii!*"

"Isn't it time you got paid what you deserve?!"

"¡*Arriba el trabajador!*"

Mamá's voice was now barely audible. The crowd had to strain to hear her, and the people pressed forward hungrily. The softness of her voice lulled them into an oasis of serenity and strength.

"All right then. Put your arms down now. Let them hang there. Let me see your *brazos caídos*, your idle arms. Let those precious arms remain immobilized by this terrible injustice you won't tolerate any longer." Slowly, her voice rose like a siren in the fog until the pitch was high and reached every corner of the plaza. "No work, *compañeros y compañeras*, no work, I repeat, without fair compensation!"

The crowd went wild. Men used empty crates as percussion instruments and beat insistent rhythms that sounded like the call of the ocean. Others pierced the air with whistles sharp as the cry of birds. Women and children danced and chanted like revelers at the Fiesta Patronal de San Juan. Julián and I stared up at the platform, where Mamá looked out at the human wave and smiled from ear to ear.

Chapter Nine

My child, what strange remarks you let escape you.

The Odyssey

I lingered at the school gate, looking back to see if Mamá would change her mind and come back to get me. She was off to another one of her rallies, and I wanted to go with her. Her anarchist activities had stepped up. I was concerned about her. Everyone was talking about a famous physician from Italy who said that anarchy was a disease. They were saying that the cure for it was to seize every avowed anarchist and commit him or her to a mental hospital. It was in all the newspapers, and I heard my mother's friends talking about it at the meetings.

With renewed vigor, I stepped up my campaign to go with her. I invoked every threat I had heard leveled against the anarchists, including the Italian doctor's. But on a school day she wouldn't hear any excuses I could muster. She walked with me to the school gate on her way to the trolley, a large bag slung over her shoulder, long skirt billowing in the breeze. Thank goodness, she wasn't wearing any of her harem skirts or, worse, men's trousers. The other kids would never let me live that down.

I liked school well enough, but sometimes it could be a drag. Compared to the books my mother gave me to read, the stories she told me, the conversations she had with her anarchist *compañeros*, most of our teachers were sleep-inducing. When Mamá and I walked past beautiful Central High School, the school I hoped to attend some day, I gazed at it longingly. When I looked at the beautiful white stairs leading up to the secondary school, its imposing Greek columns holding the large school in position, my heart ached with delight and anticipation as I thought about all the things I could learn in such a beautiful place.

In the meantime, the old Spanish soldiers' barracks at San Francisco and Luna Streets that had been made into a grammar school, with its drab gray walls peeling at the seams, would have to do.

"Hey, Marina, get over here!!" My best friend Juanita was trying to capture my attention. As I walked towards her, I could see that she was hiding something behind the skirt of her sky-blue uniform.

"What's that?"

"What?"

"What you're hiding."

I was a little exasperated with Juanita's dull game. She could be terribly immature sometimes, turning her head from side to side so her braids flicked against her cheeks. Just as I was about to turn around, overcome by boredom, she sensed my impatience and held her right arm out. With a smug look on her face, she revealed a gleaming bullet on the palm of her hand.

"Where did you get that?"

"My father had it."

"Did he give it to you?"

"Of course not, *zángana*. If he knew I had it, I'd be in big trouble."

"Where's the gun, then?"

"That's the strange thing. There's no gun. I looked all over his things and couldn't find anything else. Not even another bullet." Juanita frowned and put the bullet in her pocket.

"Maybe he found it on the street," I shrugged. The bullet story wasn't as interesting as I had hoped. "Or maybe he shot someone with it." I became excited and smiled broadly. "But what did he do with the gun?"

"*A lo mejor*, maybe." Juanita dragged this out as if I were dumb. "He shot someone and threw out the gun, and this bullet is a replacement bullet he kept just in case he missed."

"Guns have lots of bullets." I ventured into a topic I knew very little about.

"How do you know?"

"I read about Geño Bicicleta, you know," I offered knowingly.

"Who's that?"

"You know, the man who rode by some people on a bicycle and killed them. He shot his gun six times, one after another, without reloading, the article said!"

"Oh." Juanita was despondent.

"But listen, Juanita. I bet what happened was that your father shot a villain who was trying to rob a beautiful lady, and he just wanted to keep one of the bullets as a souvenir." I nodded vigorously as the story unfolded in my mind. "He threw away the gun, but to always remember how he had taken care of the villain, he removed a bullet. Whenever he looked at that bullet, he would always remember his courage."

I was beaming self-complacently, not realizing that Juanita was staring at her shoes.

"What's the matter?"

"My father's a good man. He'd never kill someone. We shouldn't say things about him."

"I'm sorry, Juanita. You're right, but we were just having fun, making things up."

Luckily, the bell rang, and we rushed to class. The school day began with its usual routines. *La señora* García examined us from head to toe as we entered the classroom, making sure our uniforms were clean and pressed, our black shoes polished to a shine, our scalps free of lice. It was our daily inspection. Not long after she had checked the attendance rolls and we had settled into our science lesson for the day, the oddest thing happened. To this day, I have no explanation for it.

I sat in the second row, next to Juanita. Juan Suria was in front of me. Sometimes I got distracted staring at the large flap-like ears that protruded, like bat wings, from his head. *La señora* García was drawing planets on the board and talking about orbital revolutions. Juanita stared, mouth agape, pulling at one of her braids. This was her favorite subject. She often talked about going to a famous university in southern Spain, where the Moors had great astronomical observatories, and becoming as good an astronomer as anyone. She was further inspired by *la señora* García's story about Ana Roque de Duprey, a woman who had been born in Aguadilla in 1853. By the age of three, Ana Roque could read, write, and solve arithmetic problems. At nine she finished school and at eleven became a teacher. When she was informed that there was no textbook available to teach geography, she wrote one. She also wrote a book on botany and many other books, articles, and pamphlets, including thirty-two novels.

But Juanita was not even mildly impressed by these accomplishments. What impressed her the most was that Ana Roque was the only woman in all of Puerto Rico who had a telescope on the roof of her house. As a result of her research in astronomy she was made honorary member of the Astronomical Society of France. She was the first woman in Puerto Rico to accomplish many other significant achievements, but Juanita couldn't stop talking about Ana Roque de Duprey's ownership of a roof-top telescope.

The teacher turned around, and just as she did, Juan Suria stuck a finger in one of his huge bat-wing-like ears.

"What're you doing?" Señora García pointed at Juan Suria, wielding her chalk like a whip handle.

And poor Juan Suria, instead of promptly removing his finger, sat there, struck with surprise at the teacher's assault, paralyzed with fear, finger firmly secured in his ear.

A wave of hilarity surged from my stomach to my chest. I placed one hand on my mouth and the other on my stomach, but these attempts to control myself couldn't stem the explosion of laughter that burst through my mouth. Señora García scowled. Juan Suria turned around, finger wedged in his ear. This had the unfortunate consequence of inducing even more paroxysms of laughter. I struggled out of my seat, heaving. My stomach hurt by then, but I couldn't stop laughing, even when I heard señora García's shrill voice scolding over the peals of my laughter.

Then I heard Juanita begin to giggle, and I knew that I was doomed. I bent over, wheezing. When I looked up and saw Juanita's face, contorted and shiny with tears, a reinvigorated wave of mirth afflicted me. Señora García stomped out of the room, threatening to bring the principal in, but that did not deter the other girls, one by one, from breaking out in seizures of laughter. When the principal arrived, all forty of the boys and girls in the class were rolling around the floor, clutching at our aching stomachs. Whenever I opened my eyes, the sight of a student's face gleaming with tears and perspiration would set me off again. Even Juan Suria laughed.

"What is the meaning of this?" El señor Rodríguez stood in the middle of our merry mayhem, frowning. His large black eyes narrowed angrily. I glimpsed señora García's white sandals behind his trousers. "Get a grip on yourselves. Get up from the floor this minute. What in the world has gotten into you today?" He and señora García pulled at our arms and thrust us against the desks that had been knocked down.

Our collective laughter subsided, and there came a lull.

Thank heavens, I thought, *this is the end of it.*

I clutched at my aching ribs. Something inside me hurt like the devil, but the moment I looked up into one of my classmate's faces or saw Juan Suria, who was to blame for all of this with his huge bat-wing ears, the heavy laughter would swell inside me and explode. Again and again, we kept setting each other off into volleys of laughter. We were screeching with hilarity and stomach ache.

Then, the principal made a fatal mistake. Rather than containing the attack in the classroom, he ordered señora García to herd us into his office so he could take care of the matter.

As we stumbled down the corridor, hands pressed firmly against our mouths, giggling softly, señor Rodríguez, who was several steps ahead of us, exclaimed, "This is a disgrace! In all my years as an educator, I've never seen anything like this."

For some reason, the way his large shoulders were set so stubbornly on his back and the heavy swing of his buttocks as he hurried down the corridor ahead of us reminded me of a rhinoceros. I'm sorry to say that fresh peals of laughter were unavoidable at that point, and my other classmates, inevitably, followed suit.

Students in other classrooms heard the raucousness, and their paroxysms of laughter joined ours and rolled through the school. Every single one of us, without exception, was affected, and no amount of threats or entreaties could stop us. We were sick with laughter, and the affliction was highly contagious. We could hear laughter ringing through the corridors in tidal waves. After futile attempts to break the contagion, señor Rodríguez closed the school for the day and we were sent home.

I still don't know how I made it home. Every muscle in my body ached. My throat felt as if it had been rubbed with the hottest chili peppers. I was relieved that Mamá wasn't home from the rally yet. Maybe I could control myself before she returned so she didn't have to know about the disturbance I had incited.

That long afternoon, I forced myself not to think about Juan Suria's bat-wing ears. I wished that in his travels Odysseus had suffered an attack like mine, caused by an evil sorceress determined to destroy him. Then I could learn from his experience and find an antidote to my sickness. Despite the uniqueness of my situation, I read from *The Odyssey* anyway, for solace. Soon I was immersed in Odysseus' conflict with Polyphemus. When I read the part where the cyclops reached out, picked up one of my hero's men, and crammed him into his mouth, I was quickly sobered.

Until the next day.

The moment I passed through the school's wrought iron gate and saw Juanita laughing with two other girls, I was like one possessed. In no time, all the students, even the little first graders, gathered around the shingled trunk of the old *ceiba* and laughed so loudly and relentlessly we weren't allowed into class. After a few hours, we were sent home and the school closed again. By the time I reached the house, I was only giggling slightly, but Mamá had already heard the news.

"What is going on in school, Marina?"

"I don't know, Mami, it's like a sickness. The moment I get to school and see one of my friends, I start laughing and can't stop. We all do."

Mamá frowned and stared at me, trying to decide whether this was a ruse to get out of school. Her thick eyebrows were drawn into a seam.

"Mami, I swear I can't bear laughing any more. My belly hurts so badly, even my ribs. Imagine!" I said this in earnest, and my mother believed me.

"Well, I guess we'll have to wait until it passes, like a fever."

The school closed for the rest of the week. When we returned on Monday, to my relief everything was back to normal. I didn't laugh once, even when I reluctantly glanced at Juan Suria's ears.

Chapter Ten

*From every side they came and sought the pit
with rustling cries; and I grew sick with fear.*

The Odyssey

Things became too serious anyway. Mamá continued her work spreading the message of pacifist anarchism, and, unbeknownst to us, her enemies planned to square accounts with her. It was early afternoon, and she had finished cleaning. I grew suspicious because she was in an inordinately good mood, humming under her breath and attempting a few dance steps as she swept the floor with the palm frond broom. She was never this lively on a Sunday morning unless she was up to something. If she was, I suspected it wasn't something I would be pleased with.

"Aren't we lucky to live in such a tiny house?" she said. Her voice resonated like fresh water from a spring. "All we have to do is wipe the floor and dust the books. Then we can spend our time on important things."

I knew there was a point to what she was saying. She always had a point to make, a lesson to teach. So I was not entirely surprised when she announced her participation at a worker's strike. Not La Colectiva strike, which was nearby, but one that was far from home.

"You'll be staying with Luisa," she announced with a smile. I burst out crying and fell on the floor, thrashing in a fit of desperation.

"Marina, *por favor!*" she said, her voice choked with frustration. "You know children shouldn't go to strikers' marches."

"Why not?" I stamped a foot and squinted hard until purposeful tears rolled down my cheeks.

She didn't want to admit the march was dangerous, but she wouldn't lie to me either.

"It's a big crowd with lots of angry people. No one knows what can happen in that situation. You can fall and someone can step on you. That's why it's not a place where children should go."

"I know what happens," I said petulantly. "You're giving a speech and everyone's going to yell and get angry. You're the one who makes them angry! And then the police get mad at you and they put you in jail for making other people angry." I dove into the big bed; this time my tears were genuine. "And I'll never see you again."

"Oh, Nana, please understand." She sat at the edge of the bed and stroked my hair. "You'll be bored to death listening to speeches, especially mine. It's the same speech I gave yesterday. You don't want to hear that boring speech again, do you?" I could hear the lightness she tried to suffuse into her voice. "Wouldn't you rather stay at Luisa's and play with Angelina? Show her that nice book I got you for your birthday last year?"

It was *The Odyssey*, the beautifully illustrated book I was never too tired to look at or read, even though I had it for so long. Every morning before going to school, I brought it down from the shelf and spread its pages out in front of me. Odysseus stood valiantly at the red prow of a ship that pitched and rolled in the wild and uncontrollable waves of a ravenous sea. Or he struggled, muscles tense with pain, to escape the six-headed lizard. Or he turned his back on Circe in search of the Dog Star, in search of his home. Odysseus was the first man I ever loved.

When my mother mentioned the book that morning, the thought of it gave me a bolt of pleasure. The anticipation of reading it out loud to Angelina while she stared at me, wide-eyed, taking in every word I breathed was, frankly, quite enticing. Even little Gloria might enjoy the pleasures of my splendid reading. Luckily, I caught myself before revealing that I had almost weakened.

"No, no, no!!" I squeezed my eyes shut and pressed my fists to my ears. I wouldn't let her get to me with her wiles, her sweet words of consolation.

"Well, Marina." She rose and shook her skirt out. When she called me Marina, I knew I had lost. "Kick and scream all you want, but you're staying with Luisa for a couple of days. I'll be back from Yauco on Wednesday. I promise."

"Don't promise me anything. I know what's going to happen. You'll end up in jail and I'll never see you again," I repeated for emphasis.

Just as she stepped toward me, a troubled look crossing quickly over her face, we heard the roll of drums, the surge of a trumpet, the rumble of a trombone. At intervals, we could hear the scratch of maracas and a cowbell resonating dully. A voice rose over the music. The stridency of the vocal flights and slides increased as it came closer. At first, we found it difficult to unravel the words. The voice pushed forward hard and unforgiving, skipping around the beat like a tired boxer. Other voices mingled with it, chanting and singing. As the loud voice advanced, its brutal push tore into the deepest recesses of my head. The sharp edge of sarcasm in its tone frightened me. Sensing my fear, Mamá opened her arms and then held me close to her heart. Soon we could decipher the insistent harangue, rude and mocking. We rushed to the entryway in time to see Pedro Mauleón y Castillo, his blue eyes flashing as angrily as the scars on his body, marching toward the main road, two policemen dancing with the band behind him and a bunch of followers repeating the refrains: "Long live the people's rights" and "Down with the despots."

The followers proudly held up a portrait of President Theodore Roosevelt, donning a wide navy blue tie and sporting an unruly moustache that drooped toward his chin. I shivered when I thought of all the disgusting things that might cling to that moustache. Instead of *el Presidente*, my mother always called Roosevelt *el imperialista supremo*.

Pedro's jacket had been torn into shreds. His plaid trousers were dirty and too large for him, held up with green suspenders wide as a man's hand. A clown's red wig covered his dark hair. A hastily scrawled sign was pinned to his back.

"*¿Qué pasa?* What's going on here?" Luisa huddled close to us, tightly grabbing Angelina's hand, little Gloria hitched on her hip. Julián inched toward me and put an arm over my shoulders. "Why's Mauleón dressed like a nut?"

Luisa pointed at Mauleón's back and squinted. "What does that sign say?"

"*El loco de Caguas*. The crazy man of Caguas," I read over the cold brass of the trumpet that lifted high above the drums.

"Who?"

"He's saying that Luis Castro is a crazy man," my mother responded, shaking her head. She shifted her weight like a bamboo leaning in the wind.

"Who's Luis Castro?"

"A journalist at *El Diario*. He just published an article criticizing not only the Republican Party, but President Theodore Roosevelt too."

"*Eah rayo*, we all know that's Mauleón's god," Luisa laughed.

"That's right." Mami's face contorted, and she pressed her lips tightly together. She didn't see the humor. "This doesn't look good."

Luisa became serious. "Yeah, Mauleón's a dangerous man. I'll never forget what he did to you. Even Eugenia couldn't get him off your back."

I was reflecting on this, ready to ask Mamá what Mauleón had done and in what way the barrio spiritualist was involved with him, when the two dancing policemen turned toward the marchers, stepping high and bringing their arms up, urging the crowd to chant louder. My heart lurched when I realized they were the same policemen who had arrested my mother. I pulled at her skirt while we hurried to the street, trying to capture her attention, to point them out, to warn her about them, but we were thrust forward by the surging crowd and unintentionally joined the rear guard of the demonstration. Mamá held my hand tightly. I looked back at the wave of people pressing against us and saw how far behind Luisa, Gloria, and Angelina had fallen. Julián, I was comforted to see, was right behind me, elbows flared out to keep the demonstrators at bay.

The crowd rushed forward. Mamá, Julián, and I were jostled and shoved. A pointy elbow dug into my face, and my cheek throbbed with pain. Angry men yelled so loudly, my ears rang. After awhile I couldn't hear the band or distinguish what all the voices around me were clamoring. The smell of anger and adrenaline was thick, and my stomach churned. Mamá kept repeating something, and I could see the consternation in her eyes.

"What's Mamá saying?" I turned to Julián, who held onto my arm while I squeezed my mother's hand on the other side.

"She says we better get out of here."

"But we're stuck." The moment I said this, a pair of iron hands gripped my waist and lifted me into the air. Wrenched from my mother's hand and Julián's grasp, I disappeared into the mass of angry men. The last I heard before being propelled above the straw hats and uplifted fists was my mother yelling my name.

As I sailed over the waves of upturned faces and grasping hands, the chanting became denser, harder. I closed my eyes and listened closely. Through the sustained note of the trumpet and roll of the trombone, I could hear the *chiki-cha*, *chiki-cha* of the maracas, but the deep, mournful bong of the cowbell broke through the coiled paths of my insides. I let out a scream, hard and sustained, pushing it to the highest pitch until my throat ached. The hands that held me high brought me down on a man's hard shoulders, and I straddled him like a horse.

My eyes were tight seams. I screamed and shook my head violently as the man's rough fingers tightened on my thighs and prevented me from climbing down. I kicked my feet forward, and I opened my eyes to see the backs of the men drawing out machetes and sticks. From the height of the man's shoulders, I could see Mauleón, the red yarn of his wig bouncing, leading the mob into the El Diario building in Puerta de Tierra. The newspapermen, heads bent over solid desks, and the printers operating the presses looked up and were stricken for a second by immobility. When they made a mad rush to protect the doors, their effort was like a drop of water attempting to end a drought. Mauleón's mob was a hundred men strong, fueled with rum and rage. Mauleón flung his wig on the floor and turned menacingly to the men, waving a machete. The mob plowed steadily forward, and the newspapermen bolted out the massive side doors and jumped out the windows, leaving the shutters knocking in the breeze.

"Let's show these lying fools a lesson!" Mauleón struck a desk with his machete, and splinters, sharp as razors, sliced the air.

The wild horse of a man I had been riding released my legs. I wobbled and swayed, suddenly unbalanced. He shrugged roughly as though dislodging a pair of hostile hands clenched to his shoulders, and I fell with a thud against a wall. He turned quickly away and yelled, "*Vamos, muchachos*," before joining the mob of men who with machetes, bats, and bare hands smashed typewriters against the wooden floor, threw chairs out the windows, and cracked desks into pieces. I never saw his face.

Paper fluttered in the air like birds. Bewildered, I crouched in the security of a dusty corner, temples throbbing as I held my head between clenched fists. Outside, I could hear gunshots. My heart hammered violently. Inside, there was the deafening clamor of enraged voices, breaking glass. Wood smashed and cracked. My ears rang with pain. The dust rising from stamping feet sifted through the sunlight that streamed through the doorway, creating a hazy unreality in the large room. I wasn't sure whether I was awake or in the terrible throes of a nightmare. I stared at the dappled sunlight resting so serenely over the mob and pushed away the sounds of seething indignation, the violence of intransigence.

Mamá found me there staring at the beams of light, reaching for the motes that fluttered, like butterflies, in the air.

"For as long as I live," Mamá said angrily, "I will never forgive Mauleón for this!"

That night I had trouble sleeping. In the darkness, I felt Mamá's soft breath on my cheek when she turned over in bed.

"I'm going to tell you a story now."

I didn't say anything. I didn't need to. Mamá knew I was awake, and she knew I was listening.

"Once there lived a beautiful young princess. Her name was Ursula."

The moment I heard that name, I sat up so fast I made the bed creak. I could see the faint outline of Mamá's face. This was a story I wanted to hear without distractions.

"Ursula lived in a beautiful land of green meadows and wild flowers that bloomed for as far as the eye could see. Her father, the king of Britain, called her one day to his private chambers. Once Ursula had kissed his ring and sat at his feet, he told her the terrible news. The kingdom needed to form an alliance with a pagan country, and she must marry the prince to consolidate the bond. Ursula jumped to her feet and, with tears streaming down her cheeks, told her father she would never marry someone who was not a Christian. She turned her back and ran out of the sumptuous room. The king was very angry. No one was ever allowed to leave the room without facing the king. Subjects had to walk backwards, always facing the king and bowing until they were out of the room. Even Princess Ursula wasn't exempt from this requirement. But he was even angrier because Ursula would not obey his orders.

"Well, Ursula cried and cried. Her tears were so copious and thick that they flooded her bedroom. Soon her tears flooded the entire castle. Finally, her father relented. 'I grant you three years,' he said, 'and then you must marry the prince I have chosen for you.'

"Ursula was so happy, she immediately stopped crying. The castle was soon dry and comfortable. A three-year postponement of marriage was enough time, she calculated, to make her pilgrimage to Rome. Once there she could seek advice, perhaps from the Pope himself, on how to extricate herself from her predicament.

"The King of Britain agreed to her pilgrimage. He thought that a long journey might be just what the princess needed to come to her senses. So with ten ladies in waiting, each attended by a thousand maidens, Princess Ursula set sail on her long journey across the North Sea. With her entourage she sailed up the Rhine to Basle, Switzerland, and from there journeyed by land to Rome. In Rome, the Pope granted Ursula an audience. Under no circumstances, he informed her, could she marry a pagan. Greatly encouraged by the Pope's words, Ursula immediately set out on her long return home. She was never to see her homeland again.

"On the way back, the fiery Huns forced them to stop in Cologne. They quickly recognized that Ursula was a princess and took her, her ladies in waiting, and all the maidens to their chieftain. The chieftain knew immediately that this was a great opportunity for him to consolidate his power, and he asked Ursula to marry him. When she refused, Ursula and the other maidens suffered the most terrible of fates. All eleven thousand virgins were massacred without pity and without remorse. Some time later, a Roman senator built a basilica in Cologne to honor the martyred virgins."

Mamá was quiet. She knew the legend was racing through my mind in a full blast of sound and colors. At first I wondered why Mamá told me this story, despite its religious slant. But as I thought about it, I realized this was a legend my mother would identify with. Ursula died because she would not surrender to a barbarian—just as my mother refused to surrender to Mauleón.

Mamá tucked me under the sheets again and kissed my forehead.

"You know, Nana," she said, "maybe *doña* Eugenia's *once mil vírgenes* protected you tonight."

Because my mother could read, we were more prosperous than most at La Perla. Literacy was a precious inheritance my grandmother had worked so hard to give Mamá, and Mamá passed it on to me. Rich girls were expected to learn to read and write in those days, not us. So what was a given to some to us was a luxury. I remember exactly how my mother taught me to read when I was only three. She used a reading system that was based on love. That's why it was so effective.

After she taught me the vowels, which in Spanish can only be pronounced one way, Mamá taught me the letter *m*. Then she strung words together, combining the *m* with the vowels, in large print. The first thing I learned to read was the most beautiful sentence in the world: *Mi mamá me ama*. My mother loves me. The second most beautiful sentence in the world flows from the first: *Amo a mi mamá*. I love my mother. Then I learned, *Mi mamá me mima*: My mother pampers me, followed by *Mimo a mi mamá*: I pamper my mother. These first four sentences I learned to read, quickly and effortlessly, reinforced the overwhelming love my mother and I felt for each other. To read at that initial stage was to discover the immensity of love etched in visible symbols I could touch.

Literacy helped us survive. When my father was killed in the war, my mother was forced to find additional work to help her sustain us both. She set up a bench and table by the yellow house my father had built to read and write letters for people; they traveled long distances for her services. The war that had wrested my father from us increased Mamá's earnings, for with so many Puerto Rican men sent to war there were always letters to be sent and received. On many occasions, she would read the terrible news of a death of a father or a son or a brother. Then she consoled the recipient by bringing her to our small house for a cup of coffee or some orange leaf tea to settle her nerves. After the war, most of the people who sought her out could only pay with a few eggs from their backyard chickens, a jar of goat milk, or a bolt of cloth. But it was enough to help us get by.

One day, Mamá sat on a crate reading a letter to a woman whose husband had immigrated to Hawaii to work on a macadamia nut farm. I was never far from my mother, either scrawling letters with a stick on the ground or hopping over stones I had shaped in geometrical designs. On this particular day, I was sitting on the steps playing with a rag doll one of my mother's customers had given me. Of course, I listened to everything that was said. The woman was thin and wore a flower-print dress. Her name was Providencia

Agostini Matos. She was born in Yauco, where she and her husband had worked on coffee plantations until North American companies bought all the arable land for sugar cane. She surrendered the envelope to my mother, and her hand trembled. She looked away in embarrassment when her eyes filled with tears. My mother studied the envelope closely and lifted her eyes.

"The letter was sent from New Orleans. That's Louisiana, not Hawaii," she said quietly.

The woman's face showed her confusion.

"What's that? Is that New York?" Suddenly she became agitated. "What's he doing in New York?"

Mamá shook her head. She tapped one end of the envelope on the table and held it up to the sun so she could confirm that the letter had slipped to the other end. She carefully tore the edge of the envelope, blew into it, and pulled out the folded paper.

"Your husband might explain. Let's see." She cleared her throat and read the stiff, formal voice of someone not accustomed to dictating his thoughts. She stumbled a few times, because the handwriting was coarse and difficult to read. As she became accustomed to it, her voice became soft and modulated

My dearest wife,

I pray to God that when you receive this letter you and the children and the rest of the family are well. Especially healthy, because if you have health, you have everything. I'm all right, thank God. I asked a friend on the ship to write this letter. I have nothing to give him in return since what little money I brought has been spent on food. But he said it was all right, that writing helped him keep his mind entertained and not die of boredom. He is now smiling as I say this. His name is Joaquín Acosta Jiménez and he's from Adjuntas. When you receive this letter you will be surprised to hear that I am not in Hawaii. We have anchored in a port called New Orleans. When we left Guánica, all four hundred of us were filled with illusions about earning money for our families after we were left with no work. The Hawaii plantation people made many promises about the money we would earn and how they would pay our fare to Hawaii, and after our contracts were over in a couple of years, they would pay our fare back home. I don't want to worry you, but I am now filled with dread because the trip here was terrible. They put us in the hold of a tramp steamer. For

days and days and days, we could not see the light of the sun.
The air was filled with smells from our own bodies. After what
seemed like an eternity, we reached this port. We were charged
for everything, our fare and every bite of bad food we put in our
mouths. If we can't pay, they have a notebook and write down
everything to take it from our earnings on the plantations. I am
already in so much debt, I can't sleep at night. Fifty men escaped
as soon as the ship hit port and now the Hawaii plantation men
are watching us like hawks, waving their guns at us, so we don't
get any ideas. Joaquín and I will move on, what else can we do?
We ship out tomorrow morning, and if I have enough money
for the stamp, I will send you another letter when we get to the
next port. This trip to Hawaii is taking forever. I miss you and
the children very much and I send all of you my blessings, kisses,
and hugs. May God be with you until I see you again.

Your beloved husband,
Justo

Mamá finished the letter, folded it, and handed a handkerchief to Providencia, who was wiping her face with her hands.

"I'm sorry, *doña* Isabel, but I can't pay you today." Providencia's face was flushed with embarrassment.

"Whenever you can, Providencia. Don't worry about that."

Providencia hesitated and shifted uncomfortably in the chair. She cleared her throat.

"Some people say your poems are very potent. I apologize for my boldness in asking you for one more favor, but could you give me one of your poems so I can take it home?"

My mother raised her eyebrows. "But I thought you couldn't read."

"Oh, no, I can't. But I don't have to read it. You see, a friend of mine, Arcadia Ruiz, she was at one of the demonstrations where you talked to the workers and you gave out a poem to everybody and you said that poems can make people free, that they can heal people's hearts. So Arcadia, who wasn't feeling well for months after her miscarriage, well, she took the poem and boiled it in water and made some tea. After she had that tea, she swears by God and the blessed Virgin that all her maladies disappeared."

I remember how Mamá turned to me, with a slight smile on her lips.

"Nana," she said. "Get me my box." I knew what box she was talking about. It's my memory box now, but at the time it was the receptacle for her intimate thoughts.

She rummaged through the papers and pulled out a scrap on which she had hastily written some verses. She reached across the table and handed the poem to Providencia, who grasped it eagerly.

"God bless you, *doña* Isabel," Providencia smiled as she turned the paper in her hand.

The thought of my mother's medicinal poetry tea still makes me smile.

Chapter Eleven

She must not tear her lovely skin lamenting.

The Odyssey

The second time my mother was arrested, she was accused of subverting public morals by wearing a man's suit. Her picture appeared in the front page of *El Diario*. She was rarely concerned about the rabid sexism of her day, except to denounce it. As with many other isms of her time, sexism was something that would not stand in her way. If it did, she was perfectly capable of tearing it down with her bare hands.

In the photo, her left arm is held firmly by the arresting policeman, who according to the article said he had no choice but to detain her for causing "a scandal." Her white linen man's suit, not meant for the full contours of a woman, creases at the knees and waist. A white shirt blends in so perfectly with the suit it seems sewn into it. The dark tie, knotted neatly at the throat, hangs over the length of the suit jacket. Fixed on her head is a dark, wide-brimmed hat, jauntily tilted to the side. Her long hair is tucked under the hat. She doesn't smile, but looks straight at the camera, daring it to contradict her.

Many times I watched dreamily as she sat in the sunlight, confidently wielding needle and thread, pins held between her pressed lips, sewing harem-style trousers to her skirts, precursors of the pant-skirts and culottes of the sixties, pulling out the straight pins and stabbing them into a darning sock, demanding to know in her solid, unwavering voice why women couldn't be as comfortable as men. Undeterred by her arrest, she insisted that trousers were more hygienic than skirts, and she would wear them regardless of who was offended.

Because of her trousers, we finally met the American reverend.

Rumors about the Reverend had been swirling around the shantytown for months. He had shown up at La Perla one day, out of nowhere it seemed, having decided that there were enough Papists in the shantytown to secure salvation for an entire flock once he had converted and rebaptized them.

He had brought in a building crew to erect the largest structure in La Perla, and he consulted a flurry of blueprints as he ordered the men around. The two-story structure was the size of ten shanties and made of solid oak. The workers painted the wood white and attached a white cross to the top. Services for shantytowners were held in the large hall on the ground floor. On the second floor, according to Julián, who had observed the Reverend's comings and goings with curiosity, were the living quarters and an open area where the Reverend held private religious services, attended by three or four men at most. Julián heard him tell a neighbor in his heavily accented Spanish that he'd have us all baptized in seawater before we knew what hit us.

The new church had recently been finished when the shantytown became lively with rumors of an approaching hurricane. All omens were promptly dissected as people zig-zagged through the shantytown describing the dark signs they had witnessed or been told of by others.

A spider web floated into Luisa's house.

Swallows returned to ground seeking shelter.

Doña Eugenia's plants didn't flower that month.

Even I had noticed that the roosters had neglected to sing in the morning, and when I contemplated the wide expanse of ocean, I could see a *guaraguao*, voluminous black wings swinging smoothly as he circled the shore.

Finally, Tomás came to warn us that there had been a meager avocado crop that year. He looked up at the morning sky, nose sniffing,

"Look at those clouds," he said sorrowfully. "See the reddish tint. That's a definite sign." Then he pointed with his finger, and Mamá and I turned our eyes upwards. "The clouds are drifting from east to west." He nodded several times. "The hurricane's coming. It's coming, all right."

"We better get ready," Mamá said.

"I'll hammer these boards for you," Tomás offered. "So many people died when San Ciriaco hit. That was terrible. You're too young to remember," he said, "but almost all of them drowned."

"Oh, I remember it well," Mamá responded. "I was six years old. I'll never forget all those dead bodies floating in the rivers that ran through our town—people, cows, chickens."

"I was a gold miner then, *mijita*." *Don* Tomás said this to me with immense pride. "Gold wasn't plentiful, but there was enough in the Luquillo Sierra where I was born so we could live. Humbly, you know, but at least we didn't starve." He pulled at his bony chin in reflection. "I mined for so many years, up there in Mata de Plátano, my village. But then the coffee plantations took over and we were forced off the land. And here I am, an old man telling stories to a little girl."

My mother frowned as she gathered and folded the clothes she had been sewing and put them away in a basket. Tomás busied himself shielding our windows with the planks of wood he had brought. Mamá and I were securing our belongings, placing them high on shelves, when we heard someone rapping on the entryway.

"*Buenos días.*" The words were spoken in a thick American accent.

Mamá threw a sidelong glance at the tall, thin man before responding. She gave him a sharp look. We both took in the deep grooves of his cheeks, his meager chin. He was wearing a black suit that looked like something a pallbearer would wear. A white collar, spotted with the yellow stains of salt air, circled his scrawny neck. His forehead was red and peeling from sunburn. He held a soft-covered Bible in his fist. A slender red ribbon dangled from the book and flapped as he breathed. When he came up the steps, I noticed his worn shoes crusted with sand and salt. Mamá stepped forward and blocked the doorway. Tomás stopped hammering and looked out. I peeked from behind Mamá's trouser-skirt. As Mamá stood protectively at the entrance, the Reverend was forced to step down.

"*Buenos días,*" Mamá said with the extreme politeness of someone who is not pleased with the person who has come to call. "Can I help you with something?"

"I wonder if we could have a word." The Reverend's voice was tight and dense. It seemed to stretch through a mouthful of pebbles. Showing excessive deference, he removed his black hat.

"Sorry I can't invite you in, but as you can see we're busy preparing for the hurricane."

Mamá stepped down, and the Reverend followed her to the cooking shed while he set his hat firmly on his head. I was a few steps behind and noticed that Tomás had come out too, hammer in hand. A menacing look hardened his face.

"*Doña* Isabel," the Reverend began. "I'm on a mission here, sent by God Almighty and the benevolence of the church to care for the souls of La Perla's residents. And I must say I'm more than worried about yours."

A rush of color flooded Mamá's face. My eyes opened wide as I glanced back at Tomás who, like me, was taking in every word.

"Pardon me? Who gave you permission to interfere with my life, with my soul, no less?"

"Well, *doña* Isabel, your recent arrest is more than evidence that you need someone to guide you toward the path of righteousness."

"Which arrest are you talking about, Reverend? I've been arrested more than once."

"Oh, I meant the time you were charged with immoral behavior."

"I don't seem to recollect ever being charged with immorality."

"As you may recall, you were arrested for wearing trousers." He raised his eyebrows and shook his head dolefully. He glanced disapprovingly at the trousers she had sewn into her skirt and faced her. "And your arrest hasn't seemed to stop you from your wayward ways. If you don't think about yourself, think about the example you're giving to your innocent daughter here, whose soul is unblemished. Up to now, that is."

"And who appointed you guardian of our souls? Who do you think you are?" My mother's voice rose dangerously. Her thick eyebrows pressed together angrily and formed a straight line across her forehead. "The sheer arrogance of your behavior is astonishing. For once, I'm at a loss for words!"

"Is this *gringo* bothering you, Isabel?" Tomás had inched closer to us, hammer in hand. The Reverend stared at the hammer nervously.

"I can handle it, *don* Tomás." Mamá waved Tomás away and turned to the Reverend. "I don't know who you are or where you come from, and frankly, I don't care. But I would advise you not to interfere in my life. Along with the state, organized religion is one of the systems that needs to be eliminated in society, if we are to progress as a species. Religion is not spirituality. It's just a system created by men to oppress without being questioned about it. So don't think you'll make any headway with me. I don't believe in the state, and I don't believe in religion."

"Humph," the Reverend snorted with a sarcastic smile. He looked around at the people who had collected in front of our shanty. "That's obvious, isn't it?"

"Yes, it is, Reverend." She stared at him unflinchingly until he was forced to look away, pulling at his collar apprehensively. "And now, if you will excuse me, we have to prepare for the hurricane."

The Reverend seemed to have awakened to an idea. "Would you allow me to help?"

My mother stared at him in amazement. When he pulled at his collar, she noticed how the skin at this neck pleated like a turkey's, with stubs of hair pushing through. She burst out laughing.

"He's still trying to convert me, *don* Tomás," she said and turned toward the house. "It's not me who needs help. *Adiós, Reverendo.*" She waved.

"What has possessed you, *doña* Isabel, to believe that society can do away with the state? Why, the very idea is preposterous!"

My mother turned to him, lips pressed together, eyes narrowing severely.

"Why is it," she said, "that people are willing to believe in the damage caused by unseen germs and bacteria, that the Earth revolves around the sun, that one day mankind can send an aircraft to the moon, and so many other things that defy logic, but they can't believe in the possibility of governing themselves? You know why? Because of people like you, who do nothing but stimulate people's sense of impotence, their hopelessness. You feed on people's fears and fan those fears so they'll be more dependent on you."

"I don't really care what you think about me. But at some point, you'll have to choose between me and *el señor* Mauleón, you know."

It was a mere whisper, and if I hadn't been lurking so closely to Mamá, I wouldn't have heard it. It was like the circling of the *guaraguao* in the wind, low and menacing. My mother flinched as though punched in the stomach. The color drained from her face.

"What did you say?"

"Pedro Mauleón will do what I tell him to do. For political reasons, you understand. That man's a heathen, and nothing but his own interests move him. But I can make it in his best interest to stay away from you."

Mamá frowned and looked around in disbelief. Tomás had gone back into the house, and we could hear the echo of his hammering in the breeze. The people who had gathered around us were walking away, planning to gather food and other necessities for the imminent hurricane. *Don* Jacinto's wheelbarrow squeaked as he drove his invalid son away. A gust of wind swirled around us, and my eyes became gritty with sand.

Mamá approached the Reverend, so close he was forced to step back uneasily.

"And what would the price be for this kindness?" I knew when Mamá was raging with fury. She became sarcastic. Some people misinterpreted it as extreme politeness.

"Stop turning people away from my church."

"I don't care a whit about your church. I haven't even mentioned your church in my speeches or talks to people."

"But you're constantly ranting and raving against religion and that's enough. I'm surprised the priests haven't gone after you."

"They have better things to do, I guess, like kissing the indolent fingers of rich ladies." Mamá shook her head. "But why would Mauleón follow orders from you? Mauleón doesn't conform to anyone's interests but his own. We want to do away with authority, the power of a few over many. What we need is not authority, but order. And Mauleón is out there fomenting disorder and chaos." She paused deep in thought. "Well, he is obsessed with the Republican Party, so I suppose he would obey the party leadership."

Something kindled in her mind. The muscles in her face twitched ever so slightly, and her eyes became deep and dark with realization.

"Listen, Reverend," she said abruptly and sucked her teeth. "I'll think about your proposition. Now, I really must get back to the house."

The Reverend was taken aback by her response.

"I'm pleased that you've come around to my way of seeing things."

"That's what you think," my mother said under her breath as she walked away.

The wind howled menacingly as Hurricane San Ciprián pushed through La Perla. My mother huddled in a corner, lost in thought. A low rumble approached, like an angry dog, followed by a sudden bang. My heart pounded against my ribs. Mamá rubbed her eyes with the heel of her hand; I knew she was tired. But she wouldn't sleep. Something the Reverend said had troubled her, and her disquiet was worse for me to witness than the gales that roared through the boards of the shack, the pounding rain and thunderbolts that lit up our darkness. The ocean rumbled at a distance, the waves gathering strength, high as mountains. Mamá pulled me to her and sat me on her lap. As she smoothed my hair back, she told me in a voice that brought peace to my heart the Taíno myth of how hurricanes were born.

"In the beginning, the universe was asleep and empty. There was no sun or moon. Stars did not exist. There was no night, nor was there day. The only thing that existed in the universe was the great goddess Atabei. She created her two sons, Yukijú and Huracán. Atabei's favorite son was Yukijú, and she gave him the power to create the world. So Yukijú became the architect of the universe.

"Yukijú created the sun and the moon and the Earth. When the sun shone over the mountains, plants and trees bloomed. But when Huracán saw the marvelous things his brother Yukijú created, he was blinded by jealousy and disappeared into a darkness, where no one could find him.

"In the meantime, Yukijú saw four precious stones on the earth, and he set them up in the sky. The stones became stars, and they multiplied into millions of stars that would guide the gods through their journeys in the universe. Then Yukijú created animals and birds, and he put them to live in the forests and in caves. Finally, Yukijú created the first man, whose name was Locuo, and the first soul, named jupía, which resided within Locuo.

"Locuo was the first Taíno. He rejoiced at all the beauty that surrounded him. He crushed flower petals and leaves to make dyes, and he drew patterns on his copper skin to bring him into harmony with the world.

"Yukijú taught Locuo how to make fire, and he taught him how to make bread and how to heal. But Locuo was very lonely. Despite his beautiful surroundings, he was not happy. So Locuo opened his navel, and from it two creatures emerged. They were as beautiful as he was. He called the man Guaguyona and he called the woman Yaya.

"Yukijú created other gods to help him with the difficult task of protecting the world. But one day Yukijú realized that there was something wrong in the world. While he created harmony, something created destructive winds. While he created light, there was something creating darkness. Then he realized that it was his brother, the powerful and rebellious god Huracán, who was releasing destruction into the world.

"Locuo and the other Taínos felt threatened by Huracán, the powerful god of the winds. Huracán emerged from his hideout in the form of a terrible wind, and he vented his fury on all the plants and animals that Yukijú had created. He attacked the bohíos that Locuo and the other Taínos had built with palm fronds. Now the Taínos could not live in peace. They were always worried that Huracán would strike them with his ferocious winds. Huracán, the terrible god, shook the earth until the four corners of the world trembled.

"A fierce struggle began between Yukijú and Huracán.

"Huracán sent torrential rains, floods, and deafening winds that swept away people and animals and everything that lived. Yukijú opened the earth in many places so that Huracán's winds would flow into the seas.

"Many Taínos took their canoes and escaped to the tops of the mountains. But many people and animals died. Everywhere, there was only death and destruction. Finally, Yukijú cast Huracán to the farthest corner of the universe where even today Huracán hides in darkness.

"Every year when Huracán remembers how Yukijú cast him away, so far from the light, Huracán gathers his winds and darkness and attacks the earth with all of his fury. But Yukijú, protector of the Taínos, is always present to vanquish Huracán's ire, and he sends him once more to the darkest recess of the universe."

The next morning it seemed that Yukiyú had barely been the victor. The tired sky was washed clear of color. The shantytown was silent. Tomás came early to see how we were and to remove the boards from our window. Mamá and I looked down at the shacks near the shore, whose residents had been forced to flee to higher grounds. Piles of wood marked the shacks where people had lived. Many took refuge in the Reverend's church, Tomás told us with a grunt of disapproval. The sand was sucked out to sea, and the ocean was gray and exhausted. I burst out crying when I saw that the palms that were still erect had had their fronds torn off by the wind. They looked as sad and forlorn as Mamá.

"This is awful, *don* Tomás," she said, shaking her head. "We better organize some food distribution. If anyone needs to stay in our place, tell them to come over."

"I don't know, *doña* Isabel." Tomás was looking warily to the top of the hill. "I think the Reverend has taken charge."

My mother grew pale as the sky. I clung to her hand, pulling her down so I could kiss her cheek. Maybe that would make her feel better, I hoped.

Next door, Luisa, Julián, and Angelina were on their knees, mopping the floor with rags.

"Still got those holes in the roof, Luisa?" Tomás poked his head into the shack. "I'll come back when I'm done helping some people down there and plug those holes up for you."

"*Gracias, don* Tomás." Luisa pushed her hair back from her eyes. "You're a blessing from God Himself."

Mamá and I got rags and mops from our house and began wiping Luisa's floor. When my mother's voice lowered to a whisper, I knew she was ready to confide a secret, something she didn't want me to know.

"I'll go get more rags," I said to Julián, but when I went out I moved quietly toward the back of the house and listened to my mother's voice coming through the spaces between the wallboards.

"....it's too much," she was saying, and she paused for a long moment. "I suddenly figured it out. Can't believe it took me so long. The Reverend is in control. Mauleón gets his funding from the same source that sent the Reverend here. "

"Mauleón's party?"

"That's right. So the Reverend can tell Mauleón to back off, but only if I agree to his terms."

"What're you gonna do?"

"Nothing. I can't let these people silence me. I'll just keep doing what I'm doing and see what happens."

"Isabel, you need someone to protect you."

"Don't worry. I can take care of myself."

Chapter Twelve

And when long years and seasons
wheeling brought around that point of time
ordained for him to make his passage homeward,
trials and dangers, even so attended
him even in Ithaka, near those he loved.

The Odyssey

"Now, behave yourself, Nana," my mother warned while she stuffed her pamphlets in a bag. "And remember to always stay by my side, even when I'm up on the platform giving my speech."

I was so happy to be allowed to attend the demonstration in nearby Cataño that I would promise her anything she wanted.

At San Miguel Street a white, chrome-heavy sedan waited for us. The car had a red flag tied to the antenna. A long banner on the hood proclaimed: *Arriba Los Trabajadores. Don* Demetrio sat next to the driver, another member of La Federación de Trabajadores.

"Buenos días, Isabel. Hello, Marinita. I'm glad to see that your mother's training you early for the struggle." He squeezed my cheek and smiled expansively. I didn't like to be called in the diminutive, but *don* Demetrio always brought me sesame seed sticks or caramel drops and said, "Sweets for a sweet," so I forgave him.

Mamá and I squeezed in the back with two tobacco rollers who I recognized from La Colectiva. Wide-brimmed hats carefully poised on their knees, they nodded and smiled. One of them had a thin and angular frame. Sharp cheekbones almost cut through his skin. He was young and well-dressed in a cream-colored linen suit. He had been sitting by the window and immediately got out of the car.

"Por favor, *doña* Isabel," he bowed slightly. "Sit by the window. It's on the shady side." His eyes were brown and deep as an inkwell. He looked at my mother with an indefinable longing that made me feel uncomfortable.

I had seen that look before in the boys at school. I was not at all pleased with the way this man gazed at my mother.

Mamá smiled and patted her hair. I couldn't believe she was flirting.

"Oh, thank you, Juan Carlos," she said sweetly. "That's so kind of you."

Once we got into the car, I was determined to keep an eye on Juan Carlos and an even closer one on Mamá. At my young age, I had already discovered to my horror that there were men capable of being attracted to my mother. I especially remembered a guy named Raúl, who was some kind of anarchist big-shot. He was tall and handsome, even by my standards, and I was terribly afraid my mother would fall for him. She did, actually. She even allowed him to come visit her at home, the very house my father built with his own hands. I was embarrassed and angry. Why did she need someone else in her life? Didn't she have me? Wasn't that enough for her? What in the world could this Raúl give her that I didn't? I sulked for weeks, maybe months. Every time he came to the house, with flowers for her and a doll or candy for me, I'd scowl and made sure I showed off my worst behavior. I was especially angered when she left me at Luisa's while she went strolling to Old San Juan, hand tucked in his arm.

One evening I was working on some math exercises for school when I heard them arguing outside. I tiptoed to the window. Mamá was standing, fists firmly anchored at her hips. It was one of her fighting stances, and even though I couldn't see her face, I could clearly detect the anger in her voice. When she accused him of fomenting violence, I knew Raúl was in big trouble.

"We can't make any compromises with the government. It maintains its very existence through the use of violence and force. There's a lot wrong with a government like that." My mother turned her head toward the sea. She shook her head, and I could see the sorrow in her shoulders as they sagged toward her chest.

"But listen to me, Isabel." Raúl opened his large palms, and I saw the glint of his gold ring. "We're not getting anywhere with the 'non-violence under any circumstances' rule. They're striking at us left and right."

"Don't you understand that violence breeds violence? In the long run, the proponents of violence will be destroyed by their own weakness. Our strength lies in the creative force of pacifism, because it builds rather than destroys. It's so much easier to destroy, isn't it? That's why states depend on it. It's easy and has the added advantage of feeding on people's fears. Recourse to violence is really an indication of great weakness." Mamá paused, then she turned to face Raúl. "I'm disappointed in you, Raúl. I didn't know you were a weak man."

Raúl threw back his head as if he had been slapped. Mamá continued. She spoke so softly I had to strain to hear her.

"You know, hatred isn't the opposite of love, as most people think. The opposite of love is fear. Fear is at the bottom of all the ills of the world, of society, of individual human beings. And fear manifests itself in so many ways it's often difficult to recognize. Hatred is one manifestation of fear. Fear of losing authority, fear of failure, fear of fear itself. We are all afraid of each other and that's what stands in the way of love. We should be loving each other, together creating a just society where everyone shares the resources of the world. Instead, we fear and we hate and we kill and we destroy. A few have the power over many, and because of the need of these few to remain in power, they create artificial laws to coerce, exploit, and oppress."

"How are you going to dismantle the state?" There was desperation in Raúl's voice. "It's impossible to survive without it!"

"I'm so tired of hearing that! What's so impossible about governing ourselves? Are we imbeciles?"

"It's just not possible, Isabel. We need the state to control our activities, to enact laws, because unfortunately we need to be ruled or else it will be complete chaos with the greedy nature of human beings."

"The only reason human beings are dishonest, brutal, and greedy is because of the state. It's not because of their human nature, but a consequence of oppression by the state, by the few who have the wealth and the power."

"We can accomplish our goal of a just society by eliminating the current state and establishing a fairer one."

"And this establishment is achieved through violence, I suppose."

"It's inevitable."

"Faure once said that it is not always possible to do what one should do, but he knew that there were things that on no account can one ever do. I agree with that. Violence is one of those things that one can never, ever condone or engage in. Man is good by nature. Institutions corrupt us. I don't agree with the Communists—they're just another group that wants to take power."

"I'm sorry you won't join us, Isabel."

After that evening, Raúl never returned. Sometimes I heard her crying in bed at night, and I knew that he was history.

And, here she was, smitten again, glancing to the side and smiling at Juan Carlos unashamedly. I was ready to get into one of my serious snits, the ones reserved for desperate times, when *don* Demetrio, hat firmly set on his head, turned around, winked, and handed me a brown paper bag.

"Sweets for the sweet," he said, distracting me completely. When I opened the bag, my mouth watered. Inside were the most enticing candies I had ever seen. They were little parcels wrapped in silvery foil, tied at the top with a red paper thread. I looked up at Mami and she nodded. Though she often objected to my eating sweets, that day she was in a good mood and generous with her approval. I rummaged carefully through the parcels, trying to see if any candies were larger than others. In that case, I would certainly choose the largest, but they all seemed the same size. With index and thumb, I picked out one of my treasures. When I undid the red thread and foil, I was rewarded with the most perfect chocolate nugget I had ever seen. It was wide-bottomed and tapered into a point at the top. When I popped it into my mouth and bit into it, I couldn't believe the taste. It was like biting into a piece of heaven.

"Those are called kisses, Marinita. Do you like them?" *Don* Demetrio asked, and I nodded, my mouth packed with delightful morsels.

Mamá poked me in the ribs. "Aren't you going to offer any to the *compañeros?*" she said peremptorily. I knew it wasn't a question.

My first instinct was to crush the bag against my chest and defend it with my life. I wanted all those bits of chocolate for myself. But when I looked at Mamá and saw the way her face threatened, I reluctantly held my treasure forward. My joy knew no end when the men said, *no, gracias*, almost in unison.

"*No, muñequita*," *don* Demetrio declined also. "They're all for you."

Smiling, I leaned back against the seat, but I noticed that my mother was still staring at me, disapproval written all over her face.

"Oh, sorry, Mami, do you want one?"

"No, thank you, Marina. It was very kind of you to offer." She enunciated evenly, her disapproval clear.

As the car reached the main road to Cataño, we fell behind a long line of cars and trucks honking their horns, passengers waving red flags from the windows. A truck packed a band playing *plenas* and *bombas*. The musicians wiggled their hips as the trumpets, bongos, and maracas beat the rhythm. People ran out of the houses that lined the roads and either waved flags or stood impassively, frowning in disapproval.

We paraded noisily along the roads through the cane fields. The car that led the procession had a bullhorn strapped to the top, and a speaker announced the strike. Cane workers bordered the roads, machetes at their sides, and the speaker invited them to stop working and join the demonstration. Many cane workers dropped their machetes and ran toward the cars and trucks, where they boarded the caravan. When we reached the plaza of Cataño, thousands of people already congregated around the platform.

Mamá finished her speech and smiled to the crowd. Standing behind her, I saw Juan Carlos looking up at her with romance in his eyes. Though I was relieved that Mamá didn't believe in marriage, I still worried about romantic entanglements. I knew I was being selfish and wondered if that made me a bad anarchist. My thoughts were quickly curbed when I saw the police, weapons in hand, circling the crowd. Mamá reached out to hold my hand. Police horses, cars, and vans blocked the roads surrounding the plaza. The wave of people surged back. Some bent down to pick up rocks from the ground and hurled them at the police. Mayhem broke out as the police moved forward like a dangerous sea mammal, their black helmets shining in the afternoon sun.

Mamá pulled me to the back of the platform.

"Hide under that table, Marina. Hurry."

When I squatted under the table, she leaned several chairs and boxes around me protectively. Then I watched her, through the chair slats, as she took hold of the microphone and addressed the crowd.

"*Compañeros y compañeras*, don't let the violence of government forces incite you to violence. We must respond to their oppression with a calm demeanor, show them that it is we who will overtake them, without any need for weapons or force. Let's show them what nonviolence can create. With pacifism we can achieve our freedom. *Calma, pueblo.*"

Some people turned back to listen. Reluctantly, I was forced to admire Juan Carlos, who with *don* Demetrio and the other men we had come to Cataño with, leaped onto the platform and stood by my mother. They were there, arms at their sides, while she exhorted the people to stay calm, not to react to the violence of the police.

My heart beat wildly as I knocked down the chairs and ran to Mamá's side. *Don* Demetrio put his arm around my shoulders. While Mamá spoke into the microphone, the platform began filling up with people responding to Mamá's request. We stood still, listening to Mamá's voice coming through forcefully, while some hurled insults and rocks at the police and others scrambled desperately to get away. Finally, the police reached us, waving clubs menacingly. *Don* Demetrio faced them.

"Are you attacking unarmed citizens who are doing nothing but exercising their right to speak?"

"Shut up, *viejo.*"

"I may be old, but I'm not having my rights subverted."

"Shut up, I said." The policeman lifted his club. He turned to Mamá. "And you, big mouth, you shut up too."

My mother looked at him stonily. The look reminded me of the time she spoke to the Reverend. The policeman had only strengthened her resolve.

"*Compañeros y compañeras,* don't let them silence us!"

The policeman shoved Mamá to the side, took the microphone and hurled it from the platform. He grabbed Mamá's arm and pulled her forward. At that moment, Juan Carlos jumped on the policeman from behind and wedged his forearm under the man's chin in a choke hold. The policeman fell to his knees. Mamá spun around.

"Stop it, Juan Carlos. Don't …" while another policeman clamped her with handcuffs and dragged her away. Four others fell on Juan Carlos with clubs and rifle butts and knocked him unconscious.

While the police were distracted with Mamá and Juan Carlos, *don* Demetrio steered me toward the side of the platform and down the steps. Friends of *don* Demetrio had gathered there, and they whisked me away to a car. I was stunned with grief and fear.

"We can't leave without Mamá."

"Someone will drive you to Luisa's house," *don* Demetrio assured me. "Then we'll bail your mother out of jail. Don't worry, Marinita, we've done this before. Your mother will be home before the cock crows."

I think that was the third time my mother was arrested. Or maybe the fourth. I can't be sure. She had been in jail so many times it became a blur in my mind. What I do remember about this time was that Mamá was placed in solitary confinement at La Princesa. Without formal charges or a trial, she was imprisoned for a month.

Luisa and I shambled down the dark tunnel as we followed the fat guard. The prison smelled musty and unclean. I sneezed into my hand, and when I brought my head up, I heard my mother's voice.

"Nana, is that you?" The question echoed from a cavern of a cell. My heart went wild with happiness. She was alive, her voice was strong. They hadn't beaten her down. All would be well, I believed, if only she would now stop the activities that angered the police, learn her lesson, and leave all of her politics behind.

"Mamá, you're so skinny."

"Oh, I'm on a diet. The food here isn't great anyhow."

Luisa recovered from her shock at seeing my mother's gaunt face and how her prison garment hung on her slight shoulders.

"Here." She handed her a bag. "Rice and beans. *Don* Demetrio brought me a chicken, so I made some *fricasé* too. But I know you don't eat meat so I didn't bring you any."

My mother's eyes welled with tears.

"Do you mind if I eat now?"

"No, no. Eat, eat. You're going to disappear if you don't eat. I'm sorry we didn't visit earlier, but they didn't let us in. They said you were in solitary confinement, that you were a dangerous criminal and didn't deserve to be seen with decent people."

Mamá frowned and shook her head.

"Not in front of *la nena*, Luisa, *por favor*."

Luisa glanced down at me.

"Oh, sorry. But you know, she knows everything that's going on. She's too smart to keep things from her anyhow."

I hated it when they talked about me as if I weren't present.

"Ahem. I'm here, you know."

Chewing on a mouthful of rice and beans, my mother put her arm around me.

"Do you want some?"

"No, I'm stuffed."

"We ate before coming." Luisa looked around at my mother's cell. She was about to say something, but she glanced back and saw that the guard was waiting. She shrugged her shoulders.

"What's going on?" I whispered. "When're you coming home?"

Mamá kissed me on the top of the head. Her breath was redolent of garlic and tomato sauce.

"The Federación sent a lawyer to represent me. I should be home soon, *mi linda*. Just be good and do what Luisa tells you."

I wasn't exactly thrilled with this. Why was she being so vague? I knew there was something she wasn't telling me.

"Thanks for the food, Luisa. It was delicious." I noticed that Mamá had something in her hand. Her fist was slightly pulled in, and she glanced up at the guard. When she saw that he had turned his head to the side, she slipped a folded paper in one of the *fiambreras*. Luisa clasped the two round aluminum food carriers together and placed them in the bag.

"Thank you, Luisa."

Our skin turned ashen when the guard took the paper bag. He looked at Luisa and then at me suspiciously. My heart was pounding wildly. I could imagine how nervous poor Luisa must have been. Her hands were shaking, and she plunged them into her pockets.

The guard looked in the bag.

"Any food in here?"

"No," Luisa's voice managed to squeak. "She was hungry and ate it all."

"Too bad. I could use some good homemade food. What they serve around here isn't fit for pig swill."

Luisa smiled coquettishly.

"Next time, I'll bring you some."

"That would be real nice," the guard grinned, and he patted me on the head.

"So, is this the anarchist's daughter?"

"Oh, yes. She's her only child." Luisa volunteered.

"Good thing she didn't bring any more troublemakers into the world. We got enough problems with the likes of her."

Luisa looked out the window.

"*Virgen Santísima*, look how time flies," she exclaimed. "It's gonna be dark soon. We better get home."

"Hope you visit us again."

"Oh, yes, *por supuesto.*"

Once out on the street, we rushed to La Perla, *fiambreras* firmly secured against Luisa's chest.

Night was falling quickly. I lit a candle while Julián, Gloria, and Angelina crowded around us. Luisa unfolded Mamá's scrap of paper.

"Here," she said to me. "You read it."

My hands trembled as I held the paper. It was brown and very coarse. It looked like something Mamá had torn from a cardboard box. I knew she always had a small pencil tucked into her pockets. She probably managed to hide it in her hair. The writing was shaky and almost illegible, unlike Mamá's normally neat script. The letter was written in very small writing so it would fit on the paper. My eyes welled with tears as I read. The letter wasn't addressed to me, as I had hoped. She had written to *don* Demetrio.

> *Dear don Demetrio,*
>
> *I hope that this letter reaches you so you may be aware of my situation. A day after my arrest, I was interrogated by an FBI agent, and my circumstances have greatly deteriorated since then. I was kept in solitary confinement for three weeks. I was only given stale bread and filthy water to drink. There is no window in the solitary cell, and because of the light deprivation I have suffered from serious disorientation. I don't know what they want me to tell them. They say I am inciting the overthrow of the government, but that's ridiculous. Or is it that they need a scapegoat and I'm the most accessible prey?*
>
> *Any help you can give me will be greatly appreciated. I don't think the attorney who represents me knows what's going on.*

*Thank you for your generosity toward Luisa and my little girl.
I'm very grateful.*

Yours sincerely,

Isabel

"Oh, my God," Luisa crossed herself many times. "What are they doing to her in that place?"

"Luisa, please, let's get her out of there," I pleaded.

"But how, *mija*? I don't have money to bribe the guard." Luisa was wringing her hands. "Right now, we have to get this letter to *don* Demetrio. He can help, I know he can."

"I'll take it right now," Julián volunteered.

"*Sí, mijo,* but be very careful. I think we've got lots of spies around here. Like that *reverendo* and Mauleón. Those two are up to no good." Luisa shook her head dejectedly.

Julián tucked Mamá's letter into his trouser pocket.

"No, wait," Luisa said. She pulled out an old basket from a wooden crate. "Take your shirt off, Julián."

Julián, the girls, and I watched closely as Luisa undid a seam in Julián's shirt, put the letter in, and sewed the seam again. She cut the thread with her teeth and put her sewing things away. Then she looked out the door.

"Okay, Julián, go now. But don't run or anything. Just pretend you're minding your own business." Just as he was about to leave, she took him in her arms and hugged him. "Take care of yourself, my boy."

Our eyes were wide with fear as Julián ran out into the night. We waited for hours. The shantytown noises became muted as people secured their windows and went to sleep. From afar, we could hear an occasional automobile roaring on the main road. When I poked my head out the window, a crescent moon glittered in the night, and the sky was filled with stars. Luisa put the girls to bed. Soon I had unwillingly fallen asleep, huddled in a corner on the floor. Luisa sat upright on her hammock, eyes firmly placed on the door.

When the night was at its darkest, Julián raced in. I woke as he closed the door.

"*Muchacho!*" Luisa jumped to her feet. "Where in the devil's name have you been? We were worried sick about you." She hugged him tightly, tears streaming down her cheeks, and she filled his face with kisses.

"Ay, Mami, *don* Demetrio's dead."

"What? Where's the letter?"

"It's right where you put it, Mami. I never gave him any letter. Didn't have the chance."

"What happened, *hijo mío? Por Dios*, don't keep me in this terrible suspense any more."

My legs had fallen asleep and I stumbled forward. My head was spinning with confusion and dread.

"I ran to *don* Demetrio's house, but when I got close I was real suspicious because two men were hiding in the bushes outside the gate. So I hid too, behind that abandoned shack right across the street. My heart was pounding and I didn't know what to do. So I thought I'd find a way to warn *don* Demetrio about these men. But while I was trying to figure out what to do, I saw *don* Demetrio's silhouette as he walked past a window. A kerosene lamp was lit on a shelf, and I saw his bald head when he bent down to get something from a table. Then, he turned around, facing the window." Julián bit his lower lip and shook his head forcefully.

"What happened?" I whispered.

"One of the men took a gun out and shot into the house. *Don* Demetrio fell, and the men ran off toward Puerta de Tierra."

"And what did you do?"

"I heard *don* Demetrio's wife scream, and all the neighbors began crowding around the house. When the police arrived, I ran back. Couldn't risk having the police take me in with this letter."

"Ay, *Virgen Santísima*, what're we going to do now? How can we help Isabel?"

"I don't know, Mami." Julián sighed, and I began to weep uncontrollably.

The next morning the shantytown was abuzz with the news. *Don* Demetrio had been killed, and Mauleón's *turbas republicanas* claimed responsibility. Right after we had our coffee, I was surprised to see Juan Carlos at the entryway.

"*Buenos días*," he said to Luisa, who was putting away the sleeping mats and hammock. I came out to the doorway with Luisa. If there was anything he could say to us about my mother, I wanted to know about it.

Juan Carlos turned his hat over in his large hands as he spoke softly. His dark brown eyebrows furrowed. He threaded his thick hair with his fingers.

"You probably know that *don* Demetrio was killed last night."

"I heard," Luisa said. "*Que en paz descanse*, may he rest in peace, he was such a good man."

"The worst thing is we can't bring the culprits to justice."

"Why not? It's about time they put that Mauleón and his thugs behind bars!"

"Mauleón's just a little fish. The people behind him are too powerful, too well-connected. Those are the real criminals, and we can't touch them."

"*No entiendo*, I don't understand," Luisa pressed her lips together.

"What about my mother?" *Don* Demetrio was very nice and I was sorry that he was dead, but I had more important things on my mind.

"*Don* Demetrio was working on her case with a *Federación* lawyer. I'll take over now."

"Can't someone pay off those guards or the judge or whatever? Isabel's not a criminal, she shouldn't be in jail."

"I know, *doña* Luisa."

"She doesn't believe in violence, not even in self-defense." Luisa grasped Juan Carlos's arm and brought her head to his ear.

"I have something to show you," she whispered. She went into the shack and tore out the letter from Julián's shirt. She checked to make sure no one was around and gave Juan Carlos the letter she had smuggled out of the jail.

Juan Carlos read the note, folded it carefully, and tucked it in his pocket.

"Now I see what they're trying to do. They're trying to break her so she'll talk."

"Talk about what?" I wanted to know.

"Give them names of other anarchists and Communists."

"But Mami isn't a Communist."

"They can't tell the difference. Anarchism, communism, socialism—it's all the same to them."

"But it's not!" I knew very well what the differences were, and I couldn't understand how grown-ups would confuse them.

"Let's say they don't want to understand." Juan Carlos wiped his forehead with a handkerchief. The sun was hot, and little beads of perspiration dotted his face. "The main thing is that we have to get Isabel out of jail." He paused. His next words chilled me to the bone. "She may be in more danger than we thought."

A week later, Mamá was home, pale and weak but happy to be free. Juan Carlos had brought her home.

"Mami, mami," I cried and ran to her open arms. I almost knocked her over, she was so weak.

"Ay, Nana, I've missed you so much!!"

"Me too. What happened to you? Tell me everything."

"Well, the police wanted information I couldn't give them. So they tried to force me into talking."

"How did they force you?"

"By not giving me food, putting me in a dark cell. It wasn't so bad, Nana. Look, I'm here and I'm well."

I knew that wasn't true. She was only saying that to assuage my fears. She was so thin and pale, I almost broke down crying again.

"How did you get out?"

"The Federación got me out, with Juan Carlos' help. They couldn't get a peep out of me."

"Do you know about *don* Demetrio?"

"Yes, Nana." Her eyes welled up with tears.

"So tell me, please tell me, how did you get out?"

"I'll let Juan Carlos tell you that part of the story."

I turned to Juan Carlos. He looked handsomer than ever, and, for the first time, I was willing to acknowledge his kindness.

"We sent out a plea to all the members of the Federación asking for donations to help your mother." He smiled at my mother tenderly. "People from all over the island contributed whatever they could to the cause. Before we knew it, we had enough funds to pay off the judge. He acquitted her of all charges."

"What charges? My mother didn't do anything!"

"The trumped-up charges. When they can't charge someone for real violations, they just make them up."

As long as I live, I will never forget that lesson. The implementation of justice in the wrong hands can lead to the grossest of wrongs. I've never trusted the justice system since then. I never will.

Chapter Thirteen

... at last we went,
bowed with anguish, cheeks all wet with tears ...

The Odyssey

"Why won't you have some of this delicious *salmorejo* I made, Isabel? It's good for you."

"You know I don't eat living beings."

"These aren't animals, *muchacha*. How many times do I have to tell you? Crabs have no brains; they're just shell and claws." Sometimes Luisa became exasperated by Mamá's beliefs. She shook her head and left with the fragrant plate of *salmorejo de jueyes* in a tin bowl. "Besides, they sure as hell ain't living any more," she mumbled as she left.

Julián often caught saltwater crabs in the marshes by the beach. He put them in a tin pail with a lid on. The pail screeched as the crabs scraped pincers against the sides, trying to escape. I used to go crab hunting with him until I saw what Luisa did to the crabs after she fattened them up in a cage.

Luisa kept a small cage covered with reticulated wire in front of her shack, where she could keep an eye on them. There she fattened and cleaned out the crabs by feeding them corn, bread, and coconut meat. It was worth the expense, since she could sell the crabs live. Even more profitable, she made *salmorejo de jueyes*, a favorite local dish made with fresh crabmeat, garlic, sweet red peppers, olive oil, and the juice of a lemon. People came from as far away as Puerta de Tierra to savor Luisa's specialty.

One afternoon after school, I was standing around Luisa's house trying to decide whether to do my homework early or postpone it as long as I could before Mamá came home. The decision was made for me when I saw Luisa come out of the cooking shed with a gourd full of moistened bread and corn. Any thought of doing homework vanished from my mind.

"Marina, you scared me," Luisa said. "I didn't know you were standing there quiet as a ghost."

I wasn't too pleased about the comparison, but I followed Luisa to the crab cage.

"These *jueyes* are getting nice and fat, aren't they? And look at this. The females are full of coral. They're going to be real tasty." She pointed out the brightly colored coral on the undersides.

"Are they all females?" I asked while Luisa poured a pail of water into the cage to clean the debris.

"No, that one over there, see him? That's the male." Luisa sprinkled the cage with bits of bread and kernels of corn. "You can only have one male in a cage with females. Otherwise the males will kill themselves fighting over the females."

Maybe my mistake was naming them, but I couldn't help myself. I looked in on them every afternoon and began to distinguish among them. I called the females Gertrudis, Carmencita, and Martita. The male was Felipe. I could watch them for hours as they uncurled their hairy feelers and wiped their eyes, which were perched on slender stalks. When I poked a stick into the cage, Gertrudis would often back up into a corner, but Felipe invariable stood his ground, bringing up his pincers menacingly. It's true that their heads were small, but I would never believe they had no brains like Luisa claimed.

One day, when Gertrudis, Carmencita, Martita, and Felipe least expected it, Luisa decided it was time.

"Time for what?" I asked with dread in my heart.

"Time to boil them, *muchacha*. Do you think I've been spending all this money fattening these *jueyes* for decoration?"

I looked into the cooking shed. On the smoky pile of coals and kindling rested a huge iron pot. Smoke billowed from the pot. A terrible fate awaited my crustacean friends.

"Ay, no, Luisa, you can't do that. Please don't kill them!" I began to cry.

"What's gotten into you, Marina? Are you crazy?" She turned around and began plunging the crabs into a pail. "Wish Julián was here," she mumbled under her breath, "so he could help me. This is the part that I hate doing."

"Wait until Julián comes, then," I said quickly. There was hope of a reprieve yet. If she waited for Julián to come home from the hospital where he worked, maybe I could somehow save my friends, set them free in the natural world where they belonged.

"No, *mija*, I can't do that. Someone's coming for *salmorejo* this afternoon. And believe me, I could use some of those pesos right now."

I pulled at her skirt as she carried ill-fated Martita, Felipe, Gertrudis, and Carmencita, who was my favorite, to the boiling cauldron. It reminded me of the Inquisition my mother was always ranting about when she attacked the Church. It reminded me of people being burned at the stake.

"Please, Luisa," I sobbed. "Don't kill them."

Luisa plucked my hands from her skirt, turned toward my house, and yelled.

"Isabel, Isabel. Get over here pronto!"

My mother ran towards us, bewilderment on her face when she saw me wailing and trying to clutch at Luisa's skirt.

"What is going on here?"

"Mami, she's killing them. Tell her not to do it, Mami. I can't bear it."

"I'm sorry, Luisa. *Lo siento*. She's really sensitive about killing animals. Whenever the slaughter starts down there," she pointed toward the seashore, "she sticks her fingers into her ears so she won't hear it."

Mamá turned to me.

"Nana, let go of Luisa. Let's go home."

"But, Mami, she's going to boil them to death. Like in the Inquisition. You keep saying that was wrong."

"*Muchacha*, how many times do I have to say that crabs have no brains. They're just shell and claws. That's it. They won't feel a thing." Luisa positioned the pail over the boiling cauldron and turned it upside down. For many months I was haunted by the sound of claws skittering at the sides of the pot as the crabs tried desperately to escape.

During my childhood I was frequently thwarted in my efforts to write poetry. One day, I attempted to compose a poem on a scrap of paper. Writing always helped to take my mind off the ugly things that often happened in La Perla, like the squeals of pain from the slaughterhouse and Mauleón's insults. I was concentrating hard on my verses when the hum of Mamá's voice came through and distracted me. I looked up. She was standing by the window, mumbling to herself. Whenever she talked to herself, I knew she was practicing a new speech. She stood by the window and looked out, arms stretched outwards, the palms of her hands facing the ceiling, as if ready to receive a blessing from an angel or something. Or maybe it was she who was imparting the blessing to all who listened. She spoke quietly. At first I could not understand what she was saying. Gradually, like turning up the volume on a radio, her voice got louder, stronger, more emphatic. By the time she had revved up her declamatory motors, she was out the door, face flushed, arms alive with purpose.

Unfortunately for me, she found several unsuspecting neighbors outside. With eyes that sparkled in the early sun, she called them to her. She had a reputation for her oratory fervor, and the neighbors approached with alacrity, eager for the excitement Mamá always provided with the combination of speeches against the established order and the sultan-style skirts she frequently wore, which got her into so much trouble.

"You'd think I could go to the police, wouldn't you? Hah! They're all in it with Mauleón, including the Reverend!"

More people began gathering around us. Mamá was invariably a good remedy for the tedium of shantytown existence. The neighbors could always tell when there was a good speech coming. They were particularly partial to the anti-government, anti-police, and anti-Catholic Church speeches. By her flushed cheeks and fiery look, everyone could see Mamá was fired up, that she was ready to wage battle. They all knew that Mauleón had sent his gang to throw rocks into our house the night before, prodded perhaps by the Reverend and his supporters. They may not always join the protests Mamá initiated, but as they listened to her speak, they encouraged her with applauses and cheers. It was clear that they disapproved of Mamá's persecutors.

"There's a lot wrong with a society that maintains its existence through the use of violence. That's why we have to do away with authority, the power of a few over many. It's unjust, and it's time to do away with it."

People began to applaud, and I rolled up my eyes to the sky. How could I possibly be inspired to write any poetry when there were so many distractions around? I stomped into the house, though it was unbearably hot. Before writing a poem, I always liked to listen to the silence of the world or be lulled by the roll of the surf. But that day, there was no silence to be found in La Perla. Mamá was outside, fired up and encouraged by her listeners. There was no stopping her.

Just as I had given up on my creative efforts, Julián appeared, holding a rusty tin can in his hand.

"Look at this. It's almost full. Feel it."

I took the can and hefted its weight. For such a small can, the old tomato sauce can without a label was surprisingly heavy. The grooves circling the can were rusted, as were the small slits that had been made with the tip of a knife at either side of the top. One slit was to let the air enter so that the sauce would pour out easily through the slit on the other side. In the center, Julián had made a slot with his pocketknife. I rattled it and realized it was full of pennies.

"What's this?"

"When I grow up, I'm gonna marry Mami. So I'm saving money to buy her a beautiful wedding gown."

"Julián, you can't marry your mother!" I was shocked.

"Why not?"

"She's too old."

"My mother's not old." He was furious and hurt at the same time, and I realized I should have kept my mouth shut.

"I'm sorry, Julián, I just didn't know you could marry your mother. But if you can, if there aren't any laws or anything against that, it's great."

"What kind of laws?"

"You know, it's what my mother says, all those laws that some men make up so that we, the poor people, can't do anything. I bet the rich can marry their mothers with no problem." I was becoming more and more convinced of my own arguments.

"Yeah, that's why I wanna go work with your mother to bring down those people who make the laws. They're all a bunch of lice, sucking our blood."

"Well, she's out there now giving a speech. Mauleón's gang attacked us again late last night, but the police won't get involved."

"They're in it with him."

"Yeah, I know. And so's the Reverend."

"What?"

"Yeah, I heard Mami telling your mother that Mauleón and the Reverend are in the same group or gang or something. So they're both out to get her. We can't trust those guys, you know. They're bad news."

"What do you think they'll do?"

Suddenly gripped with a terrible fear, I shook with dread.

"I don't know," I said and began to cry.

I was the only one awake on the mat that night, listening to the wind while the ocean rolled in; its huge waves rumbling like one of the wild animals in my stories, a wild animal with horns and claws and an angry roar. My mother hadn't come home. I was still at Luisa's, waiting for her return.

Luisa slept deeply. I knew what she saw in her dreams; she cried out, and I could hear her calling the dead baby. I heard her calling the men who had left her. I heard her accusing God.

When she cried out, she thrashed around in the hammock, and the shanty rocked. I always woke up to listen to her secrets and her pain. Life, for some reason, had made me a listener.

Julián also slept deeply, though he tossed and turned and thrashed. Sometimes he woke up with his head where his feet had been when he went to sleep on his mat. It was a straw mat, pounded down under years of bodies dead tired from so much work that they collapsed on it, tamping down its buoyancy. The mat had become hard where those bodies had worn it down. It prickled, and its broken shoots pierced skin, seemingly in retaliation for the abuse it had suffered. But Julián was too tired to feel anything. He had worked all day at the Presbyterian Hospital, mopping and cleaning disgusting things that he wouldn't name. His mother Luisa was just as tired. Her fingers cramped up every day, but she had to keep up the steady pace of slipping the knife into the folded tobacco leaf and pulling out the thick central vein. She often said she felt like those tobacco leaves, like someone was piercing her insides and pulling them out.

Little Gloria slept peacefully, sucking her thumb, her small head leaning against Angelina's rounded back. Angelina was fast asleep too and smiling sweetly. I was convinced she was an angel, one of those innocents in life that you wonder about because they don't seem human. I asked myself why she didn't have wings and flit around instead of walking. She was so trusting and forgiving. I spent many hours each day with her, and, more times than I care to admit, I would get angry and pick fights with her. Sometimes I even yelled at her. Even when I behaved the worst, she just smiled at me. I often wondered if her mother knew that Angelina was really an angel when she named her.

After all her absences, Mamá always returned. I was always so happy when she came back that I forgot that I was angry at her for leaving. I forgot my tears and the tantrums I invariably staged before she left. I forgot how lonely I was when she was away. Then when she returned my heart sang for joy and my eyes were like lamps, like the bright flames of candles, because she was my everything.

I knew I had to share her with her beliefs, with her party, with the people who took her away from me. But I also knew that she always returned to me, and she always told me when she would be returning.

That's why I was so anxious that night. Why wasn't she back yet? She told me she'd be back before nightfall.

"Five at the latest," she said. "I'll be home, and we'll have dinner together."

Where could she be? Where?

I decided finally to go to sleep, with the hope that by morning, with the light, after I had traversed those long hours in darkness, all would be well. I imagined she would be there caressing my head.

"Nana, don't cry. Why are you crying? I told you I'd come back." She would soothe me and then I would be so happy, I would forget that night ever happened. I fell asleep whispering her name.

Mamá.

In the morning, the shantytown was lively as usual. The sun was bright in the cloudless sky, the air dense with humidity. The neighbors complained as they always did about the heat of the August sun. Perspiring, they brought out their cardboard hand fans and took hearty swipes at the flies that swarmed lazily in the heat. The wind brought an unfamiliar odor to the shantytown that morning. It wasn't the fresh odor of sea salt or new palm shoots. It wasn't even the harsh odor that rose from the abattoir when the animals were butchered.

Something fell from the sky. I looked up. It wasn't rain. I put out my hand; it turned black with tiny particles. When I examined my arms and clothing, they were black with ashes. Ashes rained from the sky. I rushed into Luisa's shack.

"Luisa, Luisa, look! The sky is raining ashes!" I yelled.

She looked at me and smiled.

"Don't worry, Nana, there must be a fire somewhere far away, and those are the ashes brought by the wind."

"Ay, but I'm scared, Luisa," I said. "I'm so scared. Maybe this means that something terrible is going to happen. Maybe the sky is burning and it's going to fall with a terrible crash and crush us."

Luisa threw her head back and laughed.

"Ah, Nana, you think too much. You have such an imagination. If I thought as much as you did, I'd always have a headache. Or worse, I'd go blind. The problem with you is that your mother has given you too many books to read."

"Oh no, Luisa, I don't have too many books. You should see all the books in the workers' library! I have to write my own books because I don't have enough."

"That's even worse! You're making up all these stories. Nana, you have to begin to step firmly on the ground. You're always floating out there somewhere. Put your feet on the ground, *muchacha*, and step on it, step on it hard, because you're going to fly away, you're going float away with the wind, just like those ashes."

"Don't say that, Luisa." I was ready to cry as I contemplated the possibility of floating away in a whirl of ugly ashes.

Then I heard a commotion. We both rushed out of the house to see what had caused the disturbance. We saw Tomás and Jacinto, who was pushing his son in the wheelbarrow. They had such terrible faces, my heart was gripped with fear. Then *doña* Eugenia and her daughter Emilia were rushing toward us. Everybody we knew at the shantytown gathered there, with terrible faces. I started to cry because somehow I knew that something dreadful had happened. I knew that the black rain could only bring misfortune. It was a terrible omen and it had to do with my mother. Right away, I felt it in my bones. I was desperate and flew into *doña* Eugenia's arms. Her breast was soft as a giant pillow. I knew she would hold my head up when my head wanted to drop. She was a *curandera*, after all, and I was convinced that if my heart broke, she could put it back together. I knew that if I went into her arms and inhaled the rue, the sage, the *yerba buena* on her skin, all would be well. But then I noticed that she had forgotten her cigar. That's when I was certain that the news would be crushing.

I brushed my head against her big soft chest.

"*Hija mía*, my little girl, I'm so sorry," she said. "Something has happened to your Mamá."

"Where's Mamá? Where is she? I want her. I want her back. I want her back with all my heart," I cried.

"I'm so sorry, but your Mamá is with God now and with all the angels and the saints in heaven. Your Mamá had an accident."

"No, no!" I struggled away from her arms and I stood there daring them, all of them, every single one of them: Tomás, Jacinto, Emilia, Jacinto's son in the wheelbarrow my own father built, even the formidable *doña* Eugenia, Luisa. Everybody. I dared them to tell me something terrible. I dared them and with my will I tried to shut them up. How could they say something like that about my mother? Mamá was strong and powerful and she knew everything. Mamá could never die.

Then I looked out, because they all turned their heads toward the sea. And I saw four men climbing up the hill carrying a large bundle wrapped in a white sheet. They were approaching slowly, and I stood there like a block of stone. My arms became heavy, my head a dizzying ball of light, and my knees gave way under me. I fell to the ground like a tree that has been chopped from its roots.

I woke up in my house. *Doña* Eugenia was bending over me, dabbing my forehead with a handkerchief moistened in fragrant orange blossom water. Someone had brought something into the house, something I had never seen before. It was a table. A big table. And on the table was the large bundle wrapped in a white sheet that the men had brought up the hill. I stared at the bundle. I carefully studied all the folds and pleats, and I discerned the shape of a head, a small nose, and a chin. A chest. I bolted out of bed.

"My little girl, I'm so sorry that your mother is gone," *doña* Eugenia said. "This is only her body. Her soul is not here anymore. And we will bury her so that her soul can rest in peace."

That's when I knew with all certainty that my mother was gone for good, that she would never return. That's when I knew that the body in the white bundle was not my mother. It was the flesh, the body suit she wore while she was with me, while she was out there struggling and fighting and writing and giving speeches and reading at the tobacco factory and writing letters for people. My Mamá was gone. The mamá who taught me how to bridge any distance with my imagination, who assured me, every day of my life, that she loved me. My Mamá was gone.

I could never express how much I cried when the hole of my mother's absence opened in my heart. I was only twelve years old. At that young age I realized that the hardships we had endured were nothing compared to the hole that lay bare in the core of my being from that day onward. An essential part of me died.

I have been trying to fill that hole in me ever since. From that time on, I began searching through every memory and every experience for a clue that would explain my mother's death. They told me she drowned. But this was incomprehensible to me. My mother never went into the sea. She didn't know how to swim. Why, then, would she go into the treacherous Atlantic waters? I asked everyone, and no one could explain that to me. I said to everyone who would listen, "Let's go to the police. Maybe the police will find out what happened."

But *doña* Eugenia, Luisa, and Tomás said we shouldn't report anything, that the police were bad. And they silenced me with their words because I knew they were right. I knew the police could not be trusted.

Chapter Fourteen

I'm at my wits end, and my heart is sore.
You gods know everything; now you can tell me:
which of the immortals chained me here?

The Odyssey

After the funeral, Luisa threw me to the nuns. I felt like those early Christians facing hungry lions at the Roman Coliseum. It wasn't Luisa's fault, though. I know she couldn't take me in, with all her children and her many problems.

"You are too smart, Nana, and the nuns will educate you." She attempted to comfort me.

"No, please don't send me away. I hate nuns! Why can't I stay with you?"

"I'm sick, Nana, and I can barely support my own children. Nuns are good; they'll be kind to you. They'll teach you many, many things. You'll learn to read more, you'll learn to write more, and you'll be at peace. And the most important thing is that you'll eat every day and sleep in a nice bed every night."

And I had no choice. Because children have no choices.

Luisa took me by the hand one morning shortly after my mother's burial and left me at the wrought-iron gate of the convent. She pulled on a heavy rope and rang the bell. The nun who opened the gate looked like a magpie. The intensity of her black habit was relieved by the starched white of the chest shield, wimple, and collar. The nun hid her hands under the front panel of the habit. A rosewood rosary hung from her side. A cord was tied around her waist. The wimple was tight on her forehead. I was startled when she latched onto my hand and dragged me in.

"Luisa! Luisa!" I cried. But the nun shut the gate in Luisa's face. I saw that she too was wracked with tears when she turned away.

That's how my life at the convent began.

Houses rise like sphinxes, seemingly indifferent to the personal dramas of their inhabitants. The walls seem apathetic to secrets divulged in bedrooms; they may witness the loneliness of closed spaces with the impassivity of stones. But I believe that inhabited spaces retain fragments of the souls they have sheltered. Entities created from bits and pieces torn from human souls— from their desires, wishes, longings, sorrows, joys—melt into a disincarnate shadow that, like a veil, shrouds the atmosphere of the building and makes it thick and soggy. The mansion that had become the Convent of Our Lady of Perpetual Sorrow no longer echoed the false laughter and libidinous desires it harbored when it had been the pleasure-house of Governor de la Victoria. He died, everyone believes, while enjoying the unfathomable delights of a beautiful mulatta.

Before his body was cold, people said, his daughter Juana converted the mansion into a convent for Spanish and Creole women of station who had no desire for the pleasures of the world. Rumors were rife, though, about the intense heat that suffused the women's thighs as they lay on their pallets, arms pressed to their sides, attempting, often unsuccessfully, to concentrate on virtuous thoughts. Many a delivery man, mason, or carpenter was pleasantly surprised in the middle of a sweltering afternoon to find himself diverted into a dusty corner by the ardent arms of one of the recluses. The walls vibrated with ancient delights. The very air of the convent, sultry and dense, made women and men gasp with delectation. Many women awakened to an enjoyment deep in their interior folds that they had never known existed. Some discovered, nine months later, the consequence of their dauntless pursuit of pleasure, their childbirth howls louder than any they had emitted while quenching their appetites. The infants that mysteriously appeared on the bloody pallets of the women forced the Archbishop of San Juan to proclaim the Convent an orphanage, claiming the babies had been left at the doorstep. Once the lust had been scrubbed off the mansion's walls by decades of hardy penance, prayers, psalms and the sorry penury of orphans, the Convent's atmosphere underwent a singular transmutation. It took several decades, but finally the titillating spirits that haunted the mansion were replaced by souls who succumbed to the privation and hardships of religious fervor.

After the Spanish-American War, when the island became a colony of the United States, a deal was struck between the invading Americans and the Archbishop of San Juan. The convent-orphanage remained under the auspices of the Catholic Church, but the Spanish nuns, with their dove-white, wing-like wimples, were replaced by sedate North Americans in severe Dominican habits. The Spanish priests stayed, to better attend to the souls of the Spanish-speaking Puerto Ricans.

I still remember the shabby elegance of the convent's frescoed walls and ceilings and the tiny chapels stuffed with so many holy images they looked like dollhouses. There were precious statuettes, rosaries, and crowns of gold, silver, coral, diamonds, and ivory. Scores of reliquaries, heavy with the scent of frankincense, held the remains of devout nuns and priests who had died in the sanctuary of the convent. A large courtyard surrounded a fragrant garden. I was barely twelve years old when the convent became my new home.

The early morning mist seeped through the window, and the wrought-iron grills cast indigo shadows on the floor. The room had high ceilings, stained yellow by moisture, and rough white walls. As usual, I woke in the long and narrow room where we slept earlier than the others. Roosters crowed in the distance, just before dawn broke. It would be another hot and humid day. I looked out over the main courtyard. From where I stood, I could catch glimpses of the clusters of orange and palm trees that hugged the convent grounds. A maze of clematis and bright red bougainvillea crept over the stone walls. At this time of day, when the sun had not quite broken through and the outside world was filled with silence, I felt most like an alien being. Living in a convent was like living in a foreign country. This period was my age of melancholy.

The world hurt, and I tumbled into a void of terrifying aloneness. The jabber of the nuns in a language I at first did not understand exacerbated my inner emptiness. I confronted the new language, a language of angles and bones, with suspicion. Hard and relentless, its sharp consonants and unpredictable vowels betrayed the simplicity of everything I had known. Once I learned its rigid geometry and managed to climb the heights of its scaffolding, English became surprisingly supple and rich, and I recognized within it the muscle of domination.

With time, my second language became the language of disguise. After so many years of living in English, I still ask myself the question: Am I really me when I live in it? Or am I that other self who inhabits me and takes off on tangents that have no relevance, becoming tangled in its forest of exclusion?

My second language is absence. It is the perfect metaphor for exile. Weeping into the darkest recesses of the night, I was lost in its hierarchies. During the years in which I lived in it, I observed myself translating my self. I translated my true self into the one I became when I lived the second tongue. In this ceaseless interpretation of the self, I wondered how effective the translation could be, since I failed to distinguish the translation from the original. Was I expressing what was me? Or was the second language so separate from me that it failed to express who I was and what I felt? The language then arrested my truths. It became the language that censored, the language that punished my flights into the rich landscapes of metaphor. And it became the language of repression.

Often I woke up before the other orphans and watched Felicia as she slept. Something about her made me feel protective. I wanted to hold her in my arms and shield her from the hurt I knew life would bring her. Felicia was tiny as a sparrow. She had black hair, and her long black eyelashes swept against her cheeks. Her eyebrows were beautifully arched, her dark pink lips full. She had the largest eyes I had ever seen. They looked out in wonder at everything. She had arrived at the convent two years after me, and I tried to help her adjust, but I still remembered how hard it had been to arrive at this cold place that was like a foreign country. Like all of us at the beginning of our exile, Felicia cried herself to sleep every night for many months. When I looked at her that morning, Felicia's sheet was wedged in her underarms as usual. We were afraid of inadvertently tucking our arms under the sheets while we slept. Severe punishment awaited us if we were caught in this sinful position.

There were eight of us in the long room. The remaining four empty iron-framed beds had been stripped of linen. An overwhelming sorrow clutched at my chest when I looked at the stained mattresses on rusted bedsprings. They reminded me of the millstone around my neck. The beds were narrow and hard like our lives.

As I made the bed, I thought of the day ahead. There was never something new to alter the grind of our days. We prayed and prayed for such long periods of time our knees were coarse as old leather shoes. We also faced the drudgery of the menial work we had to perform for the nuns. The eight of us were between the ages of twelve and sixteen. The sixteen-year-olds, closer to an often-undesired sisterhood than the younger orphans, were usually more circumspect, more reconciled to their fates. Felicia was my age when she arrived, and she still contemplated a furtive escape. I was not ready to conform to life in a convent either.

Routine deadened our life in the convent. Sister Martha assigned me the task of scrubbing the kitchen floor every morning after prayers and every evening before vespers and bedtime. The nun was small and chunky. She had pink skin, and her cheeks were red, with a rash-like texture. Her light brown eyebrows were always knit, and long lines furrowed her forehead. I never saw her smile. As she spoke, I looked down at the large black and white kitchen tiles, which reminded me of my mother's funeral, an ocean of people dressed all in black or all in white. When I was assigned the floor-scrubbing task, I asked Sister Martha why the floor had to be scrubbed in the morning when it had been scrubbed the night before. She smacked me on the head and ordered me to do what I was told.

Sister Martha's rule was not limited to kitchen duties. Sometimes it seemed that she was everywhere and saw everything, like the many-headed monsters Odysseus fought. I soon discovered that Felicia had found a way of combating the sister's omnipresence.

That day I was delayed after morning mass because I had snuck into one of the forbidden lavatories to urinate. Only nuns could use the ground floor toilets; the girls were forced to climb two flights of stairs to separate facilities. Going upstairs would have delayed me even more. Once finished, I rushed down the corridor towards the kitchen, pleading to God, the Virgin, anyone who would listen, *Oh please don't let them see me, please don't let them see me.*

Suddenly, from the corner of my eye I saw the black fold of a skirt and heard the clatter of the rosary beads and keys Sister Martha fastened to the thick cord around her waist. Quickly, I veered toward the massive door that separated the stair landing from the corridor and crept behind it. I almost jumped out of my skin when I noticed the brown shadow of someone hiding there. When the figure looked up, I saw Felicia's ashen face.

I was afraid Sister Martha would hear the wild beat of my heart as she passed by the door, her determined steps hard on the tiled floor, her skirts swishing, keys jangling with the rosary beads. Our shoulders sagged when she passed by the door; I realized how tense we had been. I took a peek—the coast was clear. I grabbed Felicia's hand, and we rushed to the kitchen, immediately kneeling on the floor with rags, brushes, and buckets of soapy water.

"What were you doing behind the door?" I whispered.

"Same as you," Felicia shrugged. "Hiding from Sister Martha. I can recognize her steps now. When I hear her coming I hide behind the nearest door."

I mulled this over. It was a good strategy to stay out of the Sister's sight. Out of sight, out of mind, as they say.

One morning, I was still asleep when Margarita awakened me.

"Marina, wake up." She shook my shoulder until I was fully awake and sitting up.

"What's the matter?" I whispered. My heart was in my throat, I was so scared.

"Oh, my God, Marina, something horrible has happened."

"What, what?"

Margarita pointed at the bed with a trembling finger as if an ugly monster lurked under her sheets.

The floor tiles were cold; my heart was even colder when, with dread, I saw the circle of blood on Margarita's sheets.

"I'm bleeding," Margarita cried. "And it's coming from my insides."

"Don't worry, Margarita," I said. "It's your period. It happens every single month to girls. I got it just before I came here. It's not a nice thing, but you'll just have to live with it."

"What if the nuns find out?"

"You have to tell them."

Margarita's face froze in fear and confusion.

"No, no, they'll punish me."

"They get periods too, you know."

"What?"

"Every single woman in the whole world gets them. Even nuns. It's natural. And you have to tell them, you have no choice. I had to tell them because they control the amount of cloth they give us to collect the blood every month."

"That sounds so disgusting."

"I'm sorry, Margarita." I hugged her. "We better get these sheets washed. And the mattress too."

The morning bell rang, and the other girls woke up. They all gathered around Margarita, chattering excitedly.

"You're a woman now," Goyita said with admiration in her voice. "I can't wait to get my period. Then I'm telling the nuns to stick their prayers in their ears and I'm getting out of here. As fast as I can."

"You mean I can leave now?"

"I don't think so," I said. "The only way to leave this place is by escaping."

"So what have we here?" It was dreaded Sister Martha. When I heard her voice, the hairs on the nape of my neck stood on end. Margarita began to sob.

"What's the matter with you?" the nun demanded.

Margarita pointed at the stained bed again. This time she covered her face with her free hand.

The nun turned to face us.

"Everybody out!" she ordered.

The girls hurried to the corridor to wash and change into their uniforms, but I lingered and hid behind the door.

"So," I heard Sister Martha's voice, low and clear. "This is a very bad sign from God, Margarita."

"What is it, Sister Martha? I haven't done anything bad, I swear on my mother's grave."

"Well, you must have done something pretty terrible to bleed like that. You know what this means?"

"No."

"This is God's punishment. You will die before midnight."

Margarita did not say a word. She stood petrified as an old oak tree in an ancient forest. Her face hardened into a mask of terror. My mouth hung open. I wondered how nuns could lie so shamelessly. Sister Martha had a lot to confess next Saturday, I thought to myself.

"Reflect upon that today," Sister Martha said harshly, her lips tight as seams. "And repent."

My heart pounded when I heard the swish of the nun's skirts and the jangle of her keys and rosary beads as she walked past me. Once the nun went down the stairs, I ran to Margarita.

"I heard what she said." I shook her, trying desperately to get her to react to my voice, but she had a vague, distant gaze that made me shiver.

"It's not true, Margarita. You're not going to die. She just wants to make you suffer. You know how mean she is."

"But why would she say such a terrible lie?"

"I don't know, Margarita. Maybe she never wanted to be a nun, like we don't. Maybe she was an orphan and they forced her, and now she's taking it out on us. But please believe me, it's not true. Look at me, I'm still alive, and I got my period a long time ago."

"Maybe you haven't sinned like me."

"Oh, please, Margarita. I'm a lot worse than you are and you know it. I'm always running into trouble with the nuns, especially Sister Martha. I still have the bruises from the last beating she gave me when I was late for mass. Look." I pulled up my skirt. She grimaced at the sight of welts crisscrossing my buttocks.

But Margarita didn't seem convinced. Somehow a nun's word was more powerful than that of a lowly orphan like me. Like her.

"Margarita, let's do this. I'll sit with you tonight past midnight. I'll hold your hand all night if you want. You won't die, you'll see."

Margarita's eyes brightened. "You'll do that?"

"Yes, I will. I promise not to fall asleep. I'll tell you stories. If we're awake and alert, there's no way you can die. I'll hold onto you with all my might."

That night, I recited everything I remembered from *The Odyssey*, which I must admit was substantial. It wasn't until Odysseus landed on Circe's island that Margarita fell asleep. I slipped into her narrow bed, put my arm around her, and was soundly asleep before I could even think about the necessity of staying awake all night. In a restless dream I was chasing a beautiful blue bird through a forest. I held out my hand to catch it and woke with a start. It was just before dawn. When the bell rang, I was sitting on the edge of Margarita's bed. She looked up at me and smiled. We had vanquished the dreaded Sister Martha's predictions. We had vanquished death itself.

Most nuns were not cruel like Sister Martha. They were just indifferent. There was an exception, though. Her name was Sister Theresa.

I have always thanked God for books. Since my convent days I have thanked the Source of Goodness that I'm sure exists in the universe for Sister Theresa.

I had been at the convent for almost a year when I was assigned cleaning duties in the convent library. The room was large and kept dark to protect the books that lined its walls. Shelves built from floor to ceiling held leather-bound tomes with gilt titles. When I saw all those beautiful books in one room, I almost broke down and cried. I was tempted for the first time in my life to become a nun so I might sit in that grand library and read books all day long. Sister Joseph, who worked directly with the Mother Superior, had given me a flannel cloth, a feather duster, and instructions on how to dust the books with care, making sure my hands were dry and clean so as not to mar the leather when I touched the books. The minute she left me to my own devices, I sat on the floor with an edition of a book written in letters I had never seen before. The book was illustrated with ink plates. I studied the drawings and the curved letters, which were filled with the resonance of time and distance. I recognized Odysseus in the illustrations immediately and was comforted by the familiarity of my hero's struggles. I didn't hear the nun when she entered the room.

"Hello, there," she said softly, and I jumped in the air, almost dropping the precious book.

"Oh, Sister, I'm so sorry," I stammered. "It's just that this is such a beautiful book." I dropped my shoulders, expecting a cuff on the head or a pinched ear.

"It's in ancient Greek, you know."

"Really? That's the language spoken by Homer. My mother told me all about that." I blabbed on, oblivious now to any punishment the nun would be moved to mete out. "This is my favorite book in all the world. Mamá gave it to me, written in Spanish, but it got lost. I used to read pages from it every day." I held up the book and looked at it longingly. "I would love to read it again."

"Just a minute." The sister brushed her long skirt against my hand as she reached toward one of the shelves and pulled down another beautifully bound book.

"Here, this one's in English. Can you read English?"

I nodded. "But not too well."

"That's all right. Your English will improve as you practice. By the way, what's your name?"

"Marina Alomar Pagán."

"I'm Sister Theresa. How long have you been here, Marina?"

"One year."

"I've been away for a while and just returned." She smiled at me with such tenderness, I couldn't help myself. The tears that had been ready to burst from the moment I entered the library streamed down my cheeks like a torrent of rain.

Sister Theresa put her arms around my shoulders. When I pressed the side of my head against her chest, I could smell incense and rose water. I thought I was incapable of stopping my tears, that they would flow forever and flood the convent, San Juan, the island, the entire world.

"There, there, sweet Marina. Shush, don't cry now. Listen to me," she said and pushed me away so she could look at my face. "Let's make a pact, you and me. No one else has to know about it."

I was very surprised at this because somehow the idea of making a pact that no one else would be privy to seemed against convent rules. The nuns had rules against everything imaginable, and I couldn't believe making a pact wasn't a prohibited act, and a most serious one at that. Nothing less than mortal sin, I was convinced. With much trepidation for both Sister Theresa and for myself, I nodded.

"We'll have special lessons, just you and me. I'll lend you books to read, and then we'll discuss them. You'll see; books will fill your emptiness."

"But Sister Theresa," I objected. "I'm not allowed to do anything but pray and clean. And be good," I added hastily.

"Don't worry, sweet Marina. We'll find a way," she said.

And that's how it was. I remember the Sister in her severe black habit, a large medallion of the Virgin with the infant Jesus protecting her heart. She was small and slender. Her face reminded me of a porcelain doll I had once seen in a San Juan shop. Her skin was the color of ivory; she had dark eyes and eyebrows, a delicate nose, and small lips. Like the other nuns, she wore heavy laced shoes, polished to a black sheen. I remember watching from the bedroom window as Sister Theresa quietly skimmed toward the thick convent wall on moonlit nights, her hem swishing. I saw her place a package in a turnstile at the gate then push it forward. When the turnstile rotated back to her, propelled by a mysterious hand I was never to see, Sister Theresa extracted a book from the iron grill. Tucking her treasure under her sleeve, head bent in apparent meditation, she sailed into the convent like a graceful ship parting the waters.

Under Sister Theresa's tutelage, I learned about the fictional nature of history. She always said that history was a distortion of facts.

"Believe what you see and what your heart tells you to be true, regardless of the observations of the chroniclers of our times," she often said. "For they will interpret what they see through the prism of their own biases and prejudices, and many will report what they are commanded to by the powers that rule them. See the truth only as it is revealed by your heart and mind. Then, and this is the most important and difficult, live by your beliefs and, if necessary, die for them."

I always thought about Mamá and her ideals when Sister Theresa made these pronouncements.

Often Sister Theresa would sit down to sew. In her basket piled high with colorful yarn, spools of thread, and scraps of fabric, she would conceal a book for me.

Later, taking walks in the courtyard and garden, under the pretense of meditating upon the mysteries of the Church, we would discuss our readings under the watchful eyes of the stone Virgin of Sorrows. Sister Theresa taught me to read ancient Greek, to esthetically balance, as she liked to say, the Latin I learned in the prayer books.

By my fourteenth birthday, I couldn't baste a hem or embroider a simple handkerchief, but I had read the classics, including Plato and Plutarch in their original language. I had read Voltaire and Rousseau and the classical works of Spanish and English literature. To further balance my view of the world, Sister Theresa gave me current newspapers and denounced the social injustices of this Earth in spirited lectures. The Sister even ventured into an analysis of Steinbeck's indictments and in heated whispers chastised the capitalist revolution. How the nun obtained so much information when she rarely left the convent walls, and never alone, I was never to know.

When I heard about her death, I had been in the convent for three years and knew my way around the many open and hidden spaces. The vestry bell pealed vigorously every dawn, but since I always woke up before anyone else, I could be still and quiet for a few moments without having to pray or do penance or scrub the floors.

On one of those quiet mornings, I heard strange noises coming from the courtyard. Silently, so as not to be heard by the other girls, I stepped out of the room. The hard marble floor chilled my bare feet. I held my breath and padded under the *mudéjar* arches. At the top of the tiled staircase I stood under the carved cupola and leaned over the banister, which the novices kept smooth and well-polished. I heard voices and leaned forward. Mother Superior's voice, swollen with sorrow and apprehension, was so low I could not understand her words. Our confessor Father Juan spoke. His message rose up to the second floor like a tired bat.

"I wish to God I didn't have to give you such terrible news. We have just received word from Saint Francis of Assisi Sanatorium in Boston. Our courageous Sister Theresa has succumbed. After such a long struggle, the tuberculosis was stronger than she was. She died in God's grace. May she rest in peace."

The Mother Superior's sobs punctuated the priest's announcement. She murmured a response, and the priest left. I stepped softly on the glazed tiles. At the bottom of the stairs, the swirling circles etched in the tiles burst painfully in my head. Mother Superior sat on a *sillón de fraileros*, a wide, rectangular monk's chair, her back pushed into its pungent tooled leather, hands clasped on the severe arm rests. Distracted by her own sorrow, she never noticed when I crawled into a dark corner of the room. I wept for a long time.

How many mothers was I destined to lose?

Every night after I heard of Sister Theresa's death, I waited for everyone to fall sleep before I snuck out. When I reached the bottom of the stairs, I tiptoed into the library and picked out *The Odyssey*. Hugging the precious book, a reminder of the two most important women in my life, I lit a gas lamp and sat on one of the simple wooden chairs that surrounded the long library table. I put my head on the table and sobbed. Sister Theresa's passing brought back the pain of my mother's death, the terrible void left in my world.

I reread the many chapters of *The Odyssey*. I had read it more times than I could count, yet it was always a pleasure to decipher the neat letters cut into the thick paper, words flowing through its grain like a stream. The first time Sister Theresa had discussed the epic poem with me, she said that I was old enough to understand the sorrow of leaving. I grasped very little of the poem's meaning even then, though I had read it many times as a child. But as always, I was enthralled by the beauty of the words, the images of sun and sea and bags of wind that awakened in me a new yearning for home. It was only with the years and constant rereading that I finally apprehended the book's other message. For *The Odyssey* is not only a poem about the trials and tribulations of a hero who, in perilous journeys, attempts to find his way home; it is also about a heroic quest for justice. I shared Odysseus' hunger for justice in a world where punishment and retribution were as cruelly steadfast as a hungry spider weaving its web.

Chapter Fifteen

He led them down dank ways,
… past shores of Dream and narrows of the sunset,
in swift flight to where the dead inhabit
wastes of asphodel at the world's end.

The Odyssey

As my sixteenth birthday approached, the nuns, especially Sister Joseph, kept pressuring me to take my vows. But I was bitterly averse to accepting the habit. I never wanted to be a nun, not even a nun like Sister Theresa. I didn't believe in what nuns did. I only believed what my mother taught me. The endless acts of cruelty at the convent and the bitterness exuded by the nuns reinforced my resolve. I must admit, though, that there were times when I saw one of the novices weep when she prayed, and envy hardened my heart.

Why couldn't I be good, like the others? I asked myself.

At times, I even agreed with the nuns that my failings were immense and unforgivable. But then Sister Martha would demonstrate how mean a nun could be, and I would realize that, bad as I might be, I was not capable of being as cruel as she was.

Once I was on my knees scrubbing the kitchen floor when Sister Martha walked in and noticed a grease stain behind me.

"Does that look clean to you?" she yelled, pointing an accusatory finger at the floor. Her face was ashen with anger.

"No, Sister Martha," I said hurriedly and scrambled to scrub the stain that revealed my inadequacies.

"Get up and look at me," Sister Martha said. When I got up, she struck me in the face with her rosary. "Sister Theresa's not here to protect you now, so either you do your chores competently, or you'll be sent upstairs with only bread and water."

I cupped my stinging cheek. Sister Martha grabbed my wrist and pulled my hand away.

"I don't want to see any more dirt on this floor. You hear me?"

When she left, my tears mingled with the soapy water, and I scrubbed them into the floor.

"What happened?" Felicia tiptoed in and put her hand on my shoulder.

"Sister Martha again. This time she hit me with her rosary."

"Ay, that hurts. The beads are wooden, you know."

"I know." I looked up, and Felicia wiped my tears with her sleeve. "I'm terrified of those cells upstairs. I heard some novices have even died there." We were all called novices, even if we hadn't agreed to become nuns.

"Just do what she says, Marina."

But I knew there was nothing I could do to please Sister Martha.

When I turned sixteen, Sister Joseph, the nun apparently in charge of recruitment, wrenched me away from the other girls after prayers. She was a tall, skinny woman with blond eyebrows and ice-blue eyes. Her long, thin nose was sprinkled with light freckles. I knew when she had been out of the convent because her narrow forehead, her cheeks, and the tip of her nose would turn lobster red in the harsh tropical sun.

"So, Marina, have you made a decision?"

"Pardon me?"

"You know full well what I'm talking about, Marina. Don't play dumb with me, young lady."

"Oh, that." When I realized what she was talking about, I couldn't conceal the exasperation in my voice.

Sister Joseph glowered at me with pinched lips. I refused to turn away from the anger in her eyes.

"How dare you look at me like that? You're just an orphan from La Perla, a weed that grew in a slum. You're a little nothing, and you have to learn your place in life. I don't understand where you got that arrogance. You should be meek and humble and downright grateful for what we've given you, everything we've done for you. No one else wants you. Don't you understand that? Only God could possibly want a destitute orphan like you. That's why you have to dedicate your life to our Savior. It's the least you can do."

Hopelessness had forced some of the other girls to take the veil when they were fifteen, but I had refused. Many things had died in me, but not hope.

"I'm sorry, Sister Joseph. I don't mean to offend you or anyone else, but I don't want to be a nun."

Sister Joseph grabbed my forearm, and I winced.

"You better take your vows, young lady, or else."

"Or else what?" I was unable to contain the anger in my voice.

"Or else we'll force you. We can make you, you know." Sister Joseph's voice lowered dangerously, and I backed away. "Go to confession now." She tossed her head to the side. "And don't forget to tell Father Juan about your arrogance."

Padre Juan came every Saturday to hear our confessions. He was a short and stocky Galician, with dark black hair, streaked with gray, and hairy hands. Rumors were rife that his soul was in a state of grave peril because of a five-year relationship he had with a local woman. Once when Felicia and I were hiding from Sister Martha behind a door, we heard Sister Joseph discussing with Sister Claire Padre Juan's iniquity. Sister Joseph claimed, in no uncertain terms, that Padre Juan was not to blame for his situation. The culprit was the woman, who, as everyone knew, had cast a spell on him.

"You know how godless these local people are," she emphasized.

Having heard this, I was surprised that Padre Juan was allowed to hear confessions, absolve others from sin, and say mass. After learning of the priest's travails, I was comforted that my sins of disobedience and anger were quite tame in comparison, though I didn't have the excuse of someone casting a spell on me. My sins were knowingly committed and sometimes, I must admit, thoroughly enjoyed.

The church was next to the convent. An underground passageway, dark and smelling of drains, had been built so that we could enter the church without having to see or be seen by the outside world. As I waited in line with the other girls by the confessional, I wondered what I would confess to, for we had few opportunities to sin. So I always confessed to whatever the nuns, especially Sister Joseph or Sister Martha, objected to in my behavior. Through the years, I told Padre Juan that I was arrogant and angry and disobedient and a liar, because that's what the nuns told me I was. I learned to define myself with their words.

Padre Juan listened, I think, since he made unintelligible noises that seemed to rise from his throat. Invariably he instructed me to pray five Hail Marys and two Our Fathers. I hastily recited the Act of Contrition and rushed to a pew before the priest reconsidered the severity of my sins and increased my penance.

I must admit that on those occasions I enjoyed the peace of the church, the mute angels, the immobile statues of Mary, the girls and nuns silently praying. And I loved the scent of incense. It reminded me of when *doña* Eugenia burned the herbs she harvested from the plants in old tin cans on her tiny plot of land. She burned the *yerba buena, ruda, amanú,* and *tagarto* to prepare *despojos* that would clear evil spirits from houses, as well as negative entities, jealous thoughts, the evil eye, and the envy of others. Whenever I came to her house, she made sure to point out the names of the herbs she grew and what they were for so I would always remember.

Once Sister Theresa died, I grew restless at the convent. The nuns, especially Sister Martha, yelled and screamed that I was not quick enough in completing my chores. If I was lost in thought, they asked me what I was doing daydreaming, when I should be contemplating upon my sins or praying for forgiveness. A cuff on the head brought me swiftly back to my drab reality. How they knew that I was thinking and not praying, I never figured out, but they knew that my thoughts wandered to the outside world, where my mind always remained.

All those years, I longed to walk the streets of Old San Juan. I remembered the long strolls I took with my mother, crossing the old city from one end to the other, to go to the market or to La Colectiva, the tobacco factory where she read for the workers. Sometimes we stopped to watch a *paso fino* horse clopping on the cobblestones while we bit into a juicy mango or licked on a coconut ice from a roadside vendor. I longed for those days. I longed to recapture everything I had lost.

The opportunity came when I least expected it.

One morning in the kitchen, Felicia poked me in the ribs. She was next to me scrubbing the floor. She still cried herself to sleep every night, and every morning I worried that she would be blind because her eyes were swollen shut.

"Marina," she whispered. I looked up. Only novices were in the kitchen at that time after breakfast. Margarita was cooking, as usual. She had to learn to boil potatoes and vegetables and prepare meat with no other seasoning but salt. Whenever there was meat for the nuns, Margarita managed to set aside a pork chop or a round of steak and hide it in an empty can in a nook at the back of the stove. When the other girls had fallen asleep, she and Felicia would scurry to the kitchen to savor their treat. Margarita was often exhausted after cooking three meals a day for the nuns and breakfast and a mid-afternoon meal for the orphans and cleaning up afterwards. Whenever we could get away with it, we helped her.

Felicia poked me again in the ribs.

"Marina, I'll tell you a secret. Margarita has a boyfriend."

"How is it possible?" My scouring brush dropped next to my knees. "There aren't any boys here. Where in the world did she find a boy?"

Felicia giggled.

"It's easy. There's a boy who delivers the food every day from the market. Margarita goes out in the morning and collects the delivery. Then she collects her kisses."

"I don't believe this," I said, trying hard to keep my voice down. "If the nuns find out, they'll kill her. They'll lock her up in a cell for months and months and feed her bread and water. Then she'll surely die."

I sat back on the wet floor, thinking about this. Suddenly all sorts of possibilities opened before my eyes.

"I'll take care of this," I said to Felicia.

I got up and shook the novice habit I loathed. It was dark brown and made of coarse cotton that abraded the skin. I went up to the stove.

"Margarita," I whispered, and I pulled at her sleeve.

"Marina, don't bother me now. I have to cook this. If it doesn't come out right, the nuns will punish me."

"It's okay. They're at prayers now. Just keep stirring the pot."

I looked back toward the door. Felicia was stationed there, looking out for the nuns. I turned back to Margarita and put my mouth near her ear.

"I know you have a boyfriend."

She snapped her head to the side to stare at me. The cooking spoon dropped with a clank on the stove. We both looked back at the door, expecting a nun to come, arms flailing, but nobody came. Felicia shook her head, indicating that the coast was clear.

"How did you know?"

"You've been seen with the boy who delivers the groceries."

"Oh, my God." Margarita was distraught, her face as white as chalk. "What will I do now? If the girls know, the nuns are bound to find out. One of these *bochincheras* will tell just so they can get some privileges."

"No, I think it's just a few of us who know. But be careful, Margarita, be very careful."

She wiped her sweaty forehead with a dishtowel and then dried the palms of her hands with her apron. I was about to tell her about a plan I had hatched when she picked up the cooking spoon; it fell from her trembling hand again. Then she dropped the lids. It seemed that Margarita could not hold onto anything without dropping it. Suddenly we saw a stealthy shadow fall across the kitchen. When we looked up, Felicia was on her knees pretending to wipe the floor with a rag, and Sister Claire, the oldest nun, stood there with a stern look and pinched lips, staring at us.

"What are you two up to? Haven't you enough work to do, or should I assign you some more chores?"

"Oh, Sister Claire," I blurted nervously, silently saying a prayer of gratitude that it wasn't Sister Martha. "I'm terribly sorry, but I really wanted to learn how to cook. I asked Margarita how she made these wonderful boiled potatoes."

"Hah," Sister Claire responded. "I've never seen you interested in anything important in my life. Interested in cooking! You must be gossiping."

And she pinched my ear between her thumb and index finger. I yelped with pain as she dragged me to the chapel, where she shoved me into a pew, ordered me to get on my knees, and said, "You will stay here praying until I return. Make sure you pray hard for forgiveness for all those lies you told me."

My hands were still wet and cold from scrubbing the kitchen floor. This was the worst punishment for me. When I was ordered to pray for forgiveness, I never knew when the commanding nun would come back. It always seemed like an eternity. The worst punishment wasn't having to kneel for hours; it wasn't having to pray until my throat was dry; it wasn't being bored out of my mind. The worst was waiting for the nun to return.

One time Sister Martha forced me to kneel at the pew all night. It wasn't until the next morning, just before the nuns came to the chapel for their morning prayers, that I was allowed to stand up. My legs felt like wooden clubs holding up my torso. When I tried to take a step, I fell and bruised my chin. My legs were numb; pins and needles crawled up from my feet to my thighs.

Sister Martha dragged me to the convent while I wobbled painfully behind her, trying to keep up with her fast pace. She informed me that God was punishing me for being a liar.

"And lazy too!" She turned around and smacked me on the head. "And don't think you're getting away from doing your chores." She shoved me in the direction of the kitchen and, with long purposeful strides, disappeared into the parlor.

A few mornings later I arrived at the kitchen, to work. Felicia scrubbed the tables before the nuns came back from the chapel for breakfast. She was sniffling. Another girl stirred a pot of oatmeal at the stove.

"Where's Margarita?" I whispered.

Felicia pushed away a strand of hair from her eyes.

"The nuns caught her with the delivery boy this morning. She was locked up in a cell."

"Oh, no."

"Margarita thinks that you told the nuns so they wouldn't punish you any longer." Felicia said, glancing up at me. And from the way she looked at me, I knew she thought it was true.

I was hurt, because I would never tell on anyone. No matter how badly I was punished, I could remain still and silent as a rock.

But Margarita's misfortune became my stroke of good luck. Sister Claire had sent one of the other novices to get the groceries that morning, but the girl dropped one of the bags and broke all the eggs for the morning's breakfast. After supervising the cleaning up, Sister Claire, who normally seemed to be on the verge of a nervous attack, developed a severe tic. Her eyes began to blink hard and fast. She looked around the kitchen, and I happened to be scrubbing the floor nearest to her. Sister Claire grabbed my arm and pulled me up to my feet.

"Tomorrow," she blinked fiercely several times, "you go downstairs and get the groceries." She rushed out of the kitchen holding her head in her hands.

Eusebio, the delivery boy, was about seventeen. He was tall and skinny, with a round face and dark brown eyes. The sun had darkened his skin while he made the daily deliveries to the convent, *fondas,* and factories.

I watched closely as one of the nuns unlocked the gate and waited for Eusebio to enter the foyer, where I waited to carry the bags to the kitchen. The minute Eusebio reached the foyer, I whispered, "Eusebio, the nuns found out about you and Margarita and they're punishing her. She's locked up in a cell."

I stopped to see what impression this made on Eusebio.

"What do you mean, she's in a cell?" he asked with horror.

"Oh, don't worry, they'll let her out one day. In the meantime, I can sneak to her cell and give her a message for you, if you want."

"Yes, *por favor,*" he nodded energetically. "Tell her, tell her I love her. And if she wants I can rescue her."

Rescue.

The word punched me in the solar plexus and suddenly left me bereft of speech, stripped of my very breath.

Rescue.

The word reverberated throughout my brain. A bolt of realization blazed a path of possibilities in the mazes of my mind. I could almost see my brain light up, like an electrical storm.

I grabbed Eusebio's shirt and pulled him forward desperately, though he tried to back away.

"Eusebio, listen to me. I know how you can save Margarita, and you can save me too. I'll arrange everything."

"How?"

"All you have to do is when you go out now, leave the gate unlocked. Pretend that you close it behind you, but don't pull it too hard so the latch doesn't take."

"But they're the ones who lock it," he said. "The nuns."

"All right, that takes care of my plan." I was despondent. If nuns unlocked and locked the gate, then there was no hope for Margarita and me. A tear ran unexpectedly down my cheek. The walls surrounding the convent were could not be scaled. I looked around me. I had another idea, born out of desperation and want.

"Eusebio? Does the same nun open and close the gate?" I asked.

"Yes, of course, it's the same one."

"I know what we'll do, then. Just before dawn tomorrow, before anyone gets up, I'll take the keys from Mother Superior's office and let Margarita out. We'll sneak outside and hide somewhere in the bushes. When the nun comes and opens the gate to let you in, you have to distract her. Remember, just as she opens the gate, you distract her. Then Margarita and I can run away. She can wait for you at the Plaza de Armas. I'll show her the way. And I'll go home. I'll finally go home."

That night, I was so nervous I couldn't eat. I developed a fever, and the nuns thought I was sick. They put me to bed early, which surprised me, because it was Sister Martha, my archenemy, who insisted on it, though not until after I had finished my chores. Maybe she thought going to bed was a good punishment. I washed the stack of dishes after the nuns and novices had eaten, and I scrubbed that hateful kitchen floor again. But I was spared from the nightly prayers. I was so tired that I struggled not to fall asleep when my head hit the pillow. That night I thought of freedom, of running away, of my ugly habit and how strange I would look, an unescorted convent orphan in a brown habit, hair cropped closely to my scalp, running through the streets of Old San Juan. But I didn't care.

It must have been midnight when I woke Felicia.

"Shh," I said and pressed a finger to my lips. "Listen carefully. Margarita and I are going to escape in the morning. Do you want to come with us?"

"Where will you go?"

"I'm going back home, and Margarita's running away with her boyfriend."

"But I have nowhere to go."

"Come with me, Felicia. To La Perla. I know lots of people there."

"No, I can't." Tears shimmered on her cheeks. "This is my home now. I'm going to take the habit as soon as the nuns let me."

"Listen to me, Felicia." I was desperate. "You don't have to do this. You can get out and be free. Don't you want to be free?"

"No, I don't. I'm afraid of being here, but I'm even more afraid of what's out there." She put her arms around me, and her body shook as she wept.

"Maybe I shouldn't go either," I said softly. I loved Felicia like my own blood and couldn't bear the thought of leaving her behind.

"No, no, Marina. Don't say such a thing! You must go with Margarita. I'll pray for your safe journey."

Dawn came quickly, and a rooster crowed in the distance. I tiptoed out of bed, careful not to make any noise because Felicia, who was asleep in the bed next to mine, was a light sleeper. Any noise would startle her awake and she would cry out, until she realized where she was and that nothing had changed. With a heavy heart, I bent down and softly kissed her good-bye.

I slipped into Mother Superior's office. On the wall by the door was a row of hooks where she kept the long keys to every room in the convent. The keys were labeled. I knew where the cells used for punishment and atonement were. Margarita would be in a cell on the third floor. I rushed up the stairs, gasping not so much from the climb as from the panic in my heart. I looked through the bars at each cell until I found Margarita. She was lying on a straw mat on the floor, curled into herself like an animal that needs to protect its most tender parts. I didn't know how I would unlock the heavy door and open it without making any noise.

I didn't succeed. The lock was old and clanked, and the hinges on the door groaned. I squeezed my eyes shut and pressed ahead. Margarita jumped up when she saw me, and I pressed a finger against my lips. I took her by the hand. We ran out of the cell and down the stairs. Something must have been protecting us that day, maybe the power of Felicia's prayers, because no one heard us. We looked through the window on the second floor and saw Eusebio approach the convent gate. In the time it takes to say an *Ave María*, we rushed outside and hid behind a rose bush near the gate. With my thoughts, I wanted to still Eusebio's mind so he would not act suspiciously. My heart pounded when the nun unlocked the gate. I could feel Margarita's fast breath when Eusebio pretended he was ill and fell against the gate. The gate opened wide with the weight of his body. The nun dropped the keys and the lock and released the gate, her back to us, as she tried to help Eusebio. Margarita and I leaped from behind the rose bush and ran through the gate out to the cobblestone alley. At the bottom of the street, I stopped long enough to point toward the Plaza de Armas, where Eusebio would meet Margarita later. I watched her as she turned the corner.

Then I ran and ran as if my skirts were on fire. I ran with a strength I never knew I had. Throughout my life, when I've faltered under the weight of unbearable things, I remember that flight, I remember my courage. What joy I felt to have slipped out of that gate, that horrible gate that had locked us in silence, hidden to the world. And there I was running for my life. I ran and I ran, and I didn't stop running until I saw the sea. When I saw the immense expanse of ocean, I was so happy I ran even faster, and before I knew it I was in La Perla.

There, gleaming like a coin in the sun was my house, freshly painted yellow and bright with hope.

Chapter Sixteen

He saw the townlands
and learned the minds of many distant men
and weathered many bitter nights and days
in his deep heart ...

The Odyssey

As I approached the house, I saw Julián. But Julián wasn't Julián. The boy I knew and loved was now a full-fledged man. Little Angelina was next to him, but she wasn't the small girl who followed me around the shantytown. She had grown into a lovely adolescent.

In the tableau before me, Julián was washing his face with water from a gourd bowl; little Angelina, who wasn't so little anymore, was brewing coffee and toasting slices of bread over the fire. I was shocked into immobility. I just stood there, observing the lazy morning as it slowly opened up into a sun-lit day. I looked toward Luisa's house and was surprised to see strangers there. A man and a woman I didn't recognize sat on the steps sipping from old tin cans, and four naked children wandered around the shack, playing with sticks or crouching to urinate. They stared at my habit, my old-woman's laced up shoes, my short hair, and I felt exposed and insignificant.

Then Julián turned around slowly. He shook his head and sparkles of water fanned from his hair like a halo. At that moment Angelina looked up. In unison, they yelled "Nana" at the top of their lungs, beaming the biggest smiles I had ever seen. They almost knocked me over as they rushed to hug me. It had been a long time since I felt such happiness. In fact, I had forgotten what happiness felt like.

"Where have you been? Where have you come from? Look at you, you're so tall and so skinny," Angelina said.

Something about her appearance unsettled me. Perhaps it was her unfashionable ankle-length dress or her long hair, pulled back in a severe bun at the nape of her neck. I had been at a convent for years, but even before I was put away, women wore shorter dresses and fixed their hair in shoulder-length styles, often curling the tips with strips of brown paper, torn from bags.

"And what's that dress you're wearing?" Julián asked, as he looked at the coarse brown dress with the hemline nicking my ankles, a rosary dangling from the cord tied around my waist.

"The nuns locked me up. They were pushing me to become a nun. I hated it, so I ran away."

"How did you manage?"

"The gate was open, a nun got distracted, and I ran."

"We tried to see you, but the nuns wouldn't let us in," Julián said.

"They never told me."

Angelina brought me a cup of aromatic coffee. I sipped it slowly with my eyes closed. It was the best coffee I had ever had after my mother died.

Julián hugged me again and then put his arm protectively around my shoulders, as he always had when we were children.

"Today is the happiest day of my life. I'll stop by my job and tell them I can't work today," he said. "Then we'll get you some clothes."

"No, Julián," I protested, shaking my head forcefully. "I don't want you to waste any money on me."

"Waste money! How can you say such a thing! Look, we'll all go together to *el mercado*, like in the old days, to get you some clothes and a new pair of sandals. Then you can give those clothes away. We'll have some *alcapurrias* and orange juice and a walk around the plaza. I bet they didn't make *alcapurrias* in the convent."

I shook my head.

"We'll have a great time."

"What are you doing in our house?" I asked suddenly. "Why are those strangers in your house? And where's Luisa? Where's little Gloria?"

"Gloria died of tuberculosis right after you went into the convent. Remember? She was already sick when you left. Then Mami died about a year later. We thought you were a nun by now." Julián's eyes deepened with sadness. "Anyhow, she had pernicious anemia and went into el Hospital Presbiteriano for a new treatment a North American doctor developed there. But after they injected her with the medication, she died. They said it had nothing to do with the treatment, that she was on her deathbed anyhow. Remember, that was the hospital where I was a janitor, so I was able to keep them from cutting her up for experiments. I brought her back so we could bury her."

"How did she know about this treatment? Who told her? Did you find out about it when you worked at the hospital?"

"No, I was just a janitor there, and I didn't know much. It was the gringo Reverend, remember him?"

"He's hard to forget. He always gave me the creeps. I remember how Mamá couldn't stand him."

"Well, he convinced my mother, and a lot of other people from La Perla, to go into the hospital for treatment. All of them died." He glanced quickly at Angelina, who was frowning.

"Weren't they supposed to get cured?" I asked.

"Experimented on is more like it. Some strange things happened in that hospital. I don't understand English, but the Puerto Ricans who worked there, mostly janitors and laboratory assistants, would talk. I had a feeling things weren't right. But I was too young, only a boy, so I didn't do anything about it. Especially with your mother getting drowned after I gave her that letter."

During the four years at the convent, I had searched and searched within me. I had explored every corner, every nook, every turn of my mind, trying to find an answer to my mother's death. Julián's words drove through me like a sharp knife.

"What happened to my mother, Julian? I need to know. You must tell me the truth," I said steadily.

"Okay, okay, Nana. I will tell you all that I know, exactly how it happened. It's a long, sad story and I have been living with it for so many years." He was on the verge of tears. "Come on, sit down, and we'll talk."

My heart pounded like a door against the wind as I waited for Julián to speak. When he finally did, his voice was hoarse with pain.

"As I said, I worked at the hospital as a janitor. Remember, I was only fourteen, just a boy. One night there was a big storm. I remember it too well. The storm raged right over us. The wind was hard and noisy, and the sky rumbled with thunder and lit up like daylight, though it was already dark. I was scared and wanted to run home, but I was curious because Dr. Rhoads ... do you remember him?" Julian stared at me with his big eyes. I shook my head. "No, of course not, what am I thinking? You never met him. Well, he was the doctor in charge of one of the laboratories that I used to clean. He was responsible for that new treatment for pernicious anemia. They were experimenting with a medicine that could cure it. Dr. Rhoads was the one who gave my mother the injection that did her in. That was after your mother died. A lot of other people had already died after Dr. Rhoads gave them an injection, but we didn't know that yet. We thought people were dying of anemia. Well, something kept gnawing at my insides. And I don't know ..."

Julián paused. "I had a feeling that something was not right, something was going terribly wrong in this place.

"So that night I noticed that the light in Dr. Rhoads' office was on. I could see the light shining from his office; the door was ajar. I was surprised because everyone had rushed home as soon as the storm began. Except for Dr. Rhoads."

"And you," I said.

"Yes, and me. I can't tell you what made me stay. It was like something outside of myself that held me and kept me there." Julián turned for a moment to stare at the sea. I waited patiently for him to continue.

"I tiptoed to the door. Dr. Rhoads was getting ready to leave. He had cleared his desk. His black leather briefcase was on top of the desk. For some reason, instead of leaving he sat down to write a letter. Maybe he thought he could finish the letter before the storm broke out and that he could leave in time. I don't know. But I peeked through the door, and when I saw him, head bent concentrating on the letter, I snuck into the office. I hid behind a massive upholstered chair and observed him from my dark corner. There he was, this big man, sitting at his huge mahogany desk, the kerosene lamp making a pool of light on his paper, writing. I could hear the scratch of the pen nib on the thick paper, and I wondered what he was writing. What could be so urgent that he would risk being caught in a terrible storm? Suddenly there was a huge clap of thunder, and lightning lit the sky like fireworks. He looked out the window and frowned. He picked up his briefcase. He seemed to have realized the dangers of the storm. He put on his hat, blew out the lamp, and rushed out. He closed the door and locked it from the outside with a key.

"I thought, here I am locked in this office, I'll never get out. But my curiosity was stronger than my fear of the storm, of getting caught in the important man's office. I slipped to the desk, and there was that letter. He just left it there, out in the open. He was so arrogant. He never thought somebody could come into his office and read it. Unfortunately, I couldn't, because it was in English. My heart was beating hard. I was so frightened, I thought my chest would burst. I had never stolen anything in my life, but this letter, this letter was different. There was something about it that made me cringe. I've thought so much about that night and what came over me. I can't explain it. All I know is that I sensed that the letter was important, and I had to know what was in it. Trembling, I took it and folded it up. I thought, how am I going to get this letter home without getting it soaked, without the ink running. How?

"It was dark, but every few minutes a flash of lightning would light up the room. I looked around at the shelves built into the walls. Most of the shelves had books, but on one shelf, there were bottles of medicine. I took a bottle with some pills in it, poured the pills into my pocket, and quickly folded the letter into a very small wad. I put it in the jar and held onto that jar for dear life. Then I jumped out the window. The office was on the ground floor, but I fell into some bushes and scratched my arms and face. I was stuck there, flailing like a wild animal caught in a net. By the time I got out of the bushes, I was soaking wet. I ran and ran and ran in the rain, lightning breaking over me, until I was home. That night I slept with the jar firmly clasped in my arm, embracing it, protecting it. I knew deep in my heart that something essential was revealed there.

"The next morning the storm had passed, and the sun was shining brightly as ever. As soon as I got up, I rushed to see your mother. She was mopping up all the water that had collected in the house with the storm. Your mother took one look at me and said, 'What is it, Julián? Why are you so pale?' And I said, 'Ay, *doña* Isabel, I found this letter in Dr. Rhoads office.' She frowned and said, 'Who's Dr. Rhoads?' And I said, 'The man in charge of the hospital'. 'Ah, yes,' she said, 'the man who's developing the treatment for anemia that the Reverend keeps raving about.'

"Your mother always knew everything that was going on. She was so smart and dedicated to her causes. To all of our causes. So I gave her the letter. She went inside the house, and I followed her. She sat at her writing table, put on her glasses, and very gently, so as not to tear the paper, took the letter out of the jar. 'It was so smart of you to protect the paper, Julián,' she said. You don't know how proud I felt when she said that. A compliment from your mother was like receiving a purse full of gold. I observed her carefully as she read. She was very pale when she finished."

"And where was I when all of this was going on?" I asked.

"You were reading to Angelina and Gloria on the steps of my house while my mother cleared up the mess from the storm."

"What did Mamá do with the letter?"

"She told me not to mention it to anyone. I was even more frightened because her voice was like ice."

"Did she tell you what was in the letter?"

"No, and I didn't ask."

"Why not?"

"I was afraid to know." Julián looked out at the distance. "Looking back at it now, I wish I had asked."

"She never would have told you," I comforted him. "It might have placed you in danger. But what did she do with it?"

"I don't know. She told me to go to work and pretend that nothing had happened. And I left. When I looked back, she had turned toward her shelves and was looking for something among her books. That's all I saw." Julián wiped a tear that rolled down his cheek. "Two days later, she was dead."

I looked inside the house that used to be Mamá's. And mine. All of our things were there: the big bed my father had built, the shelves with her books, her chair and typewriter. I searched through every inch of that house. I searched in the cooking shed.

"Where's the box?"

"What box?" Julián asked.

"My mother had a box, a pine box. My father made it for her to store her important stuff: papers, photographs, the poems she wrote, the newspaper articles, her journals. That's the only place where she could have put that letter."

"We've never seen any box like that, Nana." Julián turned to Angelina, who had been quietly listening to us. "Did you see a wooden box, Angelina?"

She shook her head.

I started pacing through the small house I knew so well and then went down the steps. I looked around, baffled.

"What's happened here since I went away? Nothing's the same."

Julián and Angelina sat on the steps. There were three steps. I sat on the bottom one. Julián shook his head.

"Nana, we honestly thought you were never returning. When we tried to see you at the convent, the nuns told us you were taking the vows. That's why we moved in here. If not, someone else would have taken the house and everything else."

Angelina finally spoke.

"We moved in after we heard from the nuns at the convent that you would never return. Mami was sick, and our shack was always leaking. Even *don* Tomás couldn't fix those leaks. We didn't have any papers or anything to prove that the house was ours, and before we knew what was happening those people moved into our house."

"That's the way it is here," Julián said. "If a house is empty, someone's going to move in. But we didn't worry about it because this house is nicer. But now that you're back, Nana, we'll leave, don't worry. Angelina and I can find another place."

"They say there's still some space in Puerta de Tierra. Maybe we can go there. Or maybe Villa Palmeras," Angelina said quickly. She tried to sound cheerful, but her eyes sparkled with tears.

"What are you talking about?" I said loudly. The children in the house next door stared at us. I lowered my voice.

"You'll stay here with me. It's our house now. Angelina and I can sleep in the big bed, and Julián, you'll have to put up a hammock."

"I already sleep in the hammock that belonged to my mother, and Angelina has the big bed all to herself."

Angelina looked at me shyly. I put my arm around her shoulders and squeezed her against my chest.

"Do you mind sharing the bed with me?"

She shook her head and buried it between my breasts. Her body quivered, and she began to sob. I smoothed the hair on the top of her head. When she looked up her eyes were two dark puddles of hurt.

"It's okay, Angelina. Remember all the things we used to do together? Well, we'll be a family again."

True to his promise, Julián gave notice at work and took Angelina and me into Old San Juan. The old city was as lively as I remembered it, with the clattering wheels, the clop of horses' hooves, the rhythmic clang of the blacksmith, and the lilting sing-songs of hawkers advertising their goods. The streets teemed with vendors of pork crackling, barterers exchanging mangoes for bottles, and honey sellers crying "Honey, honey, the bee with her hoooooney." I was pleased to see that Silesio, one of the honey peddlers, was still active. He was an old man blackened by a lifetime in the sun. He carried a huge wide-mouthed bottle, wrapped in straw. A large spoon hung from a cord tied to the bottle's neck. He slung the bottle on his shoulder and served half a spoon of honey to his customers. When he didn't have honey, he filled two baskets with wild mountain raspberries, hung the baskets on the tips of a long reed, and crossed it on his back. Raspberries or honey, the mere sight of Silesio reassured me that I had returned home.

Prayer and novena hawkers sold favors from heaven. Herb and spice vendors sang the virtues of sandalwood, mint, and balsam. Sweet rolls for coffee were offered, as were brushes and brooms. I breathed in the sharp smell of roasted peanuts sold by two barefoot boys in rags. They packed lit coal lumps high on the crosshatched wires wedged in a large rectangular can. They put a can full of peanuts to roast on top of the red charcoal.

I couldn't help smiling when I saw the broom seller. Tall and thin, with thick tufts of hair sprouting from his small head, he looked just like his product. We jumped out of the way of the meat vendor's horse when he rounded into the Plaza del Mercado. Cow and bull meat, wrapped in plantain leaves and tied with hemp, settled comfortably in the large baskets resting against the horse's flanks. In El Imperio, Julián bought me a pair of white sandals and fabric for several dresses. Afterwards, we dined on *alcapurrias* and fresh orange juice. It was one of the best days of my life.

The first Sunday after my return home was a day of surprises. Angelina woke up early and went outside to wash. When she came back inside, I could smell the scent of lavender soap. She dressed quietly. As she wrapped her hair into a tight knot, I realized I was hopelessly awake and wouldn't be able to go to sleep again. Since arriving I had been sleeping for ten to twelve hours straight, to compensate for the years of sleep deprivation I experienced at the convent.

"Where you going?" I asked her.

"To church."

"Oh." Her answer surprised me. Luisa had never been religious, though all her children were baptized at Sacred Heart Church on Ponce de León Avenue, just in case, she liked to say.

So on that first Sunday home from the convent, relieved not to be forced to pray for lengthier periods of time on the Lord's Day, as the nuns called it, I was mortified to find myself confronted by religious fervor once again. Maybe religion was something inevitable, inescapable, like fleas on a dog. I lifted the sheet that separated our sleeping area from Julián's hammock and peeked. I was relieved to see that he was still in his hammock, mouth slightly open and soundly asleep. The religious bug had not affected him, it seemed.

I got dressed and followed Angelina outside, where she prepared coffee. She wore a serious expression in preparation for what she thought would be an argument. But I had no desire to argue, not after all those years of Sister Martha's yelling and bullying.

"What church do you go to?" I asked.

"La Iglesia Pentecostal de Dios."

That explained her modest clothing and hairstyle.

"Is that the Reverend's church? The one he built on top of the hill?"

"No, we have a Puerto Rican pastor nearby, Reverendo Moisés Freites. He was an illiterate butcher at the slaughterhouse until he heard God's call one night. He taught himself how to read from the Bible and established a church. He's a wonderful preacher. And he lets me preach too."

"Really?" Now I was truly surprised.

"Oh, yes, I started preaching when I was twelve years old." Angelina straightened her back proudly. "You see, when Mami died, Julián was working and couldn't take care of me, so a neighbor told Pastor Moisés Freites. He said I could come to his school on Luna Street during the day while Julián was at work. When he saw me that first time, he just touched me on the head and said I was special. He said that I was one of God's chosen children and that I could preach and perform miracles, if I followed God's precepts and heeded his divine will. I didn't know anything about the Bible, so the pastor's wife, *doña* Caridad, gave me Bible lessons for three hours every day until I knew all the stories and most of the verses by heart. She was happy that I could read because that made things easier for her." She looked at me, perhaps expecting an argument at this point. But I wasn't about to give her one. "The church changed my life, you know."

To listen to Angelina preach, for the first time in my life I attended services at a Pentecostal church.. Julián sat next to me and held my hand.

"Are you ready for this?" he whispered in my ear. I nodded, sat bolt upright, and squeezed his fingers.

We were crammed in a small room at a store front on Calle del Sol in Old San Juan. A tiny table in the front of the room held a simple wooden cross and a few lighted candles. Several rows of chairs faced the table. Accustomed to the silence and introspection of the nuns, orphans, and novices during Catholic mass, I was astounded by the level of noise in the Pentecostal Church. Parishioners banged on tambourines, raised their arms to the ceiling, and yelled hallelujah at the slightest provocation. When Pastor Moisés announced Angelina as the guest preacher, the faithful sat down, greatly quieted.

Angelina seemed so small and girlish standing at the lectern in front of a room full of people. As soon as she began to speak, though, her demeanor changed. She was imbued with the self-confidence of righteousness. Julián, who had listened to her preach before, looked around distractedly, but I couldn't tear my eyes away from Angelina, her sweet voice transformed by the deep resonance of certitude. I can't tell you exactly what she preached about that day. I think it had something to do with the return of the prodigal son. I remember wondering whether she had chosen this story on the occasion of my own return home. What I do remember clearly is how she finished the sermon, closing her eyes and holding her arms out toward the audience.

"All those who seek healing from the Lord," she entreated, her voice like water flowing down a creek, "let them come forward."

Chairs scraped on the tiled floors as people rose. There were emaciated people, obviously ill with tuberculosis or malaria; a man who told Angelina he had a gambling problem and needed to be healed; and a woman who held her fist to her heart. One by one, Angelina anointed them on the forehead with a fragrant oil and held her hand to their heads while she prayed.

That night Angelina's weeping woke me. She had pressed her face against the pillow to stifle her sobs, but I could hear the little sighs and whimpers that escaped against her will. I put my hand on her trembling shoulder.

"What's the matter, Angelina? Why are you crying?"

She turned around. Her face was wet with tears, her eyes red and swollen. She must have been crying for hours.

"I'm so ashamed," was all she said.

"Why? Everything went well at church. People loved your sermon. Everyone was talking about it."

"But I didn't heal anyone," she blurted.

I had to compose my thoughts for a moment, for what she said was true. But I was expected to comfort, not agree with her.

"Well, I listened to some parishioners talk, and they were saying that the people who went up to you for healing felt much better."

"That's not what the healing was supposed to be like. I was supposed to heal them completely. It was supposed to be a miracle, like the pastor told me. And I prayed so hard, Marina, you don't know how hard I prayed. All week, I've been praying fervently for a miracle to happen." She wiped her face with the tips of her fingers and sighed loudly "I feel like such a fool."

During the long stretch of silence, I could hear the ocean swell and crash on the shore.

"You know, Angelina," I said finally. "Maybe you shouldn't try so hard. Maybe you should pray for people to heal and then leave it up to God to decide who will be healed and who won't." She said nothing and turned toward the wall.

My search for Mamá's box, my memory box, did not cease; nothing distracted me from my search. I nearly tore the house apart board by board with *don* Tomás' help. He had aged considerably in the years I was away, but he was still handy with the hammer. While he worked, he would tell a good story about his gold mining days or the treacherous Spaniards.

"*Mijita*, let's look under this floor board," he said consolingly, applying the hammer claw to the nails holding the board securely in place. "Your father was an excellent carpenter. Look at the condition of these boards. They look like they were just put in. I feel bad having to pull them up."

There was a scuttle below, and I screamed when the scorpion hiding under the board lifted its pincers.

"*Qué pasa?* What's the matter?" *Don* Tomás hurried to my side. "*Ay, Dios mío, un escorpión.* Wait a minute, *mijita.* I'll take care of it." And he promptly dispatched the scorpion with his dependable hammer.

"And what in heaven's name are you looking for? There're no more boards left to rip out, you know," he said finally.

"Mamá's pine box. My father made it for her, and she kept all her important papers there. I don't understand how it just disappeared."

"*Ay, mija*, it didn't just disappear. Someone must have taken it. You know, after she was killed."

"You know she was killed?"

"I don't know anything for sure, but that's what people are saying."

"Who killed her, *don* Tomás? Do you know?"

"No, *lo siento*. I'm sorry." He shook his head thoughtfully. "They say it was that skinny policeman, you know, the one with the crooked smile. Others say maybe Pedro Mauleón did it, because he used to hate Isabel so much. And he had already killed *don* Demetrio and a few others. But no one knows for sure. She was such a nice lady, a truly educated lady who treated everyone with the same respect, rich or poor, king or pauper. It was her politics that got her into trouble, though. Around here, you have to keep your mouth shut. Since your mother was killed, I don't discuss anything with anybody, not politics, not religion, not the weather, not even what I had for dinner the night before. *En boca cerrada no entran moscas.* Flies can't get into a closed mouth, as they say."

Chapter Seventeen

... The blow smashed
the nape cord, and his ghost fled to the dark.

The Odyssey

The summer had been mild and dry that year. A sea-borne breeze stretched through La Perla and into Old San Juan, cooling even the hottest of tempers. Nothing seemed askew except my melancholic mood. The mystery of my mother's death plagued me. There were layers and layers of want in me unrealized and with no possibility of coming to fruition. Time weighed in my hands like stones. There were stones in my throat and in my heart, which was hardened by an inability to forgive. And to forget. I think there were stones in my eyes as well, since I couldn't quite see ahead of me. There was no clarity to my wants and desires, only murky darkness.

What was it that I wanted?

I stood in the salt-sharpened sunlight wondering about my feelings towards Julián. The three of us had lived in the yellow house by the sea for two years. I often lay awake at night while Angelina breathed softly next to me, wondering what Julián was doing behind the curtain we set up at night to separate his sleeping area from ours. Suddenly, I was concerned about looking pretty early in the morning, and I spent what seemed like hours trying to comb down my hair, scrubbing my face with a dry cloth, and dressing in what would appear to be a casually thrown on garment before he had a chance to lay an eye on me.

Then an incident happened that brought it all to concrete reality. Out of nowhere, out of the sheer need to express the longing that caved my chest hollow, a glimpse of clarity flared up like a match that had just been lit.

I had been selecting a candle stub from an old can. The night tasted salty and wet. Rain always brought disintegration to the shantytown, and

I was hoping it wouldn't rain, though we had had a long drought that year. As soon as the thought popped into my head, a pang of guilt struck me in the heart. I thought of the farmers and the different prayers they might say that night. I lit the candle, sending a plea for rain into the darkness, when the match slipped out of my hand and landed on the bed. A flame instantly caught on the sheet and spread through the bed like a snake. Somewhere in my startled brain, I knew that Julián was outside with the kerosene lamp repairing the old stove and that Angelina couldn't be far away. She was the cook of the family and tended to stay close to the stove, making sure the iron grills weren't rusted, keeping the kindling and coal dry with cloth covers. But my throat was heavy with fear. As I reached for the pitcher full of water that we kept in the house, I was incapable of uttering a sound. I tripped and some water splashed on the floor, but I held onto the pitcher and threw it on the flame. Instead of continuing to crawl across the bed, the flame had burrowed deep into the mattress. The water quenched the fire and the smell of scorched cotton finally brought Julián and Angelina running into the shack. I was trembling, and Julián placed his arm over my shoulders. I sat down at the edge of the scorched bed and brought my head to his chest. He kissed my head and with his fingers gently combed my hair back away from my face. I could hear waves crashing against the rocks at the edge of La Perla, and I was comforted. When Julián and I moved away from the bed, Angelina pulled the sheets off and took them out to wash and mend. Julián smelled of breadfruit and sweet mango. I could have stayed pressed against his heart forever. He tugged at my shoulders and I stood up, my chest bursting with the acrobatics of my heart.

It was a dream, I was convinced, until Julián pressed his soft lips against mine. I had never been kissed on the lips by a man before, and it felt odd to taste his saliva, to smell the coffee and tobacco on his breath. Then I realized his arms were around my waist, and I brought my arms up to his shoulders and cradled his neck with my hands. Fear fell from me and in its place I felt the wondrous pang of want. A want that might possibility be satisfied.

I asked Angelina to go to *doña* Eugenia's house for some herbs we needed. She was surprised, but delighted to go run an errand on her own. I knew *doña* Eugenia's daughter Emilia would keep her busy for a while, regaling her with the latest shantytown gossip.

In a bed covered with ashes and smelling of scorched cotton, Julián and I sealed our pact of love, a pact that, we were convinced, would last forever.

I often wondered how different our lives would have been if we hadn't gone to Ponce that Palm Sunday.

Sister Theresa's admonitions about historians and their distortions of the facts echoes through my mind. Everything she said about how history was written was true. Today, very few people from the island know what happened that Palm Sunday in 1937. Many who know better interpreted what they knew to be true through the prism of their own prejudices. Others reported as they were commanded by the powers that ruled them.

"See the truth only as it exists in your heart and mind. Then, and this is the most important and difficult, live by your beliefs, and if necessary, die for them."

The sister's voice moved through me like the wind lifting a leaf.

The joy of anticipation flooded me as we rushed to the Plaza de San Cristóbal in Old San Juan at dawn and joined the hundreds of people who boarded buses and folded into idling cars that shimmered under the sun. Julián gripped my hand tightly when we boarded the bus. I took a seat by the window. Weeks before this moment, we had been busy working with the party organizers for the great event. *Don* Pedro Albizu Campos, the great nationalist leader we loved, would speak that day.

We had never taken such a long trip and were impatient to get going. Julián and I had tried to leave Angelina at *doña* Eugenia's house, but we hadn't counted on her tears.

"Why can't I go too?" she asked and stamped her foot.

I smiled when I remembered the times I had asked Mamá the same question. But Angelina was better behaved than I was. Instead of stamping my foot, I usually rolled on the floor, arms and legs flailing, banging my head against the floor, pleased to detect Mamá's worried expression. Angelina cried profusely, but Julián and I were steadfast and she finally accepted defeat. Grudgingly, she went to church and later to *doña* Eugenia's house and was saved from witnessing the grim events of that day.

Entire families boarded the bus and carried on noisy and lengthy discussions about who would sit where and with whom. There were children, parents, grandparents, aunts, uncles, cousins, godparents, and godchildren. Everyone in San Juan seemed to be headed toward the cavalcade of buses and cars that would wind up and down the winding roads of the Cordillera Central, climbing from the northern city of Arecibo and coasting down to Ponce, *la perla del sur*. We all looked forward to the parade.

"Sit down and be still, *niña*," a woman in the front row ordered her daughter with a severe look. The little girl obeyed without question. She turned her face toward the window and put her hand out to catch the wind.

Treacherous curves rounded along the steep road, and the bus lumbered slowly, honking like a goose before each turn. White crosses on hairpin curves reminded us of the people who had died in accidents at those spots. The feathery leaves of *flamboyán* trees shimmered in the bright sun as the bus scaled higher and deeper into the mountains. A honeycreeper warbled vigorously on a branch. When I stuck my head out of the window to hear it better, the bird took wing. Julián moved to the front of the bus to discuss the events of the day with some of the other men. There were last-minute details, he said, and kissed me on the cheek before getting up from his seat. I had plenty of time to sit back, feel the cool mountain breeze on my face, and enjoy the scenery.

Screeching brakes woke me from a brief doze. I realized that we were cautiously descending from the mountains toward the southern coast, the driver's foot on the brakes and the bus under tight control. Once on the straighter roads of the flatlands, I felt the dry heat on my face and looked out at the acres of sugarcane swaying under the punishing sun, the blond spears humbled by the weight of the dense air. In the distance, smoke stacks smudged the blue horizon. The air was thick with the odor of burnt earth and charred stalks from the *ingenios*, the mills where the cane was crushed. My stomach turned.

The noon light swept the dawn coolness aside and, swollen with humidity, cast its heat everywhere. Into sharp corners, through gaping pores, in the restless dust, the silent heat searched relentlessly. The passengers fanned themselves with pieces of cardboard and folded paper. I noticed that the woman who sat across the aisle had come well prepared for the trip with a handbag full of bread and cheese and a thermos. She must have seen the longing in my eyes because she dug into her capacious bag and handed me a slice of bread with a chunk of *queso de hoja*. I chewed on the bread with a layer of the delicious leaf cheese. Lazily I looked out toward a landscape that changed dramatically as we approached the coast. Wooden houses and thatched huts or *bohíos* crowded together in thick patches on the flatlands. I was admiring the bustling port when the shimmering city of Ponce captured my attention. In the late morning light, its immense white plaza and grand cathedral dazzled.

Aurora Street teemed with people of all ages. That bright Palm Sunday morning, the sun towered over the Ponce Plaza, and light bounced from the glittering asphalt. Automobiles shone like pots of oil. Puerto Rican flags and Nationalist Party ensigns flapped against tall masts in the harbor. My heart lurched. It was illegal to fly the Puerto Rican flag; only the Stars and Stripes was allowed. Decades later, this type of resistance would come to be known as civil disobedience, but at the time it was a definite act of rebellion, punishable with prison sentences. With anticipation, Julián and I searched through the throng for a shady spot to watch the parade. Later that evening, Julián was scheduled to attend a meeting at the Nationalist Party headquarters. But at that moment, we were excited about the prospect of a marching band and the impassioned speech for freedom that the party leader *don* Pedro Albizu Campos would give.

"When does the parade start?" Julián asked.

"At twelve, *en punto*, on the dot. We have to keep strict discipline. Now more than ever," *don* Demetrio said.

"That's right," I agreed and smiled. "Can't give them any excuse to throw more of us in jail."

"When they want an excuse, they just make it up." *Don* Demetrio shrugged and strode toward the plaza.

Julián stuck his pointy elbows out and charged through the teeming spectators to the edge of the sidewalk, where we would have an unhindered view. People slipped through the ropes set up by the police to cordon off the area and waited eagerly for the parade to begin. Many spectators came to the plaza right after the late morning mass, still in their Sunday finery, holding the palm fronds that had been blessed and handed out by the priest in commemoration of Jesus' arrival in Jerusalem. House balconies were packed with people waiting for the festivities to begin. People climbed onto automobile hoods and wooden crates. They sat up high on horses and donkeys.

I watched with excitement as the marchers, about one hundred men and women, began to congregate on Aurora Street. The Cadets of the Republic wore immaculate white trousers and black shirts that represented mourning for the colonial bondage of the island. Military-style caps protected their eyes from the blazing sun. Members of the Women's Auxiliary Corps wore white skirts, black blouses, and caps. A band of eight uniformed musicians milled around, tuning their instruments.

Laughter and high voices permeated the plaza. People's exhilaration was contagious, and I found myself smiling broadly at nothing in particular. I glanced behind me and saw a woman put her hands to her face. After a loud drum roll, the mood of the crowd shifted, and I cringed. The laughter and bantering tones dissipated. Instead, a silent pall, edged with fear, settled on the crowd. Even the birds stopped chirping.

Hundreds of policemen, faces like weathered leather, fanned out into the street where we waited. With shoulder thrusts, they adjusted their gleaming rifles; revolvers were clipped to their belts. Some, armed with police clubs, squinted in the sun; their eyes lined with cruelty. As in a nightmare when the juxtaposition of the improbable sharpens the senses, I could smell the salt mist and hear a shutter slamming in the wind. And then I saw uniformed men posted on truck beds, bent over a ruthless configuration of submachine guns trained on the crowd. Clusters of policemen raised the truncheons in their fists and positioned themselves around the crowd. I realized that we were hemmed in, cornered. The sun roared, and I was stunned with fear and anger.

I turned toward the parade commander to see what he would do. He was a small, slender man, immaculately dressed in freshly pressed white trousers and coat over a black shirt and tie. He wore a white officer's cap. After surveying the situation, he wiped his face, wet under the strain of his difficult decision. With a sweep of an arm, he ordered the cadets to line up and march in columns three deep. The women were already behind the cadets. At their rear, the band began to play the original national anthem, *La Borinqueña*. The marchers stood at attention, faces gleaming under the hot afternoon sun. For the few minutes during which the anthem played, the crowd forgot the presence of the police and sang with vigor.

> *Despierta borinqueño*
> *que han dado la señal.*
> *Despierta de ese sueño*
> *que es hora de luchar.*
> *A ese llamar patriótico*
> *no arde tu corazón.*
> *Ven nos será simpático*
> *el ruido del cañón.*
> *Nosotros queremos la libertad*
> *nuestros machetes nos la darán.*
> *Vámonos borinqueños,*
> *vámonos ya*
> *que nos espera ansiosa,*
> *ansiosa la libertad.*
> *La libertad, la libertad.*
> *La libertad, la libertad.*

The music stopped, and the men and women began their scheduled march on Aurora Street. The musicians started playing again and the marchers approached the plaza; a police officer ordered them to halt. The musicians were silent. The marchers obeyed and stood quietly, hands by their sides, except for the flag bearer, who held the Puerto Rican flag high in the air.

That's when I heard the first shot.

Policemen, weapons drawn, pushed towards Aurora Street, thrusting steadily forward. Confident in their strength, they charged into the plaza. Without a warning call, they opened fire on the Nationalist marchers. Within seconds they were shooting at everyone in the crowd, marchers and bystanders alike. The town exploded in chaos. People staggered, shrieking and covering their eyes, stinging with tear gas. Glass sparkled on the white plaza. The day turned hard as flint.

The cadets still stood in silence, motionless, hands hanging at their sides. At their feet, the commander lay crumpled on the ground like a discarded garment, his body ripped apart by bullets. Two young boys stood at the edge of the sidewalk near the marchers. The details of the scene were sharp as if they were in a photograph. One placed a skinny arm around the other boy's shoulders, and they stood woodenly, eyes wide open in shock and confusion. By the time the boys reacted and broke into a run, volleys of bullets pelted like hail from all around the plaza, injuring, maiming, killing, as people screamed and fled, waving their arms, trying to fend off the unspeakable horror. Seconds later a hand grenade exploded, and one of the boys was on the ground. A hole, the size of a man's fist, red and blackened by burning pieces of shrapnel, flared in the back of his shirt.

The day was streaked with the blood of innocents and shafts of bold sunlight. Women, men, and children groped to the surface amid clouds of smoke. They bolted in every direction to escape the shots that whistled through the air, past them and into them. The air, thick with the sickly smell of tear gas, the hard stench of lead, and clouds of somber smoke, brought tears to our eyes. Corralled, the government's prey had nowhere to go, and many were slaughtered like animals.

A man and his young sons stood in front of a shoemaker's shop. When the shooting started I heard one of the brothers moan, "Ay ...!" His father quickly caught his fall and cradled the boy's bleeding head in his lap. Before I knew what had happened I realized that both boys had been killed. The father sat on the sidewalk, wounded.

The well-armed predators fired ruthlessly while they plowed into the crowd. Scrambling for shelter, I was blinded by tear gas, and my watery eyes stung. Through the curtain of tears, I couldn't see Julián, but I felt his hand holding mine. I tripped and fell. He dragged me to my feet, and we searched, maddened by fear, for a refuge that would protect us from the terrible siege. My temples throbbed violently as I slipped into a daze. Each time a shot rang out, my stomach quaked and my ears rang painfully. I wanted to crawl out of the din, make time start again so this nightmare would be over. Instead, my heart slammed like a shutter in the wind. Julián and I ran and ran, and I pressed a hand hard against my mouth.

People hid inside houses, under automobiles, behind fences. Terrified mothers held small children to their breasts and turned their backs against the bullets. The submachine-gun squad bore into the crowd in a roar of fire. Cries of terror and pain tore through the air. Those screams cut into my memory forever. The screams and shots merged into deep, dark thunder, the color of midnight. The echo repeated itself, tolling like a call to hell, over and over, and turned into the color of madness. I will never forget the infernal spectacle of tin-roofed homes in flames and the streets choked with the mangled bodies of the hunted as they fell.

Madness, madness all around. And there was nowhere to go.

Julián and I huddled in a corner, shrinking into ourselves, folding our bodies into miniature angles. Julián had shoved me behind him protectively, but I peeked behind his shoulder. Through the haze, I saw the flag bearer dragging himself to the sidewalk, bleeding from bullet holes all over his body. I wondered how, with the loss of blood, he could still be alive. He slid down and reclined against a brick wall. His face was ashen. He dipped his finger in a chest wound and, with his own blood, wrote on the wall.

"What is he doing?" Julián whispered before the flag bearer collapsed.

I tried to scramble out from behind, but Julián pushed me back.

"Stay right here. I'll go see what it is."

I paid no attention and followed him to the fallen man. We read his scribbled words, still dripping with fresh blood: "Long live the Republic! Down with the assassins!"

Later I found out that the flag bearer's name was Bolívar Márquez. Like my father, he too died as a result of bullets fired by an American's command.

Julián crawled to the dead man's side and tried to rescue the flag from the pavement where it lay collapsed in a sorrowful pile. Just as he took the flag, a policeman turned his gun toward him and shot him twice. I screamed when I saw Julián, with ugly holes in his shirt, fall like a broken doll. I was certain that at that moment the policeman would train his gun in my direction. My mouth went dry. I closed my eyes and prepared to die. But the policeman turned away, suddenly distracted by someone's scream, and aimed wildly at another target. I sank to my knees in a pool of Julián's blood. I clawed desperately at his chest, but his eyes stared at a distance I knew I could not reach. I sobbed and pulled at his arm. I pinched his cheeks and shook him. I gripped his blood-stiffened sleeve and whimpered like a small animal in a trap.

Suddenly, a small girl of about twelve darted out of the smoky confusion, picked up the flag from the pavement where Julián had dropped it, and ran off, flag waving in her lifted hand. Bullets hurtled madly around her as she ran away from the plaza into the safety of the maze of alleyways.

Chaos closed in on me as I tried to waken Julián. I looked around beseechingly, trying to identify a familiar face among the terrified people who scattered in all directions around me, fleeing from the carnage. Finally,

I collapsed over my Julián's chest. Broken bodies stretched out like a field of wild poppies around me. A policeman passed by a fruit vendor, turned back and cracked the vendor's skull open with a truncheon. I dropped off the edge of the earth.

The last thing I remember seeing after Juan Carlos pried me from Julián's body was two policemen picking up the wounded man whose sons had been killed in front of the shoemaker's shop. His mouth was a soft shapeless hole. They threw him like a sack into a police wagon. Juan Carlos's face was soiled, his shirt in shreds, but he was not wounded. He helped me carry Julián's body to a car waiting in a side street. Juan Carlos' brother clutched the wheel as he looked around. We waited for two more party members to pile into the car and took off cautiously, Juan Carlos's brother making sure we didn't arouse any suspicion. The tires crunched on the lake of broken glass.

"All along they were planning to butcher us," Juan Carlos said, trying to control his rage. "I just heard that Winship was behind it."

"What do you mean?" one of the men asked.

"He directed the police *comandante* to give his men orders to shoot."

"Oh, so the American governor keeps his hands clean while the Puerto Rican lackey does his dirty work for him."

"That's how repression works," Juan Carlos nodded. His fury was a form of grief. "There's a good reason why assassin Winship was sent here by Washington. It's no coincidence that he's an Army general."

"U.S. military occupation is kept alive and well while *el general* Winship wipes out the opposition."

"That's right."

"All is darkness," Juan Carlos said. His eyes glittered with tears. "In political life, what is real is often not visible." He looked out at the fields of sugarcane and the smudges of smoke on the horizon. Evening would soon fall, and darkness would hit us hard, as it always does in the tropics.

"This too will be covered up."

Chapter Eighteen

I came by ship, with a ship's company,
sailing the wine-dark sea for ports of call
on alien shores.

The Odyssey

I have been told that I am gifted, and I often wonder what that gift might be. Is it the gift of languages, of patience, of keeping questions to myself, of exuding the semblance of inner peace when my insides tremble with fear and anger? Or is it the gift of words, well tempered like Bach's clavier, haunting me because the real words I want to pronounce stay stuck in my throat like stones? I am gifted at the art of dissimilation, the art of repressing my truth. That is not an art, really. It is a yielding of everything that I truly am. Enough of that. My silence has not served me well. And now, with these words, I break it like squeezing an egg in my fist.

Poverty-stricken and heartbroken, I arrived in New York after a long voyage in the steerage compartment I shared with a family with two children. It was comforting to find another woman on board. Most of the passengers were men who had left behind their families to venture out and seek a better life. They hoped to send for wives and children when the luck that had always eluded them finally struck.

Cardboard suitcase in hand, I stepped from the *S.S. Borinquen* at the Brooklyn docks, sick from the harrowing stretch off Cape Hatteras during a terrible storm. We rocked like a paper boat in an ocean of high waves. At times I was convinced that we would all die. If there hadn't been so many innocent people in the boat, I would have wished it to go under so I could be delivered mercifully to its watery depths. Julián's lifeless eyes haunted me. Choking with tears, I recalled Angelina waving a white handkerchief at the Puerta de Tierra pier when I left. My heart broke when I was forced to leave her with the pastor and his wife. I had no choice. Being with me put both our lives at risk.

My eyes were wide with astonishment at this city built in a frenzy of steel and cement. A gregarious crowd surrounded the passengers as we came ashore. Relatives and friends hugged the new arrivals. It was April 7, 1937, and I had just turned twenty. I never felt so alone.

"Marina, there you are. I was looking for you." It was *don* José, whose family had shared a compartment with me. A typesetter from San Sebastián, he decided to escape the poverty of the island. During the four-day voyage, he often talked about the money he would make in the *gran urbe* and how he would return to his hometown the proud owner of a printing press.

"Is someone picking you up?" I shook my head. "*Venga, entonces,* come with us. My brother came to get us."

In the dingy cavern of the subway station, people rushed through the platforms like waves of bees flitting in all directions. Even in the crowded streets of Old San Juan, the market teeming with merchants and buyers, I had never seen so many people. The strident noise of trains scraping along the tracks rang painfully in my ears. *Don* José's wife and children pressed the palms of their hands against the sides of their heads. One of the girls began to cry. I looked at her sympathetically, for if I hadn't been a twenty-year-old woman, I'd be crying too.

When we entered the subway, I saw ourselves reflected in the hostile eyes of the other passengers as they took in our colorful clothes, the cacophony of our language, the poverty written on our cardboard suitcases, the cheaply cobbled shoes. For too many years, I would confront those mirrors daily.

Juan Carlos had given me money from his own pocket for my voyage to New York. He gave me a little extra so I could get by until I secured employment. He had slipped a folded piece of paper into my hand as we said good-bye.

"Here's the name and address of a good friend. He's a *tabaquero*, like me, like your father. Stay with him and his wife until you get settled. You can trust them, they're with us."

When I knocked on the door that cold April day, my heart lifted when I saw the face of one of the kindest men I would ever know. He reminded me of Julián, of how I imagined my father would be in his middle years. Miguel Walker Rosario welcomed me with open arms. He was a small, slender man. His surprisingly large hands bore the familiar stain of cigars. I was immediately comforted by the sharp scent of tobacco on his skin. One of his eyes sparkled with tenderness and concern, while the other remained unfocused and still, staring straight ahead.

Miguel was in his early fifties. He often talked about the time he left his native Mayagüez, where he learned the cigar-rolling trade. Jobs were hard to come by even in San Juan, so he sailed with his wife and their young daughter to New York. Soon he joined the ranks of Spaniards, Cubans, Russians, Belgians, Jews, and Italians—all expert cigar makers—in cigar-making shops throughout the city. He learned that his craft of making perfect cigars entirely by hand was no longer economically feasible, and he was forced, against his aesthetic inclination, to use a prosaic mold that made cigars quickly, but without character.

"I hear your father was a *tabaquero* like me." Miguel smiled and held up his tobacco-stained hands with pride.

"I hardly knew him," I said. "He died in France in the war."

"I was sent out to fight in that awful war too. I was wounded and died from my wounds. But then I came back. Like Lazarus. That experience made me change my views on everything."

"What happened?" I was intrigued.

"It's like this." Miguel settled into his armchair, his unfocused eye staring impassively forward. "I was badly injured when a land mine exploded right next to me. I remember that I knew I was dead, but I was lying there thinking, 'This isn't so bad.' I was surprised that I wasn't scared or upset about being dead. I was ... how can I describe it? Relieved! When I fell, I heard this loud ringing, like a bell, right in my ears. Then I saw my whole life like pictures in front of me, so clear and colorful, starting from the time I was a baby through my whole life up to then. I remembered everything, everything, so clearly. All of this happened almost at once. It wasn't long at all. And it wasn't difficult either. I didn't feel regrets. I didn't feel bad about anything that happened, anything I'd done. I was just interested in it. It was like going to school and learning lessons about myself, about my life.

"The next thing I know, I was on some kind of beautiful ship sailing to the other side of a huge lake, and on the other side I could see all the people I loved who were dead. My grandparents were there, cousins, my brother who died of tuberculosis. They were waiting for me to arrive, to welcome me. Then I kind of remember thinking, 'Oh, no, I don't want to die. Not yet.' By this time the ship was close to the other shore, but just before it got there it turned around and came back.

"Then I'm in the veteran's hospital without my eye. I was glad that I came back, even if it was so beautiful on that other side. But now I know that it's there, you see, that there are people waiting for me, especially my little girl. I had a second chance, a resurrection. Since then I've lived my life like a different man."

Miguel's wife, Luz Cáceres Guevara, nodded and said nothing. She was short, plump, and friendly. She had greeted me at the door with a luminous smile that opened up like a sun. Her teeth were unusually white, and they gleamed whenever she graced us with her beautiful smile. She had been Miguel's sweetheart since the eighth grade, and it never occurred to either one of them that they would ever be apart. At the time, she was a seamstress in the garment district. While Miguel spoke, I noticed her eyes becoming dark with distance.

Their railroad apartment was on the fifth floor of a six-story walk-up in the Lower East Side, an area called Loisaida by Puerto Ricans. Miguel took my suitcase and I followed him from the living room straight into a bedroom. Luz led the way.

"This is the extra bedroom. Ours is the next room facing the street." Luz lifted a pretty pink curtain in the dark room. "This window faces a wall," she said, revealing the brick side of the building next door.

The room was narrow, with barely enough space for a small bed pushed against the wall where the window was. A small table with a lamp stood between the narrow bed and the doorway. A tall armoire stood opposite the wall.

"You can put your things in here." Miguel opened the doors and pointed to the hangers and shelves.

"Get yourself settled," Luz said. "I'll heat some water so you can wash, and then we'll have some lunch. Made some nice rice and beans for you." She smiled and turned to her husband. "Miguel, go get us some soda at the bodega. And remember to tell Fermín about the *lechón* we want for Sunday."

Miguel and Luz left the room. The bed springs squeaked when I sat on the edge of the mattress. Fear pressed against my chest. No amount of comforting thoughts could persuade me that I would survive in this world of grayness and bone-chilling cold. This lifeless prison of walls and confinement was not what I had anticipated for myself. It is true that during most of my life I had lived in a tiny shantytown shack. But the world opened, luminous and warm, right outside the door. All I had to do was look out the window or step into the light of the enormous sky. The sky, the glittering sand, the shimmering sea all opened up in front of me, vast and sparkling with the unmistakable pulse of life.

Shakespeare's words, "But look, the morn in russet mantle clad," kept me from dying. The first dawn of my new life in New York, poised at the farthest reaches of darkness, I remembered those words and said to myself: *Do I really never want to see another dawn, another sunset? Dawn or sunset, it's all the same. I've always loved that edge of light. I won't die*, I said to myself. *Not yet.*

Every morning I got up before Miguel and Luz so they wouldn't have to tiptoe through my bedroom when making their way to the bathroom and kitchen. I made sure the narrow bed was neatly made with the pink chenille spread Luz had provided. Shivering, I stumbled into the tiny bathroom to do my ablutions just before they got up. When I finished I wiped clean the toilet seat, sink, and bathtub.

One of my clearest memories of those early days in New York was the unrelenting chill in my bones. In the mornings, I dreaded coming out from under the warm covers into the frigid morning air, stepping on the frozen linoleum floors, and holding my breath and clenching my teeth as I splashed cold water on my face. Luz said I had thin blood because I had just arrived from Puerto Rico. My blood would thicken soon enough, she assured me, and I would be more tolerant of the cold. She showed me how to heat water on the gas stove to wash myself.

"Truth be told," she confessed, "my blood never thickened enough. No matter how many layers of clothing I wear, I'm always cold. And I've been here for fourteen years!" She emphasized her statement with one of her radiant smiles.

"Let's buy you a coat and some warm clothes, *muchacha*. You'll die of pneumonia if you don't bundle up."

We sat at the kitchen table sipping steaming cups of the fragrant Puerto Rican coffee *don* Fermín bought at the bodega.

"*Ay, no, doña* Luz," I protested. "I need to find work first, then I'll worry about buying clothes."

"Listen to what I'm telling you," Luz insisted. Her index finger sliced through the air. "Buying clothes isn't a luxury; it's a necessity in a place like this. If you get sick from the cold, then you'll be in big trouble. No work, no nothing." She folded her arms firmly across her ample chest and shook her head. A glint of sorrow passed across her eyes, and I winced.

"What's the matter, *doña* Luz."

"Nothing, *mija*, just memories."

"I'm sorry." I waited until she wiped her eyes and cheeks. "Can I get you some water?"

"No, it's okay." Luz struggled to compose herself. I stared at the floor uncomfortably.

"It's my daughter," she said finally, and she hurried from the kitchen through the living room and my bedroom into the bedroom she shared with Miguel. When she returned, she was clutching the framed photograph of a pretty girl. Luz passed the tips of her fingers over the glass tenderly.

"Sometimes I miss her so much. She would be about your age right now. Almost twenty. I should be having grandchildren." Luz pressed her lips together, trying to keep the howl of pain at bay.

"She died of pneumonia the first winter we were here. Right there in the room you have now. She was only six years old, too young to die." She dropped her eyes, and tears rolled down her cheeks. She flicked them away. "That's why we can never leave this place. The soul of our only child is here."

Evening settled heavily. Through the office windows, I could see the first flutters of snow. I had worked as a cleaner at Luz's dress factory for two years. Luz tried to teach me how to sew on a machine, but it was hopeless. The moment I tried to wedge the fabric between the presser foot and what's called a feed dog, the fabric rebelled. When I pressed my foot on the pedal, trying at the same time to straighten the fabric, it bunched up like a misshapen accordion, and I was forced to stop. Even Luz lost her characteristic patience. Though I was demoted to the cleaning brigade, my cleaning experience at the convent allowed me to keep the factory clear of fabric and thread remnants without much concentration. All day, as I swept, mopped, and cleaned the toilet, I was able to observe the plight of the seamstresses. Not to mention my own.

One cold winter day, a bearded man waited outside the factory as we went in. He handed out some flyers. Most of the women refused to take the flyer, but I, who read anything that came within range, read it greedily. It was almost like reading one of my mother's leaflets. It was in English, but the spirit of the words was so similar. The flyer denounced the oppression of women working in sweatshops—the bitterly long days, the hunger wages. I was fired with enthusiasm and hope. Finally I had found a reason to be in this cold dank universe of indifference and want.

A week later, the bearded man returned. Luz clutched at my arm.

"Don't talk to that man," she whispered urgently. "He'll get you fired."

"But you're in the anarchist movement, Luz. Why don't you want contact with others who are struggling for the worker's freedom?"

"They're not like us, Marina." She pulled me aside so the other women couldn't hear us. "They're Communists!"

"How do you know?"

"Everybody knows." She nodded knowingly.

This, of course, did nothing to deter me. If the Communists were willing to fight for the workers' rights, then I could work with them. I would never join the party because, like my mother, I didn't believe in their ultimate goals. But they could help me better understand the union movement. I could learn what I needed to learn from them. Then, I would move on.

Gilberto, the bearded man, took me under his wing immediately. A Galician by birth, he had a long family history of rebellion. As a result of trying to organize a union at the dress factory, I was fired. But Gilberto kept me busy writing flyers and pamphlets for workers all over the city. My writing caught the eyes of the editors of both *The Daily Worker* and *Libertad,* and I found myself reporting and writing articles on the worker's struggle for both publications. I met regularly with an anarchist group. Whenever I could steal some time away from meetings and work, I wrote poetry.

My work table faced a window streaked with soot and dirt. In the large room at *The Daily Worker* were several other journalists, all men, clanking on old typewriters or scribbling furiously on yellow tablets. Crumpled papers littered the floor around waste paper baskets, a testament to the careless aim of the men.

"Hey, Marina," Tony yelled over the din of typewriters, the loud telephone conversations, and the clang of the printing press in the adjacent room. "You know what Winston Churchill said?"

"No," I responded emphatically, rolling my eyes toward the ceiling.

"He said that order is in the mind." He laughed. "Maybe the opposite applies too. Your desk is so neat you must have the messiest mind around."

"And by the look of your desk, your mind must be a clean slate."

I was about to turn around when the door opened and Nicholas Poseidon ambled in, with a cigarette wedged firmly between his fingers. He walked confidently, as if he owned the place. He was in his mid-thirties, of medium height and average build. His only physical distinction was a generous nose, which had a definite Balkan slope. When he first saw me, his dark eyes narrowed with suspicion. He stared rudely at my face, heavy brows set like handles over his dark eyes. Then his eyes lingered on my breasts and slid down to my legs. When he had taken in all he wanted, he turned to one of the men.

"So, Georgie. The article's ready, right?" His voice was not as deep as I had anticipated, but it was raspy with smoke. I turned away from him, but I could still feel his gaze roaming toward me as he spoke. An uncomfortable chill ran up my spine, and I knew, without looking, that he was approaching my desk.

"Hey, who's the new lady reporter?" He sat at the edge of my desk and puffed on his cigarette.

"I'm Marina Alomar, if you must know."

"Oh, yeah, I know who you are. Read some of your articles. Not bad, not bad ... for a woman. And an anarchist at that." His eyes twinkled slightly. He was attempting, successfully I must admit, to rile me.

"Well, thank you for the compliment, mister," I said, feigning as much indifference as I could muster. I continued typing, but my heart was thumping loudly and my hands had begun to perspire.

"I'm Nicholas Poseidon. My friends call me Nick. I'm a union organizer for sailors."

"With a name like Poseidon, what else could you do?"

One of his eyebrows shot up, despite himself.

"So, you know about Greek gods. What else do you know?" he goaded. "I'm curious."

"Nothing I'd want to tell you."

"Oooh!" The room came alive with the hoots and whistles of the men.

"You've met your match," Georgie said.

"Yeah, be careful. This one bites," Tony laughed.

"Ah, women. All the same," Nick slipped his buttocks off the desk, smooth as a snake, and walked out the door.

If one man was the furthest from any romantic ideal I may have nurtured, it was Nick. And it was this most unlikely of men with whom I fell madly and irrevocably in love. I must have been charmed or, more likely, hexed.

I've often wondered what it was about Nick that caught my eye. I reached the conclusion, finally, that falling in love had nothing to do with him. Women often fall into this trap. We attribute to a man the qualities we yearn for and convince ourselves that this man is the sole possessor of the desired characteristics. It's merely an invention. The man's perfection, sensitivity, passion, intelligence, goodness are all a product of our imagination and usually have no basis whatsoever in reality.

That's what happened to me with Nicholas Poseidon, the taciturn, mocking Greek who rarely smiled and still lived with his widowed mother in a cold-water tenement on 138th and Second Avenue. I was lonely and in desperate need of something that would give me some measure of hope. So I invented him. There was the added factor that he was Greek, like my hero Odysseus. That clinched it in my eyes. Now that I throw my mind back through the decades of experience that lay behind me, I can see him clearly as he truly was: an unremarkable man who desperately wanted to be a hero.

Chapter Nineteen

... we two were swept
by waves of longing.

The Odyssey

Whenever I had bad dreams as a child, my mother would always exhort me to say "Cómetelo, tapir. Cómetelo, tapir." (Eat it up, tapir. Eat it up, tapir.)

I didn't know what a tapir was until she explained that it was a South American animal with a nose like an elephant's trunk, eyes like a rhinoceros, a cow's tail, a tiger's legs, and a bear's body.

"Its favorite dish," my mother said seriously, "is bad dreams."

She waited to see what effect this information would have on me. When she saw that she had my undivided attention, she continued. "Some people sleep with the drawing of a tapir on their pillow so they can sleep in peace. But you don't have to do that. All you have to do is say 'Cómetelo, tapir. Cómetelo, tapir,' and your nightmare will be gone, devoured by the hungry tapir. Will you remember?"

Shortly after I met Nicholas Poseidon, I had a terrible nightmare. I was desperately searching for a little girl, but she had been eaten by a cannibal. The cannibal was a large, pale man, with blond hair and light blue eyes. Just as the cannibal trained his ice-blue eyes on me, I woke with a start.

"Cómetelo, tapir. Cómetelo, tapir," I whispered, wondering whether I'd be eaten alive and by whom.

"Well, hello, Marina." I looked up to see Nick, smiling like he owned the world, ready to settle his bottom on my desk again.

"Good morning, Nick. Listen, you'll have to excuse me, but I have a tight deadline, and I'm nowhere near finishing this article."

"What's it about?"

"The appalling working conditions in the garment district."

"Again?"

"Yes, again. For as long as it takes to effect some changes."

"So, when're you writing about us?"

"Who?"

"The Sailor's Union."

"Give me some facts and I'll write it up."

"Okay! It's a deal then."

"Sure."

"But keep that anarchist crap out of it, okay?"

"Pardon me?" I could feel my face reddening with anger.

"Sorry to offend you, but anarchists are nothing but losers. Communism's the way to go."

"Nick, I'm having a hard time understanding you. What is it that you object about anarchists?"

"You don't have a workable program to seize power and establish the society you want. The Communists at least were prepared for the revolution and took over, established the dictatorship of the people."

"We don't want to 'seize' power, as you say. We are not obsessed with power. We want to do away with the state, with government, in a peaceful way."

"Yeah, yeah, and how's that gonna work? Tell me that. We need some kind of structure at the top to make things happen."

"No, we don't. That's the problem with Communism. They've done away with private property and put it in the hands of the state. I shudder when I think about it. The people wind up with nothing."

"Oh, come on, Marina, anarchism will never work, especially the anti-violent kind you're always babbling about in those articles. It hasn't worked and never will."

"Wait a minute. You're forgetting the Spaniards. Anarchism was an enormous success in many parts of Spain. It was the greatest social experiment in the history of humanity. The anarchists took over land and factories, and the workers managed themselves and actually improved not only working conditions, but productivity. Ordinary people in Cataluña, people like you and me, managed themselves in the workplace. Whole towns and regional economies were transformed into federations of collectives. The peasants created self-managed cooperatives. There was health care, education, machinery, and investment in infrastructure. People were free. It was a dream come true, and it worked."

"Until Franco beat the pants off them!" Nick scoffed.

"The point is," I had become greatly exasperated by then, "that for a period of time, it worked. The point is that the ideals of peaceful anarchism are possible. Can't you see that? If not, you've got to be blind!"

"Yeah, possible until the next Fascist capitalist comes along with the power of well-organized force."

I shook my head.

"There's too much violence in this world. That's the biggest problem, the major hindrance to justice. There's too much violence and too much fear."

"Listen, Marina, let's change the subject. You're not convincing me of anything, and it sure as hell looks like I'm not convincing you either." He glanced around to see if the other men were listening. He lowered his voice to a whisper and moved closer to me.

"I didn't come here to fight with you. What do you say we step out for something to eat?"

"Are you asking me out on a date?"

"Well, let's see." He looked up at the ceiling and took a puff from his cigarette. "Yeah, I guess you could say that."

"Sure, then we can talk about the Sailor's Union, I guess. When?" I turned back to my typewriter and attempted to act as indifferent as he had suddenly become.

"What time do you get off tonight?"

"Not tonight," I said briskly. "I have no idea when I'll finish this. Gus will kill me if I don't get it to him in a few hours."

"How about tomorrow night?"

"Tomorrow's good."

When he swaggered out, I noticed that he threw a glance at Georgie. Georgie winked.

Nick took me to a Greek restaurant called Kleptikos. It was an evening of firsts. I had never been to a restaurant before. Mostly, my meals were consumed at home with Luz and Miguel, and Luz always packed leftovers for lunch.

When the waiter gave me the bilingual menu, the span of an eagle's wings, I glanced at the beautiful script and was surprised that I couldn't understand a word of the Greek on the menu. I always thought that with the Greek Sister Theresa had taught me, I'd be able to communicate with any Greek person easily. If I could read *The Odyssey*, I could certainly read a simple menu. But the Greek on this menu was incomprehensible. When I glanced at the English translations of the dishes that read "lamb shops" and "deep potatoes," I was still at a loss as to what to order. Finally, I decided to do what I always did when in doubt: Ask a question.

"I've never had Greek food. What's a good thing to order?"

"Everything's delicious here." Nick said. "But for your first time, let's order a *moussaka* and a *horiatiki*, a country salad. It has tomatoes, basil, onions, and lots of feta cheese with oregano and olive oil."

It sounded delicious, and my mouth watered immediately. When the *moussaka* arrived, I cut into the fragrant layers. To my dismay, I discovered that it was made with an unidentifiable ground meat that smelled pungent and strong. Carefully, hoping to be discreet, I scraped the meat off with my fork, made a little mound on the side of the plate, and wiped the fork with my napkin.

"What's the matter, you don't like lamb?"

I shrugged and shook my head. "I don't eat meat. Sorry."

"You're a vegetarian?"

I nodded.

"This is incredible. You anarchists are real nuts, you know that?"

"I've never had meat in my life. My mother was a vegetarian."

"She was an anarchist too?"

"Oh, she was the real anarchist in the family. Everyone called me 'the anarchist's daughter' when I was growing up."

"If you never had meat, why don't you try some tonight?" Nick brightened up. "Hey, maybe you'll like it?"

I wrinkled my nose as if someone had poured vinegar up my nostrils.

"We lived near a slaughterhouse, and every evening we could hear the moaning of animals having their throats cut. It was the terrible sound of fear, pain, and suffering. No, Nick, sorry but I can't."

"Well, suit yourself." I could hear the disapproval in his voice. "A vegetarian pacifist anarchist. I don't know what I'm doing going out with you."

"Maybe it's time for you to be a little more flexible," I said, and he managed to muster a smile.

On that first date, I enjoyed my first *moussaka* (ground lamb dutifully scraped off) with *horiatiki* salad and my first glass of wine. The alcohol promptly went to my head; my obvious lack of worldliness mortified me. Throughout the evening, Nick studied my every move, which made me feel more self-conscious and foolish. He was a man of the world—he had been a sailor, after all—and I was behaving like a country bumpkin.

After the main course, emboldened by the wine, I asked the waiter for water in Greek.

"*Hydra*," I said, a bit too loudly.

"What?" The waiter frowned with a look of distaste.

"*Hydra. Hydra.* Don't you understand Greek?"

Nick almost fell out of his chair laughing. "What're you talking about?" he blurted between gales of laughter.

"It's Greek. I learned it at the convent from an American nun. I don't see why you find it so funny."

"You must've learned ancient Greek. It's different. The word you want is *nero*. Water is *nero*," he repeated loudly.

"*Nero*? But that's nothing like *hydra*!" I was flabbergasted.

"You're something else." Nick laughed and slapped himself on the thigh. "Oooh, I haven't laughed so much in a long time."

Of course, I was not amused, and I let myself slide into a serious snit. This date was not working out. I should have known. Nick was an insensitive cretin, totally lacking in good manners, and I never should have agreed to go out with him.

Then another glass of red wine smoothed the ridges of my anger and humiliation. By the end of the evening, after the *moussaka*, the Greek salad, the honey-sweetened *halvah*, I was greatly appeased.

"So you gonna teach me some ancient Greek?" Nick was beset by another attack of hilarity.

I rolled my eyes to the ceiling.

"No, you're going to teach me modern Greek. I think it's more practical, don't you?"

"What do you need Greek for? You're in America now and speak English. That's all you need."

I was going to tell him about *The Odyssey* and my hero Odysseus, about the importance of having that book to comfort me during the most difficult times of my life. How I had saved money from my first year's wages to purchase a brand-new copy in ancient Greek and how I was saving money to order the Spanish and English translations at a bookstore on Fifth Avenue. And now that I had discovered another variety of Greek, how I would love to read the book in the language spoken by Nick and his mother and the restaurant waiter and the millions of people in Greece. But I knew Nick would never understand the solace of a legend. Despite his years at sea, his horizon was never far; his vision remained close to the chest, like a poker card. I wondered if he ever dreamed.

It was hard for me to concentrate on work after my date with Nick. He didn't come by the office for several weeks. Secretly and incomprehensibly, I was dying to see him again.

When I least expected it, I got my wish. I was at an anarchist's meeting at David's house in Brooklyn. When Nick walked in, I remember how good-looking he suddenly seemed to me, with his short beard, sharp cheekbones, and Balkan nose. David, the group leader, was speaking. David was in his early forties, had brown-dusted skin and a slight frame. He spoke slowly, like a doped adolescent. He chain-smoked. Even as he rambled on about dialectical materialism, his cigarette stuck to his upper lip and wobbled up and down. Although he was always railing against Yankee capitalists, he took a blond, blue-eyed Bostonian to his bed every night.

I had been seriously considering dropping out of this wing of the party but had decided to attend a last meeting, hoping our leadership situation would miraculously improve. That night David droned on and on for over an hour with his usual disquisition on Bakunin, bending his head forward, cigarette wobbling on his lips. Nothing new, just the same old stuff rehashed.

I had been asked to take notes at the meeting, and my eyes watered with boredom. I had no interest in Bakunin or Malatesta, though I tried to keep up to date on the readings David assigned every week. All I cared about was the freedom of all people. I sincerely hoped that when the anarchist revolution triumphed, I wouldn't have to run into David again. Maybe, if we were lucky, he'd be sent to export the revolution to faraway places. Antarctica sounded good. Maybe the penguins and polar bears would listen to his lengthy expositions without dying of boredom. Somehow, I wasn't convinced that David was in the movement for an ideal. It was more like there was nothing else for him to do with his life.

When Nick came into the room that night, he sat on the chair next to me and nodded as if we had just met. After the meeting, the small group gathered at the refreshment table where some of the women had set out soft drinks and sandwiches. Nick came up to me.

"Hello, Marina. We meet again."

"I suppose so," I said softly, while my heart pounded wildly in my chest. "What brings you to an anarchists' meeting?"

"I was hoping you'd be here."

"Well, I'm honestly glad to see you," I blurted without thinking. Somehow I felt depressed by this realization.

I felt pulled towards him more than ever. As we talked that evening, no one else in the world seemed to exist except him. Something long dormant had awakened in me, but I was not sure what it could be. All I knew was that I was attracted to him like a magnet.

"I went to your apartment. Luz was happy to see me. She seemed happier to see me than you are."

"Oh, she approves of you. Thinks you're a great catch. But don't take it too seriously. Anything that walks and wears pants would be a good catch for me as far as she's concerned."

Nick laughed out loud. "So she knows about your political involvement?"

"She and Miguel are very much committed. They've known David for years," I said and cast a glance at our movement leader. "They don't come to all the meetings, but their commitment is strong."

That night Nick invited me for a drink. David had been annoyed because he wanted to talk to him about organizing a meeting at the Sailors' Union. But Nick put him off, mildly but firmly. He'd see him later, Nick said. It was obvious that Nick and David knew each other from way back.

"Hey," David yelled. "What's going on?"

"None of your business," Nick said firmly. "Don't worry, I'll be back in a couple of hours."

"You better. I just got a new mission, and I need to be briefed. This whole situation is a nightmare, man," David whined, pulling hard on his cigarette. I was so enraptured by Nick's presence, it never occurred to me to ask what David was talking about.

That night at a dark bar that smelled like stale cigarettes, Nick told me his side of the story. Not all of it, of course. We were accustomed by now to hide anything that might seem significant, to keep our feelings separate from our identities: who we were, what we had been, all the information that might be useful if the person in front of you was really a mole or might be subjected to intolerable interrogation techniques. And we never knew. Sometimes it was hard to admit the truth to ourselves. As I recall, this need for secrecy was always lodged between us, like a clutch of nettles.

"I was away for a while. Just got back to New York yesterday."

"Union business?"

"You might call it that." He looked around the bar, out of habit. As always, he sat with his back toward a wall. When he turned toward me, his eyes sparkled. "Listen, Marina. I can't tell you everything I'm involved in. You understand. Sometimes I go away for a long time. One day I might have to go away for good. Alone."

Despite his warning, I agreed to see him again. With a parting kiss on the lips at the stoop of my building, we set a date. I knew another heartbreak was in store, but like a train hurtling down the tracks, I could not stop it from coming.

Chapter Twenty

The sea routes will yield their distances.

The Odyssey

On the bright morning of our first proper date, the sun towered above the world, and hints of light bounced from the dark ocean. I bent over, my arms crossed on the wooden rail, to peer into the swirling water. I could see nothing but the foamy cobwebs curled on crests of sea waves. The upper deck was packed with tourists, but I felt the loneliness that usually struck me in crowds. Maybe it was the scent of sea salt or the crest of the waves, but suddenly thoughts of Julián pushed through my mind: his smile, the way he put his arm around my shoulders protectively whenever someone threatened us at La Perla. A spray from the water dampened my face, and I squinted, wrapping a sweater around my shoulders. I breathed in deeply, one knee poised on a wooden bench, glad to be there after all, glad not to be alone.

Nick leaned against the rail beside me. Through the corner of my eye, I saw his strong profile. He put a cigarette between his lips and, cupping it with a hand, applied a match to it. The smoke curled away from us and dissolved in the wind far above the sea. We stood there, bent against the wind, feeling each other's presence through the wooden rail. A warm undercurrent fanned out through the nape of my neck and crawled up my scalp. It suffused my every pore and, annoyed, I realized that I had been blushing. "There's the lady." Nick stretched a finger in front of us as the Statue of Liberty glimmered like a jewel ahead. "America's monument to the rich."

"Actually, the United States is not all of America."

"Sorry. I forgot that you Latin Americans are sensitive about that."

"It's not that we're sensitive, we're Americans, too. So are the Canadians."

"I know, I know. Georgie keeps reminding me."

"We should call people from the United States, U.S.ers."

"I could go for that." He shrugged. "Why not?" Then he turned to me. "But tell me something, Marina. Why are you so sad all the time?"

I shrugged and looked out at the horizon.

"Don't be sad, Marina. Be happy. We have a great day ahead of us. The past no longer exists and the future may never come. I don't remember who said that, but I believe it. Let's enjoy the moment."

"*Carpe diem.*"

"Ancient Greek and Latin. Didn't you learn anything useful from those nuns?" he laughed.

A static-punctuated female voice spilled from the loudspeaker with more information about the Statue of Liberty than we could ever remember.

As we returned from the tour, I attempted to look out into the distance and pursue my own thoughts again. I looked down at the swirling waters, dark and deep, reminding me of Homer's wine black sea. The ferry sliced through the water quickly, returning to Manhattan to pick up another load of tourists.

"So, are you going to be silent all day, Marina?"

"Sorry, Nick. I was just thinking."

"About me, I hope."

"No, not really."

"I'm disappointed."

"I was just thinking that there is no true liberty, as that French lady's statue proclaims," I said, pointing at the statue. "No protection against enslavement."

"What do you mean?"

"Well, if even the mind can be shackled, what else is there? Maybe freedom is an impossible to achieve illusion."

"But wait a minute, Marina. There's a big difference between freedom and liberty. Someone can take my liberty away, but never my freedom. That's why no one can shackle your mind—that's where freedom lies."

"What if you're tortured until you can't think any longer?"

"That's temporary. That's liberty taken away, but freedom doesn't die, it just remains dormant."

"Are you saying that Pedro Albizu Campos is free in a federal penitentiary?"

"Of course, he's free. He only lost his liberty."

"But he lost everything. Not lost exactly—it has all been taken away from him. How can you make any distinctions?"

I was angry, and Nick tried to cheer me up. He turned around, back toward me, and wiggled his shoulders. Then he faced me again.

"Now, my esteemed lady," he said smiling. "I will perform a singular act of magic. For before your very eyes, I will defy the laws of physics, and you will see matter formed from nothing." Nick leaped up and spread his arms. Then he bent over, pushed his hand into an air vent and pulled out his rolled newspaper. With a great flourish, he unwrapped the newspaper and offered me an apple he had stashed away during lunch.

I laughed and took a bite of the apple. It was sweet and juicy. I was taking another bite when I noticed that the skies had become gray and large clouds were gathered over us. Before we could seek shelter, a heavy rain began to fall. Nick held the newspaper over our heads. Everyone else scrambled for shelter, but the two of us sat outside, barely protected by the paper. I was lulled by the rhythm of our breathing. I could smell Nick's skin, redolent of tobacco, aftershave lotion, and rain. My heart pounded when he let go of the drenched newspaper. He put his arm around my waist. The world shrank. Only the two of us remained in the universe, listening to our heartbeats. I lowered my head, confused by the turmoil within me, and he kissed my cheek, my ear, my neck. I retreated from him, from the passion of his kisses, and looked up into the dark intensity of his eyes. His eyes were so deep. I swam into them, not knowing what I would find or whether I would drown in them. It was dangerous territory, I felt that right away, and I was both driven back and attracted to it. He pulled me toward him as I fell into his arms.

"Let's go to a hotel," Nick said when the ferry came into the dock.

"No, I can't, Nick. I can't."

"Why not? Don't you want me?"

"Yes, but it's not right."

"What're you talking about? I'm free and you're free." He looked at me with exasperation. "What's the problem, then?"

"It's wrong. I feel that I'm betraying someone." I couldn't tell him about Julián's steady presence in my life.

"No, this isn't wrong. What we feel for each other can't be wrong. Please, Marina."

"I don't know. I'm so confused."

"Why are you confused? Come with me and you'll forget everything."

He hugged me, and his hug was gentle and strong at the same time. I dissolved in his embrace. An overwhelming lassitude overcame me. I felt pulled by Nick's desire. I stumbled into his need until it became mine.

Nick switched on the naked bulb that hung on a wire from the ceiling. We stood stuffed in the tiny room, and I couldn't avoid brushing against him. A tap dripped in the bathroom.

"Sorry this isn't a very nice hotel. But you know how things are these days. Money's tight."

"That's all right," I responded uneasily, a sinking feeling in my chest. "Excuse me, I need to go to the bathroom."

The toilet had no lid, so I sat on the rim of the bathtub. I reflected on the topography of cracked walls and tried to force my mind back into my head. But it had a will of its own and wandered back to the cracks and the yellow stains of humidity seeping through the soiled walls. I closed my eyes, breathed deeply, and sat as straight as a ruler. A vengeful flow of non-stop thoughts forcefully sabotaged any attempt to empty my mind.

Then my thoughts settled on Julián. All those years and I still felt tied to him.

No, I said to myself tentatively acknowledging my want. *I can't go through with this.*

What would Julián think if he were still alive?

That I didn't love him enough, that I had betrayed him?

But maybe he would understand. Julián had always understood even the tacit, silent parts of me that refused to reveal themselves.

I staggered to my feet and shook a numb leg. Vigorously, I massaged the circulation back. Trying to delay the inevitable, lingering, I washed and dried my hands thoroughly. Finally, I took in a deep breath and resolutely walked out of the bathroom.

Nick stood by the window smoking. I walked up to his side, and while he continued searching the dark sky, he settled an arm over my shoulders.

"You know, Marina, this is a special night for me. Since my sailing days were over, I've felt an emptiness in my life. I never even dream. I sleep an empty sleep. How can one dream when there is nothing inside? All that was mine was my anger. It was my sustenance, you see, the force that kept me alive, day by day. Now that I've met you, I feel something else, something alive. I don't know what it is, Marina. I don't know."

He turned his head and looked at me. Gently, very gently, he kissed my forehead, my eyes, the tip of my nose, my cheeks, my lips, my chin, my throat. I closed my eyes tight as seams, and a shiver of pleasure washed over me. He clasped my head between his large hands and combed my long hair back with his fingers. He kissed me deeper and deeper until my loins protested my cold passivity, and I returned his kisses with the same urgency. I felt the hardness of his body against me.

We lay naked in bed.

"Don't move, don't do anything. Close your eyes and concentrate on the pleasure I give you," he whispered.

When he entered me, finally, after pleasing me countless times, he was steady and quick.

"I love you," he whispered as he trembled and collapsed in my arms.

A few minutes later, his kisses were warm on my breasts. Then he stretched out, reached for a packet of cigarettes, puffed hungrily, and, sliding his arm under my neck, eased down to talk.

"You know, Marina, I can't sleep when I'm happy. Are you prepared for a night without sleep?"

"I can't stay overnight! You know that. Luz and Miguel will be sick with worry." I sat up, clutching the sheet under my chin.

"Okay, okay, don't get upset. We'll leave in a few hours. After we've made love again, if you want, as soon as I'm capable."

"Yes," I said hoarsely.

"You're a hungry woman, Marina. I knew that the moment I set eyes on you. And that's good because I'm a hungry man."

I turned my head and stared out the window.

"Tell me, my Marina. What're you thinking right now?"

"I'm thinking of Giza."

"Giza? I don't understand."

"The pyramids of Egypt in Giza."

"What about it?"

"That life soars upwards and we're often left behind."

Chapter Twenty-One

His life may not in exile go to waste.

The Odyssey

Since the fall of Constantinople, Tuesday had been an ill-omened day in Nick's family. It was the day we married in a brief ceremony at City Hall. Luz lost her beatific smile and cried throughout the ceremony. Miguel stood like the soldier he had been, bending stiffly at the waist when it was his turn to sign the register. Before I kissed them good-bye, Luz pulled me to the side.

"Be careful, *mija*. Some men are difficult to love," she said enigmatically. I wondered whether she sensed my own apprehension or could see what was really beneath Nick's carapace.

For as long as I live, I will not understand why we married. I had been brought up in the freedom of an anarchist's home and was always suspicious of government involvement in people's personal affairs. But when Nick proposed shortly after our first date, I surprised myself by saying yes. Everything that happened with Nick was unexpected, and after a few years, I stopped trying to understand his motivations. Or even mine.

When I moved into Nick's apartment the evening of our marriage, his mother, Kyria Varvara, appealed to my sense of self-preservation and, having crossed herself several times, right shoulder to left as the Greek Orthodox do, she entreated me to do the same.

"You must never marry or travel on a Tuesday, never move, and, if possible, don't leave your house, *then prepi*," she informed me in her thick accent.

"If you must," she recommended, "only do so after you have crossed yourself several times the moment you step out. Say a few prayers to God and the Virgin and hope the *mati*, the blue evil eye warder you are wearing, does its magic." Kyria Varvara heaved her substantial bosom and sighed.

"What evil eye warder?"

Kyria Varvara frowned at Nick. She patted her apron pockets and shook her head.

"Wait," she said. "I will find you one."

She returned, put the blue stone into my hand, and shook her head again.

"I cannot understand Nicos." She turned to her son. "Why did you never tell her about these things, Nico *mou*? Why did you have to get married in such a hurry, and on a Tuesday? I couldn't even be there. You are inviting the wrath of the gods."

Nick shrugged and steered me toward one of the bedrooms. Evil eye averter secure in hand, I followed as he brought my two battered suitcases into the room we would share for fifteen years.

Kyria Varvara was pleased when I began speaking Greek. I had a talent for languages and paid close attention when Kyria Varvara talked to Nick or to her friends or relatives when they stopped by the apartment. If I was present, they tried to speak in English, but I always encouraged them to switch back to Greek. Kyria Varvara complied by speaking slowly and gesticulating wildly. But the real reason I learned Greek quickly was because I was hungry for the language, hungry for the new vision of the world it would give me. I struggled with the formidable syntax and knew that Greek had taken hold like a fever I couldn't shake.

Often when Nick went out early in the morning or was away on his frequent trips, Kyria Varvara would knock on our bedroom door and bring me a cup of Greek coffee, scented with cardamom seeds.

"*Kalimera, Marina, ti kaneis simera?*" she greeted me, her thick eyebrows raised in anticipation, inquiring about my well-being when I opened the door.

"*Kala, Kyiria Varvara, efharisto.*" I was always well, regardless of the heaviness that had settled in my heart, the terrible loneliness when Nick was away for undisclosed times in mysterious places.

"Later, I will bring you some baklava I am making. You are too skinny, Marina, you must fill out so you can have Nico's baby." She placed her thick hands in front of her ample abdomen, palms facing upward, as if holding a bowl of egg yolks.

"And my baklava is not like that *skoupedia*, that garbage, Stelios serves in that taverna of his." She shook her head dolefully. "Mine is made with the finest ingredients. There is only one way to make it right, you know. No shortcuts." When she breathed in with great determination and raised her voice, an unmistakable sign that she was ready to explain something, I knew my coffee would get hopelessly cold.

"I use sixty phyllo leaves, sixty exactly, no less, no more, and I butter each and every one carefully with the finest butter from the Peloponnese. With moistened fingers, I layer the leaves with my special mix of minced walnut, cinnamon, the squeeze of a lemon, and honey from Hymmetos. My nephew Christos brought me the ingredients last week." She drew the tips of her fingers together and kissed them noisily. "You will see, Marina *mou*."

But it wasn't Kyria Varvara's culinary talents that kept me captive in that apartment all those years. It was her stories. Thanks to her unflagging efforts to explain herself to me, to have me understand the life she experienced, I learned demotic Greek quicker than I ever anticipated from Kyria Varvara's stories, the stories of her relatives, the stories of the other people she knew. Layers upon layers of never-ending tales flowed from the surface of her life to the core of all that she was. From these stories told with verve and great generosity, I discovered that every Greek had a story.

I remember one of the first things Kyria Varvara showed me. It was a photo of herself and her husband Giorgos, squinting in the harsh sun of the stark Attican landscape. Next to them was an old run-down moving truck with the word ΜΕΤΑΦΩΡΕΣ scrawled by hand on its side panel. In that land of white dust and beveled light, metaphor meant to move from one place to another. I could not fail to be captured by this exaltation of the commonplace.

Kyria Varvara often positioned herself regally at her upholstered chair and, after inquiring politely about my health and well-being, let out her stream of tales. At first, I was bewildered when she began weeping. In the early months, I couldn't understand her words, the source of her tears, though I understood her pain perfectly well. I would get up from the chair at the small table I used as a desk and put my hand on her trembling shoulder. She would wipe her face with a blanket of a handkerchief. Undeterred by the tears flowing down her plump cheeks, she taught me the Greek of anguish and despair.

"*Po, po*, Marina." She would wave her hand in the air dramatically and turn her eyes toward the ceiling. "I have lived a long, long life and seen many things no eyes should ever have to see. That has been God's will."

"But, Kyria Varvara, you're still young," I said.

"*Oxi*, Marina *mou*. You are mistaken. I'm sixty-two years old. That is a long time to live, *kori mou*, my daughter," she said, shaking her head sorrowfully. "And how old are you, if I may ask?"

"I just turned twenty-four."

"And without children." She shook her head again, this time in disapproval, not of me but of the situation that had caused my childlessness. "I was twenty when I had Nicos, my only child. He was born in Athens. I was so happy to give Giorgos the son that he desperately wanted."

"Did you meet Giorgos in Athens?"

"I went to Athens from Patras when I was very young. I worked cleaning houses, taking care of children. I wanted to be a seamstress, but no one would teach me. The ladies of the houses I worked in only wanted me to clean after them. And I always wanted to be a seamstress. It was my dream." Kyria Varvara's eyes misted with longing.

"I was only eighteen when my sister took me to a matchmaker. She thought I was too old to be without a husband, and the matchmaker found Giorgos for me." Kyria Varvara glanced at her hands folded on her lap, lowering her voice.

"I didn't like him at first and refused to marry him because he was so dark. I wasn't used to being around *mavri*. He comes from Asia Minor, from Smyrna, you see, and I was afraid of him. There were no dark people in Kalanistro, the village in Achaia where I was born in the Peloponnese, so I had never seen any *mavri* until I moved to Athens. When I saw him I said to myself, '*Po, po*, nothing's going to happen here.' But he was so gentle, so kind and nice to me, that I finally accepted, and we exchanged rings on my saint day, Aghia Varvara. Giorgos did not demand things, even though other men made demands from a woman. He did not ask for a dowry when my father asked him what he wanted. My father was a farmer, and we had sheep and olive groves and fields of black raisins and wheat. All that. Even though he had four daughters, my father could have given him a dowry. But Giorgos refused and said that he would work and that would be enough.

"Everything he said was true. Giorgos was a good provider for me and our son. But then my Giorgos was killed in the second Balkan war." At this point in her tale, Kyria Varvara invariably pulled out her handkerchief and wiped the tears from her face.

"Life was too hard for us after that, and there were so many days when I went to bed with nothing but hunger pangs in my stomach, only to wake up in the morning to feed my Nicos, take him to my sister's house, and then go to work at a shop that sold wedding supplies. I had a spirit stove where I used to melt the wax. When the wreaths were ready, I used to take them to the shops. I made almost nothing. I was so skinny, you could blow me away with your breath. Then my oldest sister sent me a letter from New York, saying I should come. She made the ship arrangements, and that's how we arrived here. Nicos was a small boy." Kyria Varvara wiped her eyes. "I still miss my Giorgos, you know. They say that the dead are gone, but it's not true. Giorgos is with me for as long as I live."

Chapter Twenty-Two

Here they put in, furled sail, and beached the ship.
                                                        The Odyssey

After all those years of living with Nick and Kyria Varvara, years of turbulence and want, I couldn't imagine how it was possible that time had passed so quickly and how I had never recognized the warning signs that hung in the heavy atmosphere of the apartment. I had been living one day at a time and couldn't see what was ahead of me. Nick and I had different commitments that kept us busy.

Commitments that never included the other.

I don't know what kept us together.

Perhaps the glue that bound us was my fear of being alone and his desire for an acquiescent body to warm his bed. He had gotten used to my presence in his mother's apartment, and I had become accustomed to the indifference that settled into our lives. Over time, we rarely sat together for a meal or even talked much. We made love always in the dark and in silence. When it was over, like an overwrought cliché found in every pulp novel and B-rated movie, Nick sat up with his back against the bed frame, lit a cigarette, and looked out the window. Most of the time, though, I slept alone.

"By the way, Marina, where is that son of mine?" Kyria Varvara was preparing *avgolimano,* and the sharp scent of lemon filled the kitchen. "He's been away for too long this time. *Panayia mou,* I dread to think about the things he is doing, who he is with, where he could be."

"Don't worry, Kyria Varvara, he can take good care of himself."

As I said this, I turned my head, nauseous with apprehension. Nick had left one night a month before for a union meeting, and the next day I woke at dawn wondering when he would return. He had frequently been away for weeks, but when his absence extended for a month I decided it was time to find him.

The people at the Sailor's Union were circumspect when I dropped by to inquire. David, who seemed to know more about Nick than he let on, just shrugged his shoulders when I asked.

"He's a man, Marina. He can't be tied to your apron strings all the time," David said.

The small apartment became a mourner's temple. Kyria Varvara dragged her upholstered chair to the window, and there she sat for most of the day, sighing loudly and wiping the tears from her face. I quit my job at the newspaper and took on translation work I could do at home. Our vigil continued for a month, two months.

Six months became a year of waiting and still no sign of Nick.

After a long winter day, when waiting for Nick in the small apartment had become unbearable, I took a long walk to Chinatown. It was a bitterly cold evening. I bent forward against the razor-sharp wind. Market stands full of octopus, fish, and clams, emitting the briny scent of the sea, reminded me of my island, Luisa's crabs, and, inevitably, my mother's death. I turned away from the market and looked into an alley off Pearl Street.

In the hazy mist of nightfall, I saw a Chinese woman dressed in a red tunic, buttoned at the side of her neck. She wore a round silk cap, flat at the top, with an embroidered band over the upper part of her forehead. She sat behind a makeshift wooden stand, an old fruit crate probably, covered with a yellow tasseled cloth. A handwritten sign pinned to the cloth read "Madame Zoe—Fortune Telling, Palm Reading."

I don't know how or why, but I found myself sitting on the small bench across from her. As I looked at her hands, coarse with time, inexplicably I thought of *doña* Eugenia sprinkling salt around her shack to ward off the evil spirits.

Without a word, Madame Zoe reached forward and examined my ears. Then she shuffled a deck of tarot cards, the size of a pack of cigarettes. She motioned to me to cut the deck in half with my left hand. Then she placed the left stack on top of the right and arranged ten cards on the table, face down. One by one, she turned the cards over like book pages and examined each one. There were swords and pentacles and a beautiful wheel that looked like a compass. Then she sat back and surveyed the spread as a whole, placing the palms of her hands on the sides of the table.

"You live eighty-five years, more so." Her strong voice startled me. I was expecting her words to be laced with otherworldliness, hushed and mysterious.

"But you always stay young," she said firmly. "Your life difficult, but one day you find peace." She studied the cards to her left, then to her right. "You think you alone, you not alone," she said. I looked around me, expecting to find someone else there. Her next words struck me at my core. They had the resonance of something I already knew but did not realize that I knew until she uttered them. "You are too patient, that why no success in your life. In some years you no more patient, you have success and you go back home."

As I cut through the cold night, I thought of the promise of home and wondered whether I would ever return to the island, after all I had lived through, all I had changed, all I had lost.

Soon I would lose even the freedom to return home.

One night, around three in the morning, I heard a peremptory knock on the door. As I put on my bathrobe, the banging grew louder, more insistent. When I came out of the bedroom, tying my robe at the waist, Kyria Varvara was already at the door.

"Marina, what is this? They are saying they are FBI. To open up."

"Step to the side, *mitera mou*. I'll open."

Three tall men flashed their badges in my face and shoved me aside. One stood at the door while the others combed through the apartment, turning it upside down.

"What are you doing?" Kyria Varvara yelled. "This is my home! You have no right to come here and search through my things. Making such a mess!"

"Shut up, lady," one of the agents barked. He had closely cropped hair and a pockmarked face.

"Don't talk to her like that. Do you have a warrant?"

"We don't need one. Are you Marina Alomar?"

"Yes, I am."

"Where's Nicholas Poseidon?"

"Why are you looking for my Nicos?" Kyria Varvara cried. "He is not here. He has not come home in a year."

"We don't know where he is," I said quietly.

When the other agent returned from the bedrooms, he pulled a pair of handcuffs from his pocket and pushed me against a wall. Harshly, he clamped the cuffs on my wrists. His breath was rancid, like cheese that had gone bad.

"What are you doing? What is this?" Kyria Varvara was desperate, pacing around the living room, trying to find someone who would respond to her questions.

"Hey, look at this," the pockmarked agent said as he pointed at the table where I worked. "I bet we can find some nice revolutionary stuff in this pile of papers."

"That's my work. My translations."

"Aha, this is just the kind of stuff we were looking for. It's even in a foreign language. What is this, Greek?"

"It's poetry, you idiot. I'm a translator."

"Yeah, sure. We know what you're translating. Communist propaganda."

"I am not a Communist!" Those words flooded my mind with memories of my mother's claims, her arrests, all she had been through because of her convictions.

"Communist, Communist, who are you saying is Communist?" Kyria Varvara was in tears. "Are you crazy? Marina is no Communist. She is a good girl. She is like my own daughter." She came up to me and clutched at my arm desperately. "Please do not take her away from me, please."

"Don't beg, *mitera mou*. It won't do any good."

I spent the rest of the night in a cell with no windows, a harsh light bulb burning through my eyelids as I closed my eyes against the memory of the insults, the beating. I had nothing to say about the people the agents asked about. Nick was gone. I hadn't seen David in months. And what could I possibly say about Miguel and Luz except provide a testament of love and friendship?

After two days of interrogations, I was offered a deal. Either I signed a paper stating I would not return to Puerto Rico to promote the revolution, or I'd be put in jail. On what charges? I asked, my heart thumping in my throat. They pulled out a folder with articles I had written for the *Daily Worker* and *Libertad* and lists of meetings I had attended with known anarchists. They read quotes of statements I had made at the meetings where they had planted moles. The fact that I spoke Greek was also held against me, though I still don't know why. The most surprising information in my folder had to do with my mother's activities and her arrests. They knew everything about her. They too called me "the anarchist's daughter."

Summer pulled in quickly with its sweltering heat and discouragement. By then, I had forgotten Madame Zoe's predictions, and my pact with the FBI had wiped clean my yearning for home. One morning when Kyria Varvara had gone out to the market, I looked up from my work, startled by the realization that she and I had settled into a routine of sorts, brought together always by the specters of Nick's absence, his imminent return. Kyria Varvara's empty chair by the window seemed forlorn. Even when she wasn't there, it reminded me of her pain.

That early summer morning, I had been working at my table, wondering whether I'd ever be able to translate Sarandaris' words and produce, in English, that perfectly symmetrical poem that would take one's breath away with the beauty of its images, the perfection of its rhyme. An insistent knock at the door startled me. The pen slipped from my fingers and hit the floor with a tinkle of complaint.

It was a hot day, and I wore a simple cotton shift. Our apartment had a contradictory nature and always sided with the elements. Unbearably cold all through the winter, it turned hot as an oven as soon as the summer edged in. That morning, as I looked out at the thick haze in the air, I knew it would be an unbearably hot day.

When I heard the knock, I frowned and wondered whether I should open the door. I hated to be interrupted on those days when I could work. I had been trying to solve a recalcitrant translation problem in one of Sarandaris' most challenging poems.

Again, I heard the knock.

Harder this time.

It wasn't Kyria Varvara, of course. She had her own key. It was too early for visitors, and Nick also had his own key. Mumbling impatiently under my breath, I got up and tugged at the back of my skirt.

"Just a minute," I yelled.

When I opened the door a crack, there stood Nick, clutching a small paper bag with one hand, the other sunk in a pocket. My heart lurched when I saw him, distant and serious, distorted by my tears. He seemed to soar toward the ceiling. The darkness of the hall closed around him like a tunnel. His face was frozen in what was likely a smile.

Before opening it fully, I pressed my forehead against the door while my nerves settled down, until my poor heart grew accustomed to his presence at the threshold of my world, a world that at that time had ceased to include him. Anger, relief, hurt, reproach, and joy all struggled to gain dominance in my heart at that moment.

In Greek myth, Demeter's children would be angry with her when she was gone for long periods of time, but would always be happy to see her when she returned home, forgetting that she had ever left. I wished at that moment that I could have been happy for Nick's return, that I could have laughed and flung my arms around his neck and given him wet kisses on the mouth. But I couldn't forget his unexplained absences, the suffering I endured.

I can't remember what I said then. I probably stood around nervously, tugging at my hair, staring at a point past his shoulder, saying nothing. Afterwards, when he was gone again, immersed in a world of shadows unknown to me, I often wondered how he saw me that morning, fumbling with the door, struggling to find a voice to ask him in. He seemed uncomfortable at first, glancing around the room nervously.

"Hello, Marina. I lost my key." This was delivered in one fitful breath. He attempted another smile, and again he only managed an insincere grimace.

I stood in the middle of the room, staring at him. He resembled a beached boat in the open bay of the living room.

"Oh, Nick," I said, once I had found my voice. "Where have you been? We've been worried sick about you. It's been a year, a whole year without any news. Nothing. How could you put us through this?"

He looked around the room as if he were a visitor not intending to stay long. "This is quite a welcome! Can I put my weary bones on a chair before you start nagging?"

"This is your home. I'm your wife. Why are you treating me like a stranger?"

He sank into a chair and positioned an ankle on his knee. I brought my chair to the center of the room and sat across from him.

"Coffee, tea, orange juice, water?" Not realizing how early it was, in my agitation I recall offering him some wine too.

"Coffee would be good. Thank you. Black, no sugar, please."

"I remember," I said. I snuck a look at my face as I passed by the tin-framed mirror that hung on the wall near the kitchen. I smoothed my hair down and busied myself with the brass coffee pot, scalding my fingers with boiling water, making a clatter when I dropped a spoon in the sink.

"Here you go," I said buoyantly, I hoped, but I must have sounded torpid instead. "Think I'll join you. I've been working for hours without a break."

He took in the scent of the strong coffee. I watched as he closed his eyes to sniff. Then he took a sip and got up without a comment. I supposed he had approved of the strength of the coffee. I followed him to the worktable, cluttered with papers, pens, dictionaries, and poetry books. I picked up a cap and screwed it tightly on the ink pot. I gathered the sheaf of papers I had been working on and piled them neatly on the corner of the table.

"That's my latest," I said. "A translation of Sarandaris' collected poems." My heart raced when I caught a glint of admiration in his eyes. He broke into a big smile.

"I've got to hand it to you, Marina, you've really succeeded. People are talking about your translations of Seferis and Elitis. In English and Spanish. Sometimes I can't believe that I'm actually your husband." He looked around at the cramped apartment. "How did you manage? And with my mother babbling all day long."

I remember picking up one of Sarandaris' poems while I attempted to be articulate, desperately wanting him to understand what was important to me. Instead, I shrugged and said simply, "I don't know, I just did."

"You must have some money stashed away now. What're you doing living with my mother still."

I was sincerely offended by this. I loved Kyria Varvara, her hearty meals, the life I had forged with my bare hands for both of us.

"I like it here," I responded simply.

"Are you still active? Politically, I mean."

"Could be." I was noncommital.

To steer the conversation toward my work once more, I faced my wooden book case and picked out one of my translations. I inscribed and signed it. I held it up to him. I remember how sharply the shiny book cover picked up the light as I leaned over the chair to hand it to him.

"I don't see things as they are, but as they should be. I often don't even see the parts, but the beauty of the whole. That's why I live here with your mother. That's why I write and translate poetry."

A pool of light came through the window. Nick took my hand and very gently kissed it. I swallowed hard and tried not to say anything, to keep a blank face so he'd never guess how pleasurable the kiss had been, how his lips sent a shock through my arm. As frequently happened when he returned from a long absence, I was unable to utter a word. He placed the book on the table and kissed me again, with a longing that was almost painful. We stood by the window, the white curtains billowing gently, our kisses growing more intense. The passion I felt bordered on physical agony. He reached for the skin under my dress, and I pulled back.

"Wait. Kyria Varvara might come in any minute."

Nick stood there, arms at his sides, and glanced at the door, as if expecting Kyria Varvara's key turning in the lock.

"You're right." He paused and passed a hand across his face. "You know I love you, Marina."

That's when I began to pace. I put my hands over my ears. My life had settled into a peaceful routine. I loved my work, my freedom. I didn't need Nick's hard love, his disaffected needs, his absences. I did not want to walk that path again. Yet my heart, my stupid heart, advised otherwise.

"I don't want to hear this," I said weakly.

"I don't need to tell you what you already know," he said.

"What are you talking about?" My voice quavered with anger.

He pulled the curtain back and looked out. Two men were arguing noisily on the sidewalk, and the honk of a distant car could be heard.

"You know you love me still." His eyes were bright as glass as he asked the question he had come to ask. "Forgive me, Marina. You know that there's work that I have to do. I have no choice. I have to leave again soon, and I might not be able to come back here. But maybe I will. I just can't give you any guarantees. All I can do is ask that you wait for me."

"What makes you think that after all these months, a whole year, of not hearing from you, not one word, you have the right to come back and ask everything of me."

"Love is what makes me ask."

"I don't know, Nick. I can't take another one of your absences."

He nodded sadly. "If you love me you will," he said, and he walked out the door.

I sat at my desk and caressed the cup of coffee he had just touched. I folded my arms on the table, put my head down, and wept.

Kyria Varvara came in with a string bag full of vegetables and fruit.

"He came back," I said hoarsely.

She dropped the bag on the floor, put her hands to her head. "Where is he?" She ran to our bedroom and flung the door open.

"I'm sorry, Kyria Varvara. He left again."

"What did he say? Where did he come from? Is he sick?"

"No, he's a little thinner, but fine." I attempted a smile.

"Where is he? I want to see my Nicos!"

"I'm so sorry. Maybe he'll come back later. I just don't know."

"Why didn't you make him stay, Marina?" she said reproachfully.

"Kyria Varvara." I couldn't keep the frustration from my voice. "He is my history, not my present."

"But Marina *mou*, look how he loves you. Imagine, coming back for you after all this time."

"He left again."

"He will return. My Nicos will return, Marina, you will see." She turned toward her bedroom. "I must pray to the Virgin Mary now. Thank her for keeping him safe for me. Oh, I am so happy that he's alive."

"He never said anything about returning, Kyria Varvara."

"Oh, he will come back. Men always do when they are in love."

Chapter Twenty-Three

What shall I say first?
What shall I keep until the end?

The Odyssey

Every unrealized joy, every unfulfilled dream, every frustrated desire leaves behind it a residue, a trace of bitterness that sinks slowly but surely into the heart. It becomes *kaimos*. Whatever life or death has deprived one of forms a cloud in the mind, which, in time, falls as gentle rain. This is *kaimos*. What time has not succeeded in erasing from the heart becomes a *kaimos*. The traces left by deep-felt human contacts, be it the woman—mother, daughter, mistress—who has moved on or a vanished father, friend, or brother whose going has left dark loneliness, these too are the stuff of which Greek songs are made that become a *kaimos*. A product of a philosophical outlook on life, the "pleasing pain" of *kaimos* must find outward expression to lighten the spirit; otherwise pressure builds to the point of suffocation. After living with Kyria Varvara and Nick all those years, *kaimos* had been stitched to my heart.

Hardly a day goes by when a memory of Kyria Varvara, her stories, her long days at the window, doesn't sink into my consciousness. Sometimes a patch of blue in a neighbor's curtain reminds me of her chair. Or the waft of lemon from my tea wakes me from my musings, and I can taste the *avgolimano* she prepared every Easter. I can't seem to scrub my mind free of the images, though it's been so many years since Nick disappeared.

After five years of his absence, Kyria Varvara died of a broken heart, and I was left motherless again, with yet another hole to fill, another instance of *kaimos* poised heavily in my heart. Three decades of exile later and without explanation, the FBI allowed me to return home. But there were rules I had to adhere to. I was not to join any political party; I was not to gather with more than five persons at a time; I was not to publish political writings or give speeches of any kind. I signed another paper and here I am, living quietly with my memories.

At this point in my narration, it is time to reveal the discovery I made in my mother's memory box. The letter, in English, was written in a hurried hand, the black ink cutting across the thin, yellowed paper like the trail of blood on a wound. This was the letter Julián found on the desk of Dr. Cornelius Packard Rhoads (a.k.a. Dusty) that windy night so many years ago. Dr. Rhoads was an eminent member of the medical elite doing research with human subjects at the Presbyterian Hospital in San Juan for the Rockefeller Institute. He was testing a new treatment for pernicious anemia. I later discovered that although all his subjects were dying of anemia, he treated some and placed others in a control group without treatment. All in the control group died. He never sought patients' consent, never told them what he was doing. Those in the control group did not know they were condemned to die.

When you read the letter, written on November 11, 1931, addressed to his friend Dr. Fred Waldorf Stewart, you can understand why my hands shook uncontrollably for hours after reading it and why my heart, even today, is so heavy.

Dear Ferdie,

The more I think about the Larry Smith appointment, the more disgusted I get. Have you heard any reason advanced for it? It certainly is odd that a man out with the entire Boston group, fired by Wolback and, as far as I know, completely devoid of any scientific reputation, should be given the place. There is something wrong somewhere, probably with our point of view.

The situation in Boston is settled. Parker and Nye are to run the laboratory together, with either Kenneth or MacMahon to be assistant; the chief to stay on. As far as I can see, the chances of my getting a job in the next ten years are absolutely nil. One is certainly not encouraged to attempt scientific advances when it is a handicap rather than an aid to advancement. I can get a damn fine job here and am tempted to take it. It would be ideal except for the Porto Ricans—they are beyond doubt the dirtiest, laziest, most degenerate and thievish race of men ever inhabiting this sphere. It makes you sick to inhabit the same island with them. They are even lower than Italians.

What the island needs is not public health work, but a tidal wave or something to totally exterminate the population. It might then be livable. I have done my best to further the process of extermination by killing off eight and transplanting cancer into several more. The latter has not resulted in any fatalities so far. The matter of consideration for the patients' welfare plays no role here—in fact, all physicians take delight in the abuse and torture of the unfortunate subjects.

Do let me know if you hear any more news.

Sincerely,

Dusty

Juan Carlos had safeguarded the box and its secrets. When he died in prison, Angelina unwittingly inherited the role of caretaker of my mother's memories. Everything that happened and that had been forgotten was documented in that box.

After reading the letter and my mother's diary and other writings, I realized that Dr. Rhoads asked the Reverend to arrange my mother's death, and Pedro Mauleón did the deed. Though it was Mauleón who drowned her at the bottom of La Perla at the spot where the animals were slaughtered, Dr. Rhoads and the Reverend also had her blood on their hands.

Later, I researched Dr. Cornelius Rhoads' illustrious career, and his many acts came to light. It is all public record, you see. It did not surprise me to learn that, in fact, of the thirteen Puerto Rican patients at Presbyterian Hospital, the eight who were personally treated by Dr. Rhoads died shortly after treatment. One of them was a twelve-year-old girl. As compensation for his work in Puerto Rico, Dr. Rhoads was appointed director of the Sloan-Kettering Institute and consultant at the U.S. Commission of Atomic Energy and its Brookhaven National Laboratory in Long Island, New York, where experimentation on radiation and bacteria for warfare use were carried out. He also received the Army's Legion of Merit for his contributions to the development of chemical warfare.

I also learned that *don* Pedro Albizu Campos, whom my mother had informed of the contents of Dr. Rhoads' letter and who was the only person still living then who knew of Dr. Rhoads' acts, was imprisoned at La Princesa. While *don* Pedro was incarcerated, a nuclear scientist from the Oak Ridge Institute of Nuclear Studies visited Puerto Rico. Shortly afterwards, *don* Pedro was secretly radiated while in solitary confinement. I have seen the photos of *don* Pedro at that time, his legs and arms swollen like hams, burns all over his body, his head a patchwork of scalds.

And as with my mother's death, the world was blind and deaf to *don* Pedro's torture and assassination. His executioners went unpunished. There was nothing to do but to bear the withering silence.

I began this story with the taste of revenge in my mouth. I wanted to see justice done somehow, even though the protagonists of this tale are all dead. I wanted the public humiliation of the U.S. Government, the Rockefeller Institute, Dr. Rhoads' heirs. All of them needed to be exposed and brought down.

I wanted to relay the history of my mother and the anarchist's daughter as it really happened, not as something envisioned by a stranger's eye, some hateful man's eye.

But something happened as I arranged puzzle pieces so the story became whole. The solace of weaving words soothed me and helped me to figure out the patterns of my life, my mother's life, and our place in history ... herstory.

When I was a young girl, I often visited *doña* Eugenia and her daughter Emilia. On hot lazy afternoons, we sat on the porch as Emilia, with the thick calloused hands of a peasant, would take a slim crochet needle and the finest of lisle threads to create the most delicate doilies and handkerchiefs and the finely scalloped edges of percale pillows and sheets that she would sell to the shops. She would hold a skein of thread on her lap, pull out a straight line of thread in front of her, and knot it at the end. Then she made a loop with the hook of the crochet needle, pulled through some thread, and on and on, looping and linking until she had a chain. The chain stitch was the warp and woof from which so many delicate pieces emerged in her magical hands. As I watched her deft fingers, I listened attentively. For as she crocheted, she stitched together stories, chains of family sagas, folk tales, ghost stories, the latest gossip, all linked together like her crocheted work. It was a voyage of discovery.

My story is like a chain of crochet stitches. The events are so finely stitched together that the essential knots and loops and the edges of intricate connections are made invisible by the telling., I stand back and hold my story, like a crocheted creation, in front of me, this story pieced together from memories, from the lives of those who allowed me to journey through their waters, and the indifference of history.

And as I hold this story close to my heart, I realize that I am no longer fueled by hatred, by that insatiable thirst for revenge. I have set the story down as it happened. I have revealed a truth that had been hidden and forgotten.

All my anger is spent. Now, after all these years, I can let it all rest. Madame Zoe's predictions were right, after all. I can now sit in my rocker and look out at the beautiful rainbows arching over the ocean waves. I can settle into the last days of my life knowing that I am finally at peace.

Author's Note

Several historical figures appear in this novel. Ana Roque de Duprey's achievements are accurately described. Pedro Albizu Campos was the head of the Puerto Rican Nationalist Party until his death in 1965. Pedro Mauleón was, in fact, a rabble rouser for the Puerto Rican Republican Party. The fictional character of Isabel Pagán is loosely based on Luisa Capetillo, a union organizer, anarchist, pacifist, and feminist who lived before the events narrated in this novel. Dr. Cornelius P. Rhoads' role in the Presbyterian Hospital anemia experiments and his letter confessing to the purposeful administration of lethal injections to eight Puerto Rican patients were well-documented in the U.S. and Puerto Rican press of the time. Dr. Rhoads' self-incriminating letter was not found by a cleaning boy, but by a Puerto Rican lab technician at the Presbyterian Hospital, and it was the technician who handed the letter to *don* Pedro Albizu Campos. It is believed by reliable sources, including journalist Pedro Aponte Vázquez, who has written extensively on this case, that Dr. Rhoads was the intellectual mastermind behind the torture by atomic radiation—an act of revenge for Albizu's bringing the letter to the attention of the media—of *don* Pedro Albizu Campos while he was in solitary confinement at La Princesa Prison in San Juan.

Acknowledgments

In writing this book, my resolve was greatly strengthened by the people who supported my work. I wish to thank Dr. Joan Anim-Addo, a precious witness to the stories that unfold in my heart. I thank Dr. John Brademas, who generously shared with me his original historical research and other material on the Spanish anarchist movement. I thank Pedro Aponte Vázquez for his steadfast research and writings on *don* Pedro Albizu Campos. I thank Aixa Pascual Amadeo for her invaluable assistance in unearthing the newspaper and magazine articles published in the historical period in which the novel unfolds.

I would like to thank my Greek friends, who, during my years of residence in Greece and beyond, have offered me their love, laughter, and heroic sense of destiny. I especially thank Marina Katzaras, Angela Kiosoglou, Georgia Koumandaris, Despina Meimaroglou, and Jennifer Michaelides.

I thank my Puerto Rican friends for the courage of their words and the freedom of their spirits. I am deeply grateful to Carmen Carrasquillo, Sandra Pereira, and Sara Meléndez for our friendship, which has spanned the reaches of time and the challenges of distance.

I thank my daughter Yanira Ambert de Posson for the passion, love, and compassion she brings to everything she does and to everyone around her. I wish to thank my husband Walter McCann for the love, equanimity, and peace he has brought to my life.

Finally, my heartfelt thanks to the readers who breathe life into this novel as they read.

Made in the USA